TALES OF MYSTERY &

General Editor: D...

**AUSTRALIAN
GHOST STORIES**

Australian
Ghost Stories

*Selected, with an Introduction
and Notes, by James Doig*

WORDSWORTH EDITIONS

In loving memory of
MICHAEL TRAYLER
the founder of Wordsworth Editions

I

Readers interested in other titles from
Wordsworth Editions are invited to visit our
website at www.wordsworth-editions.com

For our latest list and a full mail-order service contact
Bibliophile Books, Unit 5 Datapoint,
South Crescent, London E16 4TL
Tel: +44 020 74 74 24 74
Fax: +44 020 74 74 85 89
orders@bibliophilebooks.com
www.bibliophilebooks.com

This edition published 2010 by
Wordsworth Editions Limited
8B East Street, Ware,
Hertfordshire SG12 9HJ

ISBN 978 1 84022 641 6

Typeset in Great Britain by Roperford Editorial
Printed by Clays Ltd, St Ives plc

CONTENTS

INTRODUCTION

The first true Gothic horror story is Horace Walpole's *The Castle of Otranto*, published appropriately enough on Christmas Eve in 1764. Walpole's tale of murder, madness and supernatural vengeance set in a rambling castle in medieval Spain inspired countless imitators over the next half-century. Most of these have fallen into well-deserved obscurity but some, such as William Beckford's *Vathek* (1786), Anne Radcliffe's *The Mysteries of Udolpho* (1794), Matthew Gregory Lewis's *The Monk* (1786), Charles Maturin's *Melmoth the Wanderer* (1820), and of course Mary Shelley's *Frankenstein* (1818) have become classics of their kind. The Gothic novel was a deliberate reaction against the philosophical rationalism of the 'age of reason' and the realistic novel that dominated the eighteenth century; in his use of the supernatural and his evocation of an imagined medieval past Walpole was thumbing his nose at the social realism of Richardson, Fielding and Sterne. In this sense, it was thought that the Gothic novel was the preserve of mature European cultures with an established antiquity; Gothic literature had no place in the colonies.

A debased form of the Gothic novel emerged in the early nineteenth century in the form of Penny Bloods. Taking advantage of advancements in printing, publishers produced vast quantities of illustrated weekly serials written by literary hacks, with lurid titles such as *The Secret Cave; or the Blood Stained Dagger* (1812). By the middle of the nineteenth century the Penny Blood was targeted at a predominantly juvenile market. These Penny Dreadfuls, as they were called, usually featured a young hero, frequently on the wrong side of the law, such as Jack Harkaway, Dick Turpin and Robin Hood. There is evidence that 'bloods' were read veraciously in the colonies; early in the late nineteenth and early twentieth century, the Melbourne bookseller John P. Quaine built up a world class collection of 'bloods' from foraging rubbish dumps deposited in deserted mining claims. Some 'bloods' and 'dreadfuls' had Australian themes, such as

Jack Harkaway in Australia, *Ned Nimble Amongst the Bushrangers*, and *Blue-Cap the Bushranger*.

While the Gothic novel was suffering a long, terminal decline, the short supernatural tale emerged around the middle of the nineteenth century, fuelled by the opportunities provided by the increasing number of periodicals. The requirements of the short story form and the maturing tastes of the reading public demanded a more disciplined, naturalistic style of writing, in contrast to the gaudy excesses of the Gothic novel. Magazines such as *Blackwood's Magazine* (1817–1980), *Bentley's Miscellany* (1837–1868), *Dublin University Magazine* (1833–1877) and in particular Charles Dickens's *Household Words* (1850–1859) and *All the Year Round* (1859–1895) regularly published supernatural stories by the likes of Joseph Sheridan le Fanu, Wilkie Collins, Amelia B. Edwards, Elizabeth Gaskell and Dickens himself. Later in the century and into the twentieth magazines such as *Belgravia* (1866–1899), *The Cornhill Magazine* (1860–1975), *The London Magazine* (1900–1933), *The Strand Magazine* (1891–1950), *The Idler* (1892–1911) and *The Pall Mall Magazine* (1893–1937) carried fantasy and supernatural fiction by some of the greatest exponents of the genre such as Robert Louis Stevenson, Bram Stoker, M.R. James, Algernon Blackwood, E.F. Benson, Arthur Conan Doyle, and H.G. Wells.

In the United States, the great American supernaturalists, Nathaniel Hawthorne and Edgar Allan Poe, utilised the trappings of Gothic fiction in new and lasting ways. Hawthorne found inspiration not in the European Middle Ages but the religious excesses of America's puritan past, while Edgar Allan Poe's tales evolved and extended the genre by finding terror not in external effects but in the human soul. Poe not only produced classic supernatural tales that brought the genre into the modern age, but he also wrote some of the greatest tales of psychological terror and single-handedly invented the detective story. As in Britain, periodicals were the main source of supernatural fiction. Poe's tales appeared in the magazines he edited, such as *Burton's Gentleman's Magazine* (1837–1841) and *Graham's Magazine* (1841–1858), and ghost stories and fantasies appeared regularly in *Harper's Monthly* (1850–current) and *Atlantic Monthly* (1857–current). In the late nineteenth century the first pulp magazines appeared, so called because of the cheap, poor quality paper they were printed on. Pulps such as *The Argosy* (1882–1980), *The All-Story* (1905–1914), and *The Blue Book* (1907–1952) published the occasional fantasy or supernatural tale, but it was in *Weird Tales* (1923–1954) and its numerous imitators that many of the great twentieth-century American authors of supernatural horror and fantasy first reached a wide audience. Writers such as Clark Ashton Smith, Robert E. Howard, Ray Bradbury, and especially H. P. Lovecraft, were to have a lasting impact on supernatural fiction and prefigure the extraordinary success of contemporary horror writers such as Stephen King. Pulp magazines were also popular in Britain, and pulps like the *Red Magazine*, *Yellow Magazine*, *Green Magazine* and the *Premier Magazine* contained many fantasy and supernatural tales.

*   *   *

Australia was similar to the United States in that it was considered too young to have accumulated the necessary props for a successful Gothic novel. In his 1856 essay, 'The Fiction Fields of Australia', the critic Frederick Sinnet wrote:

> There may be plenty of dilapidated buildings, but not one, the dilapidation of which is sufficiently venerable by age, to tempt the wandering footsteps of the most arrant *parvenu* of a ghost that ever walked by night. It must be admitted that Mrs Radcliffe's genius would be quite thrown away here; and we must reconcile ourselves to the conviction that the foundations of a second *Castle of Otranto* can hardly be laid in Australia during our time.

How could Australia produce a recognisable Gothic literature without a single age-weary medieval castle replete with secret passages and trapdoors or the background of superstitious terror and ignorance that Victorians saw as characteristic of the Middle Ages? On the one hand, Australian writers could follow the British example and write about European terrors. On the other, they could find inspiration in the Australian experience; after all, colonists had to face real-life horrors of aggressive natives (which often resulted in terrible massacres of the aborigines), lawlessness, loneliness, drought, flood, and of course the fearsome deprivations of convict life. Apart from physical hardship there was a quality in the Australian landscape that lent itself to explorations of the supernatural. Marcus Clarke expressed this other-worldly quality in his preface to the collected poems of Adam Lindsay Gordon published in 1876.

> What is the dominant note of Australian scenery? That which is the dominant note of Edgar Allan Poe's poetry – Weird Melancholy . . . The Australian mountain forests are funereal, secret, stern. Their solitude is desolation. They seem to stifle, in their black gorges, a story of sullen despair. No tender sentiment is nourished in their shade . . . In the Australian forests no leaves fall. The savage shout

among the rock clefts. From the melancholy gums strips of white
bark hang and rustle. The very animal life of these frowning hills is
either grotesque or ghostly. Great grey kangaroos hop noiselessly
over the coarse grass. Flights of white cockatoos stream out, shrieking like evil souls. The sun suddenly sinks, and the mopokes burst
out into horrible peals of semi-human laughter. The natives aver
that, when night comes, from out the bottomless depth of some
lagoon the Bunyip rises, and, in form like a monstrous sea-calf,
drags his loathsome length from out of the ooze. From a corner of
the silent forest rises a dismal chant, and around a fire dance natives
painted like skeletons. All is fear-inspiring and gloomy.

Although there were literary possibilities in the Australian environ-
ment, the Australian reading public still looked to Britain to satisfy its
taste for Gothic and supernatural fiction. Australian stationers stocked
the latest British novels and Australian newspapers and periodicals
included short stories and serials by British and American authors,
including Wilkie Collins, Le Fanu, Mary Braddon, Amelia Edwards
and many others. Gothic serials were popular and the Irish-born
Australian, Mary Fortune (1833–1909), writing under her *nom de
plume* Waif Wander (often shortened to W.W.) wrote serials for
The Australian Journal with titles like *The Secrets of Balbrooke* (1866)
and *Clyzia the Dwarf* (1866). Her short story, 'The White Maniac:
A Doctor's Tale', which leads this anthology, is based firmly in
the Gothic tradition and is set in London. Fortune is best known for
her series of detective stories called 'The Detective's Album' that
appeared in *The Australian Journal*, some of which have supernatural
content. Other publications by Australians were inspired by celebrated British originals; George Isaacs's (1825–1876) *The Burlesque of
Frankenstein* (1865) is a verse drama based loosely on Mary Shelley's
novel, while the Australian politician and author, William Forster
(1818–1882), used Catherine Crow's short story 'A Story of a Weir-
Wolf', about the sufferings of a young girl wrongly accused of lyc-
anthropy, as the source his own verse drama, *The Weirwolf: A Tragedy*
(1876). Even the mummy was the subject of a popular novel by a best-
selling Australian author: Ambrose Pratt's *The Living Mummy* (1910).

The Australian Journal (1865–1962) was one of dozens of Australian
periodicals that included the occasional supernatural tale in its pages.
Others include the *Australasian* (1864–1946), *Australian Town and
Country Journal* (1870–1919), *Queenslander* (1866–1939), *The Boomerang* (1887–1892), *The Bulletin* (1880–2008) and *The Lone Hand* (1907–
1921). Most of the stories in this collection first appeared in these

magazines. The first known supernatural tale set in Australia was 'Fisher's Ghost', a well-known narrative by John Lang (1816–1864) in which the ghost of a murdered man leads the authorities to his killer. The story survives in several versions. It first appeared, published anonymously, in *Tegg's Magazine* in 1836. The basic plot of justice obtained through supernatural means is extremely common in colonial supernatural fiction; Mary Fortune wrote several stories in this vein which appeared in 'The Detective's Album'.

Perhaps the most important figure in Australian colonial fiction is Marcus Clarke (1846–1881). Clarke wrote novels, journalism and short stories including what he called 'Strange Tales' which, like Poe, he published in the magazines that he edited. Clarke's *His Natural Life*, serialised in the *Australian Journal* in 1870 and published in book-form in 1874, is arguably the greatest Australian colonial novel and is a harrowing tale of an innocent man transported to Australia and the deprivations he suffers. 'The Mystery of Major Molineux', reprinted in this anthology, is a remarkable tale in the werewolf tradition and has echoes of Stevenson's *The Strange Case of Dr Jekyll and Mr Hyde* which it predates by five years. In attempting to explain the pathology of Major Molineux in physiological terms it is an early example of the 'scientific mystery'. Another important figure in Australian literature is Henry Lawson (1876–1922), whose reputation was sealed in 1896 when his short story collection, *While the Billy Boils*, and poetry collection, *In the Days When the World was Wide*, were published by Angus and Robertson; 'The Loaded Dog' and 'The Drover's Wife' are known to generations of Australian school children and are justly regarded as classics. A number of his stories explore in simple but powerful language the tragedy and desperation of ordinary lives. Lawson preferred realistic stories and 'The Third Murder', which appeared in *The Boomerang* in 1890, is an ironic take on the conventional haunted house tale.

Ernest Favenc (1845–1908) is a name that should be better known to anyone interested in macabre fiction. A writer, journalist, explorer and historian, Favenc wrote many tales of fantasy and the supernatural that draw on his first-hand knowledge of the Australian outback. Most of his stories appeared in Australian periodicals like *The Bulletin* and the *Australian Town and Country Journal*, but a number of weird tales also appeared in *Phil May's Annual* alongside stories by Arthur Conan Doyle, Grant Allen and Barry Pain. The two stories included in this anthology are interesting in the way that Favenc translates traditional Gothic props into an Australian setting. Edward Dyson (1865–1931) is another writer who based much of his short fiction on first-hand experience, in his case in the mining *milieu* of Ballarat and other small towns in Victoria where he grew up. 'The Accursed Thing' powerfully evokes the other-worldly fears of miners working in dreadful and dangerous conditions. If Favenc and Dyson knew hardship and deprivation, Roderic Quinn (1867–1949) was a poetic dreamer who lived most of his life amongst Sydney's Bohemian society. He is best known as a poet and was strongly influenced by the Irish poetry of the Celtic Twilight, however he wrote dozens of short stories, mostly for *The Bulletin*, including the lyrical 'Sea Voices' which is included here. Dulcie Deamer (1890–1972) was also a member of Sydney's Bohemian set. She gained early recognition by winning a short story competition run by *The Lone Hand* in 1907 and the following year published a collection of historical fantasies, *In the Beginning*, from which 'Hallowe'en' is taken.

Many Australian authors found literary success overseas writing for the British and American magazines. Guy Boothby (1867–1905) was perhaps the most successful Australian *émigré*, making his fortune with a series of novels involving Dr Nikola, a mysterious figure possessed of strange powers, seemingly endless wealth, grotesque servants, and an ever-present jet black cat named Apollyon. He wrote numerous short stories for the better class of English magazine like *Pall Mall*, *The Windsor* and *Pearson's*, but tragically his life was cut short at the age of thirty-eight by pneumonia. H. B. Marriott Watson (1863–1921) also found fame with a larger-than-life leading character, in his case, Richard Ryder, better known as Galloping Dick, a swashbuckling eighteenth-century highwayman. Born in Victoria and educated in New Zealand, Watson gained some notoriety in the 1890s for a series of decadent tales published in W. E. Henley's *National Observer*, the best known of which is 'The Devil of the Marsh'. Fergus Hume (1859–1932) was also raised and educated in New Zealand; he went to Melbourne in 1885 where he wrote *The Mystery of a Hansom Cab* (1886), which became a great bestseller and made his lasting reputation as a mystery writer. Hume moved permanently to England in 1888 and although he wrote an incredible 120 novels and collections over the next thirty years he never again achieved the success of his first novel. Rosa Praed (1851–1935) led a difficult life in outback Queensland before moving to England in 1876 to pursue a literary career. This she did with gusto, producing a string of bestsellers, many of them set in Australia and featuring feisty Australian heroines. Always interested in spiritual and occult matters Praed enthusiastically joined the theosophy *milieu* that enjoyed extraordinary popularity in England in the late nineteenth and early twentieth centuries. Many of her novels, such as *The Brother of the Shadow* (1886) and *The Soul of Countess Adrian* (1891), have occult or theosophist themes. Her celebrated short story, 'The Bunyip', is an atmospheric tale that powerfully evokes the 'weird melancholy' of the Australian outback.

Although they had very different backgrounds and personalities, Beatrice Grimshaw (1871–1953) and James Francis Dwyer (1874–1952) had much in common: both wrote adventure stories set in exotic locations; both published prolifically for the popular magazines of the day; and both developed a breezy, lyrical style, well suited to the places and people they wrote about. Grimshaw's 'The Cave' and Dwyer's 'The Cave of the Invisible' were originally published in *The Blue Book*, the American adventure pulp. A writer in a similar vein was Louis Becke (1855–1913) who made his reputation with short stories set in the Pacific islands that were published in *The Bulletin*. Feted in London in 1896 when he fled bankruptcy and a messy separation from his wife, he continued to be dogged by debt, alcoholism and accusations of bigamy, and died ill and alone in a Sydney hotel in 1913.

A striking feature of the writers represented here is that so many of them died in difficult circumstances. Marcus Clarke died at the age of thirty-five leaving his wife and six children destitute; Henry Lawson's later life was plagued by debt, alcoholism and mental illness; such was Mary Fortune's obscurity that the year of her death was not known with certainty until very recently; Rosa Praed and H. B. Marriott Watson died alone, having been predeceased by their loved ones; Dulcie Deamer and Beatrice Grimshaw lived out the last years of their lives in hospices. If *terra australis incognita* was believed by early cartographers and explorers to be a fearful land peopled by monsters, Australia's early writers could well claim that it is more subtly cursed.

JAMES DOIG
Canberra 2010

LIST OF AUTHORS

AUSTRALIAN
GHOST STORIES

The White Maniac: A Doctor's Tale

Mary Fortune

Between 1865 and 1908 Mary Fortune (1833-1909), under her pseudo-nym 'Waif Wander', wrote more than 500 crime stories in the popular *Australian Journal*. Some of these were brought together in a very rare collection, *The Detective's Album* (1871). She was born in Belfast, Ireland, and followed her father to the Victorian goldfields in 1855. Her life was punctuated by several crises, including the birth of an illegitimate son, the death of her first child, and two failed marriages. As well as her detective fiction, Fortune wrote an excessive gothic serial novel, *Clyzia the Dwarf*, and a number of supernatural and horror stories in the *Australian Journal*, including 'The White Maniac: A Doctor's Tale', which appeared in July 1867. She wrote of her own work: 'I have been told by some that I tell horrible stories and by others that I am not sensational enough; and I have personally come to the conclusion that I shall tell just such stories as I please.'

In the year 1858 I had established a flourishing practice in London; a practice which I owed a considerable proportion of, not to my ability, I am afraid, but to the fact that I occupied the singular position of a man professional, who was entirely independent of his profession. Doubtless, had I been a poor man, struggling to earn a bare existence for wife and family, I might have been the cleverest physician that ever administered a bolus, yet have remained in my poverty to the end of time. But it was not so, you see I was the second son of a nobleman, and had Honourable attached to my name; and I practised the profession solely and entirely because I had become enamoured of it, and because I was disgusted at the useless existence of a fashionable and idle young man, and determined that I, at least, would not add another to their ranks.

And so I had a handsome establishment in a fashionable portion of the city, and my door was besieged with carriages, from one end of the week to the other. Many of the occupants were disappointed, however, for I would not demean myself by taking fees from some vapourish Miss or dissipated Dowager. Gout in vain came rolling to my door, even though it excruciated the leg of a Duke; I undertook none but cases that enlisted my sympathy, and after a time the fact became known, and my levees were not so well attended.

One day I was returning on horseback toward the city. I had been paying a visit to a patient, in whom I was deeply interested, and for whom I had ordered the quiet and purer air of a sub-urban residence. I had reached a spot, in the neighbourhood of Kensington, where the vines were enclosed in large gardens, and the road was marked for a considerable distance by the brick and stone walls that enclosed several of the gardens belonging to those mansions. On the opposite side of the road stood a small country-looking inn, which I had patronised before, and I pulled up my horse and alighted, for the purpose of having some rest and refresh-ment after my ride.

As I sat in a front room sipping my wine and water, my thoughts were fully occupied with a variety of personal concerns. I had received a letter from my mother that morning, and the condition of the patient I had recently left was precarious in the extreme.

It was fortunate that I was thought-occupied and not dependent upon outward objects to amuse them, for although the window at which I sat was open, it presented no view whatever, save the bare, blank, high brick wall belonging to a house at the opposite side of the road. That is to say, I presume, it enclosed some residence, for from where I sat not even the top of a chimney was visible.

Presently, however, the sound of wheels attracted my eyes from the pattern of the wall-paper at which I had been unconsciously gazing, and I looked out to see a handsome, but very plain carriage drawn up at a small door that pierced the brick wall I have alluded to; and almost at the same moment the door opened and closed again behind two figures in a most singular attire. They were both of the male sex, and one of them was evidently a gentle-man, while the other waited on him as if he was the servant; but it was the dress of these persons that most strangely interested me. They were attired in white from head to heel; coats, vests, trousers, hats, shoes, not to speak of shirts at all, all were white as white could be.

While I stared at this strange spectacle, the gentleman stepped into the vehicle; but although be did so the coachman made no movement toward driving onward, nor did the attendant leave his post at the carriage door. At the expiration, however, of about a quarter of an hour, the servant closed the door and re-entered through the little gate, closing it, likewise, carefully behind him.

Then the driver leisurely made a start, only, however, to stop suddenly again, when the door of the vehicle was burst open and a gentleman jumped out and rapped loudly at the gate.

He turned his face hurriedly around as he did so, hiding, it seemed to me, meanwhile, behind the wall so as not to be seen when it opened. Judge of my astonishment when I recognised in this gentleman the one who had but a few minutes before entered the carriage dressed in white, for he was now in garments of the hue of Erebus. While I wondered at this strange metamorphosis the door in the wall opened, and the gentleman, now attired in black, after giving some hasty instructions to the servant, sprang once more into the carriage and was driven rapidly toward London.

My curiosity was strangely excited; and as I stood at the door before mounting my horse, I asked the landlord who and what were the people who occupied the opposite dwelling.

'Well, sir,' he replied, looking curiously at the dead wall over against him, 'They've been there now a matter of six months, I dare say, and you've seen as much of them as I have. I believe the whole crew of them, servants and all, is foreigners, and we, that is the neighbours around, sir, calls them the "white mad people".'

'What! do they always wear that singular dress?'

'Always, sir, saving as soon as ever the old gentleman goes inside the gate he puts black on in the carriage, and as soon as he comes back takes it off again, and leaves it in the carriage.'

'And why in the name of gracious does he not dress himself inside?'

'Oh, that I can't tell you sir! only it's just as you see, always. The driver or coachman never even goes inside the walls, or the horses or any one thing that isn't white in colour, sir; and if the people aren't mad after that, what else can it be?'

'It seems very like it, indeed; but do you mean to say that everything inside the garden wall is white? Surely you must be exaggerating a little?'

'Not a bit on it, sir! The coachman, who can't speak much English, sir, comes here for a drink now and then. He doesn't live in the house, you see, and is idle most of his time. Well, he told me himself, one day, that every article in the house was white, from the garret to the drawing-room, and that everything *outside* it is white I can swear, for I saw it myself, and a stranger sight surely no eye ever saw.'

'How did you manage to get into the enchanted castle, then?'

'I didn't get in sir, I only saw it outside, and from a place where you can see for yourself too, if you have a mind. When first the people came to the place over there, you see sir, old Mat the sexton and bell-ringer of the church there, began to talk of the strange goings on he had seen from the belfry; and so my curiosity took me there one day to look for myself. Blest if I ever heard of such a strange sight! No wonder they call them the white mad folk.'

'Well, you've roused my curiosity,' I said, as I got on my horse, 'and I'll certainly pay old Mat's belfry a visit the very next time I pass this way, if I'm not hurried.'

It appeared unaccountable to even myself that these mysterious people should make such a singular impression on me; I thought of little else during the next two days. I attended to my duties in an absent manner, and my mind was ever recurring to the one subject – viz. an attempt to account for the strange employment of one hue only in the household of this foreign gentleman. Of whom did the household consist? Had he any family? And could one account for the eccentricity in any other way save by ascribing it to lunacy, as mine host of the inn had already done. As it happened, the study of brain diseases had been my hobby during my noviciate, and I was peculiarly interested in observing a new symptom of madness, if this was really one.

At length I escaped to pay my country patient his usual visit, and on my return alighted at the inn, and desired the landlord to have my horse put in the stable for a bit.

'I'm going to have a peep at your madhouse,' I said. 'Do you think I shall find old Mat about?'

'Yes, doctor; I saw him at work in the churchyard not half an hour ago, but at any rate he won't be farther off than his cottage, and it lies just against the yard wall.'

The church was an old, ivy-wreathed structure, with a square Norman belfry, and a large surrounding of grey and grass-grown old headstones. It was essentially a country church, and a country church-yard; and one wondered to find it so close to the borders of a mighty city, until they remembered that the mighty city had crept into the country, year by year, until it had covered with stone and mortar the lowly site of many a cottage home, and swallowed up many an acre of green meadow and golden corn. Old Mat was sitting in the middle of the graves, one tombstone forming his seat; and he was engaged in scraping the moss from a headstone that seemed inclined to tumble over, the inscription on which was all but obliterated by a growth of green slimy-looking moss.

'Good-day, friend, you are busy,' I said. 'One would fancy that stone so old now, that the living had entirely forgotten their loss. But I suppose they have not, or you would not be cleaning it.'

'It's only a notion of my own, sir; I'm idle, and when I was a lad I had it sort o' likin' for this stone, Lord only knows why. But you see I've clean forgotten what name was on it, and I thought I'd like to see.'

'Well, I want to have a look at these "white mad folk" of yours, Mat, will you let me into the belfry? Mr Tanning tells me you can see something queer up there.'

'By Jove you can, sir!' he replied, rising with alacrity, 'I often spend an hour watching the mad folk; faith if they had my old church and yard they'd whitewash 'em, belfry and all!' and the old man led the way into the tower.

Of course my first look on reaching the summit was in the direction of the strange house, and I must confess to an ejaculation of astonishment as I peeped through one of the crevices. The belfry was elevated considerably above the premises in which I was interested, and not at a very great distance, so that grounds and house lay spread beneath me like a map.

I scarcely know how to commence describing it to you, it was something I had never seen or imagined. The mansion itself was a square and handsome building of two stories, built in the Corinthian style, with pillared portico, and pointed windows. But the style attracted my attention but little, it was the universal white, white everywhere, that drew from me the ejaculation to which I have alluded.

From the extreme top of the chimneys to the basement, roof, windows, everything was pure white; not a shade lurked even inside a window; the windows themselves were painted white, and the curtains were of white muslin that fell over every one of them. Every yard of the broad space that one might reasonably have expected to see decorated with flowers and grass and shrubberies, was covered with a glaring and sparkling white gravel, the effect of which, even in the hot brilliant sun of a London afternoon, was to dazzle, and blind, and aggravate. And if this was not enough, the inside of the very brick walls was whitewashed like snow, and at intervals; here and there, were placed a host of white marble statues and urns that only increased the, to me, horrible aspect of the place.

'I don't wonder they are mad!' I exclaimed, 'I should soon become mad in such a place myself.'

'Like enough, sir,' replied old Mat, stolidly, 'but you see it *didn't* make they mad, for they did it theirselves, so they must 'a been mad afore.'

An incontrovertible fact, according to the old man's way of putting it; and as I had no answer for it, I went down the old stone stairs, and having given my guide his donation, left the churchyard as bewildered as I had entered it. Nay, more so, for then I had not seen the extra-ordinary house that had made so painful an impression upon me.

I was in no humour for a gossip with mine host, but just as I was about to mount my horse, which had been brought round, the same carriage drove round to the mysterious gate, and the same scene was enacted to which I had before been a witness. I drew back until the old gentleman had stopped inside and performed his toilet, and when the carriage drove rapidly toward the city, I rode thoughtfully onward toward home.

I was young, you see, and although steady and unlike most young gentlemen of my age and position in society, had a strong vein of romance in my character. That hard study and a sense of its inutility had kept it under, had not rendered it one whit less ready to be at a moment's call; and, in addition to all this, I had never yet, in the seclusion of my student life, met with an opportunity of falling in love, so that you will see I was in the very best mood for making the most of the adventure which was about to befall me, and which had so tragic a termination.

My thoughts were full of the "white mad folk", as I reached my own door; and there, to my utter astonishment, I saw drawn up the very carriage of the white house, which had preceded me. Hastily giving my horse to the groom I passed through the hall and was informed by a servant that a gentleman waited in my private con-sulting room.

Very rarely indeed had my well-strung nerves been so troublesome as upon that occasion; I was so anxious to see this gentleman, and yet so fearful of exposing the interest I had already conceived in his affairs, that my hand absolutely trembled as I turned the handle of the door of the room in which he was seated. The first glance, however, at the aristocratic old gentleman who rose on my entrance, restored all my self-possession, and I was myself once more. In the calm, sweet face of the perfectly dressed gentleman before me there was no trace of the lunacy that had created that strange abode near Kensington; the principal expression in his face was that of ingrained melancholy, and his deep mourning attire might have suggested to a stranger the reason of that melancholy. He addressed me in perfect English, the entire absence of idiom alone declaring him to be a foreigner.

'I have the pleasure of addressing Doctor Elveston?' he said.

I bowed, and placed a chair in which he re-seated himself, while I myself took possession of another.

'And Doctor Elveston is a clever physician and a man of honour?'

'I hope to be worthy of the former title, sir, while my position ought at least to guarantee the latter.'

'Your public character does, sir,' said the old gentleman, emphatically, and it is because I believe that you will preserve the secret of an unfortunate family that I have chosen you to assist me with your advice.'

My heart was beating rapidly by this time. There was a secret then, and I was about to become the possessor of it. Had it anything to do with the mania for white?

'Anything in my power,' I hastened to reply, 'you may depend on; my advice, I fear, may be of little worth, but such as it is – '.

'I beg your pardon, Doctor,' interrupted he, 'it is your medical advice that I allude to, and I require it for a young lady – a relative.'

'My dear sir, that is, of course, an every day affair, my professional advice and services belong to the public, and as the public's they are of course yours.'

'Oh, my dear young friend, but mine is not an every day affair, and because it is not is the reason that I have applied to you in particular. It is a grievous case, sir, and one which fills many hearts with a bitterness they are obliged to smother from a world whose sneers are poison.'

The old gentleman spoke in tones of deep feeling, and I could not help feeling sorry for him at the bottom of my very heart.

'If you will confide in me, my dear sir,' I said, 'believe that I will prove a friend as faithful and discreet as you could wish.'

He pressed my hand, turned away for a moment to collect his agitated feelings and then he spoke again.

'I shall not attempt to hide my name from you, sir, though I have hitherto carefully concealed it, I am the Duke de Rohan, and circumstances, which it is impossible for me to relate to you, have driven me to England to keep watch and ward over my sister's daughter, the Princess d'Alberville. It is for this young lady I wish your attendance, her health is rapidly failing within the last week.'

'Nothing can be more simple,' I observed, eagerly, 'I can go with you at once – this very moment.'

'Dear Doctor, it is unfortunately far from being as simple a matter as you think,' he replied, solemnly, 'for my wretched niece is mad.'

'Mad!'

'Alas! yes, frightfully – horribly mad!' and he shuddered as if a cold wind had penetrated his bones.

'Has this unhappy state of mind been of long duration?' I questioned.

'God knows; the first intimation her friends had of it was about two years ago, when it culminated in such a fearful event that horrified them. I cannot explain it to you, however, for the honour of a noble house is deeply concerned; and even the very existence of the unfortunate being I beg of you to keep a secret forever.'

'You must at any rate tell me what you wish me to do,' I observed, 'and give me as much information as you can to guide me, or I shall be powerless.'

'The sight of one colour has such an effect on the miserable girl that we have found out, by bitter experience, the only way to avoid a repetition of the most fearful tragedies is to keep every hue or shade away from her vision; for, although it is only one colour that affects her, any of the others seems to suggest that *one* to her mind and produce uncontrollable agitation. In consequence of this she is virtually imprisoned within the grounds of the house I have provided for her; and every object that meets her eye is white, even the ground, and the very roof of the mansion.'

'How very strange!'

'It will be necessary for you, my dear sir,' the Duke continued, 'to attire yourself in a suit of white. I have brought one in the carriage for your use, and if you will now accompany me I shall be grateful.'

Of course I was only too glad to avail myself of the unexpected opportunity of getting into the singular household, and becoming acquainted with the lunatic princess; and in a few moments we were being whirled on our way toward Kensington.

On stopping at the gate of the Duke's residence, I myself became an actor in the scene which had so puzzled me on two previous occasions. My companion produced two suits of white, and proceeded to turn the vehicle into a dressing-room, though not without many apologies for the necessity. I followed his example, and in a few moments we stood inside the gate, and I had an opportunity of more closely surveying the disagreeable enclosure I had seen from the church belfry. And a most disagreeable survey it was; the sun shining brilliantly, rendered the unavoidable contact with the white glare absolutely painful to the eye; nor was it any escape to stand in the lofty vestibule, save that there the absence of sunshine made the uniformity more bearable.

My companion led the way up a broad staircase covered with white cloth, and balustraded with carved rails, the effect of which was totally destroyed by their covering of white paint. The very stair-rods were of white enamel, and the corners and landing places served as room for more marble statues, that held enamelled white lamps in their hands, lamps that were shaded by globes of ground glass. At the door of an apartment pertaining, as he informed me, to the Princess d'Alberville, the Duke stopped, and shook my hand. 'I leave you to make your own way,' he said, pointing to the door. 'She has never showed any symptoms of violence while under the calm influence of white; but, nevertheless, we shall be at hand, the least sound will bring you assistance,' and he turned away.

I opened the door without a word, and entered the room, full of curiosity as to what I should see and hear of this mysterious princess. It was a room of vast and magnificent proportions, and, without having beheld such a scene, one can hardly conceive the strange cold look the utter absence of colour gave it. A Turkey carpet that looked like a woven fall of snow; white satin damask on chair, couch, and ottoman; draped satin and snowy lace around the windows, with rod, rings, and bracelets of white enamel. Tables with pedestals of enamel and tops of snowy marble, and paper on the walls of purest white; altogether it was a weird-looking room, and I shook with cold as I entered it.

The principal object of my curiosity was seated in a deep chair with her side toward me, and I had an opportunity of examining her leisurely, as she neither moved nor took the slightest notice of my entrance; most probably she was quite unaware of it. She was the most lovely being I had ever beheld, a fair and perfect piece of statuary one might have thought, so immobile and abstracted, nay, so entirely expressionless were her beautiful features. Her dress was pure white, her hair of a pale golden hue, and her eyes dark as midnight. Her hands rested idly on her lap, her gaze seemed intent on the high white wall that shot up outside the window near her; and in the whole room there was neither book, flower, work, nor one single *loose* article of ornament, nothing but the heavy, white-covered furniture, and the draping curtains. I advanced directly before her and bowed deeply, and then I calmly drew forward a chair and seated myself. As I did so she moved her eyes from the window and rested them on me, but, for all the interest they evinced, I might as well have been the white-washed wall outside. She was once more returning her eyes to the blank window, when I took her hand and laid my fingers on her blue-veined wrist. The action seemed to arouse her, for she looked keenly into my face, and then she laughed softly.

'One may guess you are a physician,' she said, in a musical, low voice, and with a slightly foreign accent, that was in my opinion, a great improvement to our harsh language.

'I am,' I replied, with a smile, 'your uncle has sent me to see about your health, which alarms him.'

'Poor man!' she said, with a shade of commiseration clouding her beautiful face, 'poor uncle! but I assure you there is nothing the matter with me; nothing but what must be the natural consequence of the life I am leading.'

'Why do you lead one which you know to be injurious then?' I asked, still keeping my fingers on the pulse, that beat as calmly as a sleeping infant's, and was not interested by a single throb though a stranger sat beside her.

'How can I help it?' she asked, calmly meeting my inquisitorial gaze. 'Do you think a sane person would choose to be imprisoned thus, and to be surrounded by the colour of death ever? Had mine not been a strong mind I would have been mad long ago.'

'Mad!' I could not help ejaculating, in a puzzled tone.

'Yes, mad,' she replied, 'could *you* live here, month after month, in a hueless atmosphere and with nothing but *that* to look at,' and she pointed her slender finger toward the white wall, 'could you, I ask, and retain your reason?'

'I do not believe I could!' I answered, with sudden vehemence, 'then again I repeat, why do it?'

'And again I reply, how can I help it?'

I was silent. I was looking in the eyes of the beautiful being before me for a single trace of the madness I had been told of, but I could not find it. It was a lovely girl, pale and delicate from confinement, and with a manner that told of a weariness endured at least patiently. She was about twenty years old, perhaps, and the most perfect creature, I have already said, that I had ever beheld; and so we sat looking into each other's eyes; what mine expressed I cannot say, but hers were purity and sweetness itself.

'Who are you?' she asked, suddenly, 'tell me something of yourself. It will be at least a change from this white solitude.'

'I am a doctor, as you have guessed; and a rich and fashionable doctor,' I added smilingly.

'To be either is to be also the other,' she remarked, 'you need not have used the repetition.'

'Come,' I thought to myself, 'there is little appearance of lunacy in that observation.'

'But you doubtless have a name, what is it?'

'My name is Elveston – Doctor Elveston.'

'Your christian name?'

'No, my christian name is Charles.'

'Charles,' she repeated dreamily.

'I think it is your turn now,' I remarked, 'it is but fair that you should make me acquainted with your name, since I have told you mine.'

'Oh! my name is d'Alberville – Blanche d'Alberville. Perhaps it was in consequence of my christian name that my poor uncle decided upon burying me in white,' she added, with a look round the cold room, 'poor old man!'

'Why do you pity him so?' I asked, 'he seems to me little to require it. He is strong and rich, and the uncle of Blanche,' I added, with a bow; but the compliment seemed to glide off her as if it had been a liquid, and she were made of glassy marble like one of the statues that stood behind her.

'And you are a physician,' she said, looking wonderingly at me, 'and have been in the Duke's company, without discovering it?'

'Discovering what, my dear young lady?'

'That he is mad.'

'Mad!' How often had I already ejaculated that word since I had become interested in this singular household; but this time it must assuredly have expressed the utmost astonishment, for I was never more confounded in my life; and yet a light seemed to be breaking in upon my bewilderment, and I stared in wondering silence at the calm face of the lovely maiden before me.

'Alas, yes!' she replied, sadly, to my look, 'my poor uncle is a maniac, but a harmless one to all but me; it is I who suffer all.'

'And why you?' I gasped.

'Because it is his mania to believe me mad,' she replied, 'and so he treats me.'

'But in the name of justice why should you endure this?' I cried, angrily starting to my feet, 'you are in a free land at least, and doors will open!'

'Calm yourself, my friend,' she said, laying her white hand on my arm, and the contact, I confess, thrilled through every nerve of my system, 'compose yourself, and see things as they are; what could a young, frail girl like me do out in the world alone? and I have not a living relative but my uncle. Besides, would it be charitable to desert him and leave him to his own madness thus? Poor old man!'

'You are an angel!' I ejaculated, 'and I would die for you!'

The reader need not be told that my enthusiastic youth was at last beginning to make its way through the crust of worldly wisdom that had hitherto subdued it.

'It is not necessary that anyone should die for me; I can do that for myself, and no doubt shall ere long, die of the want of colour and air,' she said, with a sad smile.

There is little use following our conversation to the end. I satisfied myself that there was really nothing wrong with her constitution, save the effects of the life she was obliged to lead; and I determined, instead of interfering with her at present, to devote myself to the poor Duke, with a hope that I might be of service to him, and succeed in gaining the liberation of poor Blanche. We parted, I might almost say as lovers, although no words of affection were spoken; but I carried away her image entwined with every fibre of my heart, and in the deep sweetness of her lingering eyes I fancied I read hope and love.

The Duke was waiting impatiently in the corridor as I left the lovely girl, and he led me into another apartment to question me eagerly. What did I think of the princess's state of health? Had she shown any symptoms of uneasiness during my visit? As the old gentleman asked these questions he watched my countenance keenly; while on my part I observed him with deep interest to discover traces of his unfortunate mental derangement.

'My dear sir, I perceive nothing alarming whatever in the state of your niece; she is simply suffering from confinement and monotony of existence, and wants nothing whatever but fresh air and amusement, and exercise; in short, life.'

'Alas! you know that is impossible; have I not told you that her state precludes everything of the sort?'

'You must excuse me, my friend,' I said, firmly, 'I have conversed for a considerable time with the Princess d'Alberville, and I am a medical man accustomed to dealing with, and the observation of, lunacy, and I give you my word of honour there is no weakness whatever in the brain of this fair girl; you are simply killing her, it is my duty to tell you so, killing her under the influence of some, to me, most unaccountable whim.'

The duke wrung his hands in silence, but his excited eye fell under my steady gaze. It was apparently with a strong effort that he composed himself sufficiently to speak, and when he did his words had a solemnity in their tone that ought to have made a deep impression upon me; but it did not, for the sweetness of the imprisoned Blanche's voice was still lingering in my ears.

'You are a young man, Doctor Elveston; it is one of the happy provisions of youth, no doubt, to be convinced of its own infallibility. But you must believe that one of my race does not lie, and I swear to you that my niece is the victim of a most fearful insanity, which but to name makes humanity shudder with horror.'

'I do not doubt that you believe such to be the case, my dear sir,' I said, soothingly, for I fancied I saw the fearful light of insanity in his glaring eye at that moment, 'but to my vision everything seems different.'

'Well, my young friend, do not decide yet too hastily. Visit us again, but God in mercy grant that you may never see the reality as I have seen it!'

And so I did repeat my visits, and repeat them so often and that without changing my opinion, that the Duke, in spite of his mania, began to see that they were no longer necessary. One day on my leaving Blanche he requested a few moments of my time, and drawing me into his study, locked the door. I began to be a little alarmed, and more particularly as he seemed to be in a state of great agitation; but as it appeared, my alarm of personal violence was entirely without foundation.

He placed a chair for me, and I seated myself with all the calmness I could muster, while I kept my eyes firmly fixed upon his as he addressed me.

'My dear young friend; I hope it is unnecessary for me to say that these are no idle words, for I have truly conceived an ardent appreciation of your character; yet it is absolutely necessary that I should put a stop to your visits to my niece. Good Heavens, what could I say – how could I ever forgive myself if any – any –'

'I beg of you to go no farther, Duke,' I said, interrupting him. 'You have only by a short time anticipated what I was about to communicate myself. If your words allude to an attachment between Blanche and myself, your care is now too late. We love each other, and intend, subject to your approval, to be united immediately.'

Had a sudden clap of thunder reverberated in the quiet room the poor man could not have been more affected. He started to his feet and glared into my eyes with terror.

'Married!' he gasped, 'Married! Blanche d'Alberville wedded! Oh God!' and then he fell back into his chair as powerless as a child.

'And why should this alarm you?' I asked. 'She is youthful and lovely, and as sane, I believe in my soul, as I am myself. I am rich, and of a family which may aspire to mate with the best. You are her only relative and guardian, and you say that you esteem me; whence then this great distaste to hear even a mention of your fair ward's marriage?'

'She is not my ward!' he cried, hoarsely, and it seemed to me angrily, 'her father and mother are both in existence, and destroyed for all time by the horror she has brought around them! But, my God, what is the use of speaking – I talk to a madman!' and he turned to his desk and began to write rapidly.

There I sat in bewilderment. I had not now the slightest doubt but that my poor friend was the victim of monomania; his one idea was uppermost, and that idea was that his unfortunate niece was mad. I was fully determined now to carry her away and make her my wife at once, so as to relieve the poor girl from all imprisonment, to which there seemed no other prospect of an end. And my hopes went still farther; who could tell but that the sight of Blanche living and enjoying life as did others of her sex, might have a beneficial effect upon the poor duke's brain, and help to eradicate his fixed idea.

As I was thus cogitating, the old gentleman rose from his desk, and handed me a letter addressed, but unsealed. His manner was now almost unearthly calm, as if he had come to some great determination, to which he had only been driven by the most dreadful necessity.

'My words are wasted, Charles,' he said, 'and I cannot tell the truth; but if you ever prized home and name, friends and family, mother or wife, send that letter to its address after you have perused it, and await its reply.'

I took the letter and put it into my pocket, and then I took his hand and pressed it warmly. I was truly sorry for the poor old gentleman, who suffered, no doubt, as much from his fancied trouble as if it were the most terrible of realities.

'I hope you will forgive me for grieving you, my dear sir; believe me it pains me much to see you thus. I will do as you wish about the letter. But oh, how I wish you could see Blanche with my eyes! To me she is the most perfect of women!'

'You have *never* seen her yet!' he responded, bitterly, 'could you –
dare you only once witness but a part of her actions under one
influence, you would shudder to your very marrow!'

'To what influence do you allude, dear sir?'

'To that of colour – one colour.'

'And what colour? have you any objection to name it?'

'It is red!' and as the duke answered he turned away abruptly, and
left me standing bewildered, but still unbelieving.

I hastened home that day, anxious to peruse the letter given me
by the duke, and as soon as I had reached my own study drew it from
my pocket and spread it before me. It was addressed to the Prince
d'Alberville, Chateau Gris, Melun, France; and the following were
its singular contents –

> DEAR BROTHER – A terrible necessity for letting another into
> our fearful secret has arisen. A young gentleman of birth and
> fortune has, in spite of my assurances that she is insane, determ-
> ined to wed Blanche. Such a sacrifice cannot be permitted, even
> were such a thing not morally impossible. You are her parent, it
> is then your place to inform this unhappy young man of the
> unspoken curse that rests on our wretched name. I enclose his
> address. Write to him at once.
>
> Your afflicted brother,
> DE ROHAN

I folded up this strange epistle and despatched it; and then I
devoted nearly an hour to pondering over the strange contradictions
of human nature and more particularly diseased human nature. Of
course I carried the key to this poor man's strangeness in my firm
conviction of his insanity, and my entire belief in the martyrdom of
Blanche; yet I could not divest myself of all anxiety to receive a reply
to this letter, a reply which I was certain would explain the duke's
lunacy, and beg of me to pardon it. That is to say if such a party as the
Prince d'Alberville existed at all, and I did not quite lose sight of the
fact that Blanche had assured me that, with the exception of her
uncle, she had not a living relative.

It seemed a long week to me ere the French reply, that made my
hand tremble as I received it, was put into it. I had abstained from
visiting my beloved Blanche, under a determination that I would
not do so until armed with such a letter as I anticipated receiving;
or until I should be able to say, 'ample time for a reply to your communication has elapsed; none has come, give me then my betrothed.'

Here then at last was the letter, and I shut myself into my own room and opened it; the words are engraven on my memory and will never become less vivid.

> SIR – you wish to wed my daughter, the Princess Blanche d'Alberville. Words would vainly try to express the pain with which I expose our disgrace – our horrible secret – to a stranger, but it is to save from a fate worse than death. Blanche d'Alber-ville is an *anthropophagus*, already has one of her own family fallen victim to her thirst for human blood. Spare us if you can, and pray for us.
>
> D'ALBERVILLE

I sat like one turned to stone, and stared at the fearful paper! An anthropophagus! A cannibal! Good heavens, the subject was just now engaging the attention of the medical world in a remarkable degree, in consequence of two frightful and well authenticated cases that had lately occurred in France! All the particulars of these cases, in which I had taken a deep interest, flashed before me, but not for one moment did I credit the frightful story of my beloved. Some detestable plot had been formed against her, for what vile purpose, or with what end in view I was ignorant; and I cast the whole subject from my mind with an effort, and went to attend to my daily round of duties. During the two or three hours that followed, and under the influence of the human suffering I had witnessed, a revolution took place in my feelings, God only knows by what means induced; but when I returned home, to prepare for my eventful visit to the 'white house', a dreadful doubt had stolen into my heart, and filled it with a fearful determination.

Having ordered my carriage and prepared the white suit, which I was now possessor of, I went directly to the conservatory, and looked around among the brilliant array of blossoms for the most suitable to my purpose. I chose the flaring scarlet verbena to form my bouquet; a tasteless one it is true, but one decidedly distinctive in colour. I collected quite a large nosegay of this flower, without a single spray of green to relieve its bright hue. Then I went to my carriage, and gave directions to be driven to Kensington.

At the gate of the Duke's residence I dressed myself in the white suit mechanically, and followed the usual servant into the house, carefully holding my flowers, which I had enveloped in newspaper. I was received as usual, also by the duke, and in a few seconds we stood, face to face in his study. In answer to his look of fearful inquiry

I handed him my French epistle, and stood silently by as he read it tremblingly.

'Well, are you satisfied now?' he asked, looking me pitifully in the face, 'has this dreadful exposure convinced you?'

'No!' I answered, recklessly, 'I am neither satisfied nor convinced of anything save that you are either a lunatic yourself, or in collusion with the writer of that abominable letter!' and as I spoke I uncovered my scarlet bouquet and shook out its blossoms. The sight of it made a terrible impression upon my companion; his knees trembled as if he were about to fall, and his face grew whiter than his garments.

'In the name of heaven what are you going to do?' he gasped.

'I am simply going to present my bride with a bouquet,' I said, and as I said so I laughed, an empty, hollow laugh. I cannot describe my strange state of mind at that moment; I felt as if myself under the influence of some terrible mania.

'By all you hold sacred, Charles Elveston, I charge you to desist! who or what are *you* that you should set your youth, and ignorance of this woman against my age and bitter experience?'

'Ha ha!' was my only response, as I made toward the door.

'By heavens, he is mad!' cried the excited nobleman, 'young man, I tell you that you carry in your hand a colour which had better be shaken in the eyes of a mad bull than be placed in sight of my miserable niece! Fool! I tell you it will arouse in her an unquenchable thirst for blood, and the blood may be yours!'

'Let it!' I cried, and passed on my way to Blanche.

I was conscious of the Duke's cries to the servants as I hurried up the broad staircase, and guessed that they were about to follow me; but to describe my feelings is utterly impossible.

I was beginning now to believe that my betrothed was something terrible, and I faced her desperately, as one who had lost everything worth living for, or placed his last stake upon the cast of a die.

I opened the well-known door of the white room, that seemed to me colder, and more death-like than ever; and I saw the figure of Blanche seated in her old way, and in her old seat, looking out of the window. I did not wait to scan her appearance just then, however, for I caught a glimpse of myself in a large mirror opposite, and was fascinated, as it were by the strange sight.

The mirror reflected, in unbroken stillness, the cold whiteness of the large apartment, but it also reflected my face and form, wearing an expression that half awoke me to a consciousness of physical indisposition. There was a wild look in my pallid countenance, and a reckless air in my figure which the very garments seemed to have imbibed, and which was strangely unlike my usual calm propriety of demeanour. My coat seemed awry; the collar of my shirt was unbuttoned, and I had even neglected to put on my neck-tie; but it was upon the blood-red bouquet that my momentary gaze became riveted.

It was such a contrast; the cold, pure white of all the surroundings, and that circled patch of blood-colour that I held in my hand was so suggestive! 'Of what?' I asked myself, 'am I really mad?' and then I laughed loudly and turned towards Blanche.

Possibly the noise of the opening door had attracted her, for when I turned she was standing on her feet, directly confronting me. Her eyes were distended with astonishment at my peculiar examination of myself in the mirror, no doubt, but they flashed into madness at the sight of the flowers as I turned. Her face grew scarlet, her hands clenched, and her regards *devoured* the scarlet bouquet, as I madly held it towards her. At this moment my eye caught a side glimpse of half-a-dozen terrified faces peeping in the doorway, and conspicuous and foremost that of the poor terrified Duke; but my fate must be accomplished, and I still held the bouquet tauntingly toward the transfixed girl. She gave one wild look into my face, and recognised the sarcasm which I *felt* in my eyes, and then she snatched the flowers from my hand, and scattered them in a thousand pieces at her feet.

How well I remember that picture today. The white room – the torn and brilliant flowers – and the mad fury of that lovely being. A laugh echoed again upon my lips, an involuntary laugh it was, for I knew not that I had laughed; and then there was a rush, and white teeth were at my throat, tearing flesh, and sinews, and veins; and a horrible sound was in my ears, as if some wild animal was tearing at my body! I dreamt that I was in a jungle of Africa, and that a tiger, with a tawny coat, was devouring my still living flesh, and then I became insensible!

When I opened my eyes faintly, I lay in my own bed, and the form of the Duke was bending over me. One of my medical *confrères* held my wrist between his fingers, and the room was still and dark.

'How is this, Bernard?' I asked, with difficulty, for my voice seemed lost, and the weakness of death hanging around my tongue, 'what has happened?'

'Hush!' my dear fellow, you must not speak. You have been nearly worried to death by a maniac, and you have lost a fearful quantity of blood.'

'Oh!' I recollected it all, and turned to the Duke, 'and Blanche?'

'She is dead, thank God!' he whispered, calmly.

I shuddered through every nerve and was silent.

It was many long weeks ere I was able to listen to the Duke as he told the fearful tale of the dead girl's disease. The first intimation her wretched relatives had of the horrible thing was upon the morning of her eighteenth year. They went to her room to congratulate her, and found her lying upon the dead body of her younger sister, who occupied the same chamber; she had literally torn her throat with her teeth, and was sucking the hot blood as she was discovered. No words could describe the horror of the wretched parents. The end we have seen.

I never asked how Blanche had died, I did not wish to know; but I guessed that force had been obliged to be used in dragging her teeth from my throat, and that the necessary force was sufficient to destroy her. I have never since met with a case of anthropophagy, but when I read of the rare discovery of that fearful disease I fancy I feel Blanche's teeth at my throat.

Spirit-Led

Ernest Favenc

Ernest Favenc (1845–1908) is a name that should be better known to aficionados of supernatural fiction. He was born in Surrey, England, and came to Australia in 1864. He worked on stations in North Queensland before leading a number of exploration expeditions in Northern Australia. Later he joined the staff of the Sydney *Evening News* and drew from his experiences in his literary work, which included fiction and non-fiction. He published three collections of short stories, *The Last of Six: Tales of the Austral Tropics* (1893); *Tales of the Austral Tropics* (1894), which includes the stories in the earlier collection with the addition of two others; and *My Only Murder and Other Tales* (1899). All three contain stories of horror and the supernatural, and there are other unpublished tales in contemporary magazines. I've chosen two stories from *Tales of the Austral Tropics*, both of which first appeared in *The Bulletin*, that I hope will give a flavour of this writer's fine sense of the macabre.

Chapter 1

It was the hottest day the Gulf had seen for years. Burning, scorching and blistering heat, beating down directly from the vertical sun, in the open, radiating from the iron roof which provided what was mistakenly called shade. In the whole township there was not a corner to be found where a man could escape the suffocating sense of being in the stoke-hole of a steamer.

The surroundings were not of a nature to be grateful to eyes wearied with the monotony of plain and forest. The few stunted trees that had been spared appeared to be sadly regretting that they had not shared the fate of their comrades, and the barren ironstone ridge on which the township was built gave back all the sun's heat it had previously absorbed with interest.

Two men who had just come in from the country swore that where they crossed the Flinders the alligators came out and begged for a cold drink from their water-bags; and the most confirmed sceptic admitted the existence of a material hell. Naturally there was little or no business doing and, just as naturally, everybody whose inclination pointed that way went 'on the spree'.

Amongst those who had not adopted this mode of killing old father Time were two men in the verandah of the Royal Hotel. (When Australia becomes republican it is to be presumed that a 'Royal' will cease to be the distinguishing feature of every township.)

The two men in question were seated on canvas chairs in the verandah, both lightly attired in shirt and trousers only, busily engaged in mopping the perspiration from their streaming faces, and swearing at the flies.

'Deuced sight hotter lounging about here than travelling,' said Davis, the elder of the two; 'I vote we make a start.'

'I'm agreeable,' replied his companion; 'the horses must be starving out in the paddock. We shall have a job to get Delaine away, though; he's bent on seeing his cheque through.'

'That won't take long at the rate he's going. He's got every loafer in the town hanging about after him.'

'Hullo! what's that?' said the other, as the shrill whistle of a steam launch was heard. 'Oh! of course, the steamer arrived at the mouth of the river last night; that's the launch coming up. Shall we go down and see who is on board?'

The two men got up and joined the stragglers who were wending their way across the bare flat to the bank of the river. The passengers were few in number, but they included some strangers to the place; one of whom, a young-looking man with white hair and beard, immediately attracted Davis' attention.

'See that chap, Bennett?' he said.

'Yes, Dick, who is he?'

'Some years ago he was with me roving for a trip; when we started he was as young-looking as you, and his hair as dark. It's a true bill about a man's hair going white in one night. His did.'

'What from? Fright?'

'Yes. We buried him alive by mistake.'

'The deuce you did!'

'He had a cataleptic fit when he was on watch one night. The other man – we were double-banking the watch at the time – found him as stiff as a poker, and we all thought he was dead, there was no sign of life in him. It was hot weather – as bad as this – and we couldn't keep him, so we dug a grave, and started to bury him at sundown. He came to when we were filling in the grave; yelled blue murder, and frightened the life out of us. His hair that night turned as you see it now, although he vows that it was not the fright of being buried alive that did it.'

'What then?'

'Something that happened when he was in the fit, or trance. He has never told anybody anything more than that he was quite conscious all the time, and had a very strange experience.'

'Ever ask him anything?'

'No; he didn't like talking about it. Wonder what he's doing up here?'

By this time the river bank was deserted; Davis and Bennett strolled up after the others and when they arrived at the Royal, they found the hero of the yarn there before them.

'Hullo, Maxwell,' said Davis, 'what's brought you up this way?'

Maxwell started slightly when he saw his quondam sexton; but he met him frankly enough although at first he disregarded the question that had been asked.

In the course of the conversation that followed Maxwell stated that he was on his way out to the Nicholson River, but with what object did not transpire.

'Bennett and I were just talking of making a start tomorrow, or the next day. Our cattle are spelling on some country just this side of the Nicholson. We can't travel until the wet season comes and goes. You had better come with us.'

'I shall be very glad,' replied the other, and the thing was settled.

Bennett had been looking curiously at this man who had had such a narrow escape of immortality, but beyond the strange whiteness of his hair, which contrasted oddly with the swarthy hue of his sunburnt face, and a nervous look in his eyes, he did not show any trace of his strange experience. On the contrary, he promised, on nearer acquaintance, to be a pleasant travelling companion.

The summer day drew to a close, the red sun sank in the heated haze that hovered immediately above the horizon, and a calm, sultry night, still and oppressive, succeeded the fierce blaze of the daytime. The active and industrious mosquito commenced his rounds, and men tossed and moaned and perspired under nets made of coarse cheese-cloth.

The next morning broke hot and sullen as before. Davis had risen early to send a man out to the paddock after the horses, and was in the bar talking to the pyjama-attired landlord.

'You'll have to knock off his grog or there'll be trouble,' he said; 'he was up all last night wandering about with his belt and revolver on, muttering to himself, and when a fellow does that he's got 'em pretty bad.'

'I'll do what I can, but if he doesn't get drink here he will somewhere else,' replied the other reluctantly.

'Then I'll see the P. M. and get him to prohibit his being served. It's the only way to get him straight.'

At this moment the subject of their remarks entered the bar – a young fellow about five or six and twenty. He was fully dressed, it being evident that he had not gone to bed all night. The whites of his eyes were not blood-shot, but blood-red throughout, and the pupils so dilated that they imparted a look of unnatural horror to his face.

'Hullo, Davis,' he shouted; 'glad to see a white man at last. That old nigger with the white hair has been after me all night. The old buck who was potted in the head. He comes around every night now with his flour-bag cobra all over blood. Can't get a wink of sleep for him. Have a drink?'

His speech was quite distinct, he was past the stage when strong waters thicken the voice; his walk was steady, and but for the wild eyes, he might have passed for a man who was simply tired out with a night's riding or watching.

The landlord glanced enquiringly at Davis, as if to put the responsibility of serving the liquor on him.

'Too early, Delaine, and too hot already; besides, I'm going to start today and mustn't get tight before breakfast,' said the latter soothingly.

'O be hanged! Here, give us something,' and the young fellow turned towards the bar, and as he did so caught sight of Maxwell who had just come to the door and was looking in.

The effect of the dark face and snow-white hair on his excited brain was awful to witness. His eyes, blazing before, seemed now simply coals of fire. Davis and the landlord turned to see what the madman was looking at, and that moment was nearly fatal to the newcomer. Muttering: 'By — , he's taken to following me by daylight as well, has he? But I'll blank soon stop him;' he drew his revolver and, but that Davis turned his head again and was just in time to knock his hand up, Maxwell would have been past praying for. The landlord ran round the bar, and with some trouble the three men got the pistol from the maniac, who raved, bit, and fought, like a wild beast. The doctor, who slept in the house, was called, and, not particularly sober himself, injected some morphia into the patient's arm, which soon sent him into a stupor.

'By Jove, Davis, you saved my life,' said Maxwell; 'that blessed lunatic would have potted me sure enough only for you. Whom did he take me for?'

'He's in the horrors, his name is Delaine, and he's out on a station on the tableland. They had some trouble with the blacks up there lately, and, I suppose, it was the first dispersing-match he had ever seen. There was one white-haired old man got a bullet through his head, and he says he felt as though his own father had been shot when he saw it done. He's a clergyman's son; of course he drinks like a fish and is superstitious as well.'

'I trust they'll lock him up until I get out of the town; but I'll remember your share of this. Wait until we get away and I will tell you what brought me up here, but don't ask me any questions now. Is your friend Bennett to be trusted?'

'In what way? Wine, women or gold? I don't know about the first two, but the last I can answer for.'

'It's a secret. Possibly connected with the last.'

'I hope so, I want some bad enough. I think I know where to put you on to a couple of good horses, and then we'll make a start.'

Chapter 2

The stove-like township is three days journey away; four men, Davis, Bennett, Maxwell, and a blackfellow are camped for the night by the side of a small lagoon covered with the broad leaves of the purple water-lily. In the distance the cheery sound of the horse-bells can be heard, and round the fire the travellers are grouped listening to Maxwell who is telling the tale he has never yet told.

'When I fell down on watch that night and became to all appearance a corpse, I never, for one instant, lost either consciousness or memory. My soul, spirit, or whatever you like to call it, parted company with my body, but I retained all former powers of observation. I gazed at myself lying there motionless, waited until my fellow-watcher came around and awakened the sleeping camp with the tidings of my death, then, without any impulse of my own, I left the spot and found myself in a shadowy realm where all was vague and confused. Strange, indistinct shapes flitted constantly before me; I heard voices and sounds like sobbing and weeping.

'Now, before I go on any further, let me tell you that I have never been subject to these fits. I never studied any occult arts, nor troubled myself about what I called 'such rubbish'. Why this experience should have happened to me I cannot tell. I found I was travelling along pretty swiftly, carried on by some unknown motive power, or, rather, drifting on with a current of misty forms in which all seemed confusion.

'Suddenly, to my surprise, I found myself on the earth once more, in a place quite unknown to me.

'I was in Australia – that much I recognised at a glance – but where abouts?

'I was standing on the bank of a river – a northern river, evidently, for I could see the foliage of the drooping ti-trees and Leichhardt trees further down its course. The surrounding country was open, but barren; immediately in front of me was a rugged range through which the river found its way by means of an apparently impenetrable gorge. The black rocks rose abruptly on either side of a deep pool of water, and all progress was barred except by swimming. The ranges on either hand were precipitous, cleft by deep ravines; all the growth to be seen was spinifex, save a few stunted bloodwood trees.

'What struck me most forcibly was that in the centre of the waterhole, at the entrance of the gorge, as it were, there arose two rocks, like pillars, some twelve or fifteen feet in height above the surface of the water.

'Below the gorge the river-bed was sandy, and the usual timber grew on either bank. At first I thought I was alone, but, on looking around, I found that a man was standing a short distance away from me. Apparently he was a European, but so tanned and burnt by the sun as to be almost copper-coloured. He was partially clothed in skins, and held some hunting weapons in his hand. He was gazing absently into the gorge when I first noticed him, but presently turned, and, without evincing any surprise or curiosity, beckoned to me. Immediately, in obedience to some unknown impulse, I found myself threading the gloomy gorge with him, although, apparently, we exercised no motion. It was more as though we stood still and the rocks glided past us and the water beneath us. We soon reached a small open space or pocket; here there was a rude hut, and here we halted.

'My strange companion looked around and without speaking, drew my attention to a huge boulder close to the hut and on which letters and figures were carved. I made out the principal inscription. "Hendrick Heermans, hier vangecommen, 1670". There were also an anchor, a ship and a heart, all neatly cut. I turned from these records to the man. He beckoned me again, and I followed him

across the small open space and up a ravine. The man pointed to a
reef cropping out and crossing the gully. I looked at it and saw that
the cap had been broken and that gold was showing freely in the
stone. The man waved his hand up the gully as though intimating
that there were more reefs there.

'Suddenly, sweeping up the gorge came a gust of ice-cold wind,
and with it a dash of mist or spray. Looming out of this I saw for a
moment a young girl's face looking earnestly at me. Her lips moved.
"Go back. Go back!" she seemed to whisper.

'When I heard this I felt an irresistible longing to return to my
discarded body and in an instant gorge, mountains and all my
surroundings disappeared, and I found myself in the twilight space
battling despairingly on, for I felt that I had lost my way and should
never find it again.

'How was I to reach my forsaken body through such a vague,
misty and indeterminate land? Impalpable forms threw themselves
in my path. Strange cries and wailings led me astray, and all the
while there was a smell like death in my nostrils, and I knew that I
must return or die.

'O, the unutterable anguish of that time! Ages seem to pass during
which I was fighting with shadows, until at last I saw a sinking sun, an
open grave, and men whose faces I knew, commencing to shovel
earth on a senseless body.

'Mine!

'I had felt no pain when my soul left, but the re-entrance of it into
its tenement was such infinite agony, that it forced from me terrible
cries that caused my rescue from suffocation.'

Maxwell paused, and the other two were silent.

'You will wonder,' he resumed, 'what all this has to do with my
present journey. I will tell you. You remember Milford, a surveyor
up here, at one time he was running the boundary-line between
Queensland and South Australia for the Queensland Government. A
year ago I met him, and we were talking about the country up this
way. In running the line he had to follow the Nicholson up a good
way, until finally he was completely blocked. He described to me the
place where he had to turn back. It was the waterhole in the gorge
with the two rock-like pillars rising out of the water.'

Again there was silence for a while, then Davis said musingly –

'It's impossible to pronounce any opinion at present; the coincidence of Milford's report is certainly startling. But why should this
sign have been vouchsafed to you? Apparently this being you saw

was the ghost of some old Dutch sailor wrecked or marooned here in the days of the early discovery of Australia. Had you any ancestors among those gentry?'

'Not that I am aware of,' returned Maxwell, 'but if we find the place we shall certainly make some interesting discovery, apart from any gold.'

'And the girl's face?' enquired Bennett.

Maxwell did not answer for a minute or two.

'I may as well tell you all,' he said then; 'I was in Melbourne, after I saw Milford, and I met a girl with that same face, in the street. Strange, too, we could not help looking at each other as though we knew we had met before. That meeting decided me on taking the trip up here. Now, that is really all. Are you ready for the adventure?'

'I should think so,' said Davis; 'we have fresh horses at the camp, and nothing to do with ourselves for three months or more. Please God, on Christmas Day we'll be on Tom Tiddler's ground picking up gold in chunks.'

'One question more,' put in Bennett. 'Have you ever had any return of these trances or cataleptic fits?'

'Never since, not the slightest sign of one.'

Chapter 3

There was no doubt about the strange proof or coincidence, whichever it should turn out to be. The three men stood on the bank of the Nicholson River gazing at the gorge and the waterhole, from the bosom of which rose the two upright pillars of rock. Two weeks had elapsed since they were camped at the lagoon.

'It is the same place,' muttered Maxwell, and, as the overwhelming horror of his fight through shadowland came back to him, he leant on his horse's shoulder and bowed his head down on the mane.

Bennett made a sign to Davis and both men were silent for a while, then Davis spoke –

'Well, old man, as we are not possessed of the supernatural power you had when you were last here, we'll have to get over that range somehow.'

Maxwell lifted his head. 'We shall have to tackle the range, but I expect we shall have a job to get the horses over. How about leaving them here in hobbles and going up on foot?'

'Not to be thought of,' replied Davis; 'why, the niggers' tracks just back there in the bed of the river, are as thick as sheep-tracks.

The horses would be speared before we got five miles away. I know these beggars.'

'That's true,' said Bennett.

Davis eyed the range curiously for some time. 'There's a spur there that we can work our way up, I think,' he said at last, indicating with his hand the spot he meant. The other two, after a short inspection, agreed with him. It was then nearly noon, so the horses were turned out for a couple of hours' spell, a fire lit and the billy boiled.

'What could have led your Dutch sailor up this way?' said Davis as, the meal over, they were enjoying an after-dinner pipe.

'That is what has puzzled me. I have read up everything I could get hold of on the subject of Dutch discovery and can find no record of any ship visiting the Gulf about that date,' replied Maxwell.

'There may have been plenty of ships here, of which neither captain nor crew wanted a record kept. Those were the days of the buccaneers,' said Bennett.

'Yes, but with the exception of the ship Dampier was on board of, they did not come out of their way to New Holland,' returned Maxwell.

'The *Bachelor's Delight* and the *Cygnet* were on the west coast, as you say; why not others who had not the luck to be associated with the immortal Dampier?'

'True; but the Dutch were not noted as buccaneers. However, plenty of ships may have been lost in the Gulf of which all record has disappeared. The question is, what brought the man up into this region?' said Davis.

'I firmly believe we shall find the clue to that secret, when we find the ravine. It seems incredible that a shipwrecked or marooned man should have left the sea-coast, whereon was his only hope of salvation and have made south into an unknown land, through such a range as this.'

'Well, boys, we'll make a start for it,' said Davis, jumping up; and the party were soon in their saddles.

The range proved pretty stiff climbing, and they were so often baulked, and forced to retrace their steps, that it was sundown before they reached the top.

* * *

It was a desolate outlook for a camp. A rough tableland of spinifex – evidently extending too far for them to attempt to go on and descend the other side before darkness set in – lay before them.

'Nothing for it but to go on and tie the horses up all night,' said Bennett. Fortune, however, favoured them; in about a mile they came on a small patch of grass, sufficient for the horses, and as their water-bags were full, they gladly turned out.

For a time the conversation turned on their expectations for the morrow, but gradually it dropped, as the fire died down. One by one the stars in their courses looked down through the openings of the tree-tops on the wanderers sleeping below, and silence, save for the occasional clink of a hobble, reigned supreme until the first flush of dawn.

'Well, Maxwell,' said Davis, as they were discussing breakfast, 'hear anything from your old Dutch navigator last night?'

'No, but I had some confused sort of dream again about this place; I thought I heard that voice once more telling me to "go back". But that, of course, is only natural.'

'I think we are close to the spot,' remarked Bennett. 'When I was after the horses this morning I could see down into the river, and there appeared to be an open pocket there.'

Bennett proved right. In half-an-hour's time they were scrambling down the range, and soon stood in an open space that Maxwell at once identified.

Naturally everybody was slightly excited. Although at first inclined to put the story down to hallucination, the subsequent events had certainly shaken this belief in the minds of the two friends. Maxwell silently pointed to the boulder; there was something carved on it, but it was worn and indistinct. Two centuries of weather had almost obliterated whatever marks had been there.

'They were fresh and distinct when I saw them,' said Maxwell, in an awed voice.

By diligent scrutiny they made out the inscription that he had repeated, but had they not known it the task would have been most difficult. The words had not been very deeply marked, and the face of the boulder fronting north-west, the full force of the wet seasons had been experienced by the inscription.

'This is a wonderful thing,' said Davis. 'There can be no doubt as to the age of that.'

'Let's go up the ravine and look for the reef and then get back as soon as possible. I don't like this place. I wish I had not come,' returned Maxwell.

They left the packhorses feeding about and rode up the gully, taking with them the pick and shovel they had brought. 'It was here, I think,' said Maxwell, looking around; 'but the place seems altered.'

'Very likely the creek would change its course slightly in a couple of hundred years, but not much. That looks like an outcrop there.'

'This is the place,' said Maxwell, eagerly, 'I know it now, but it is a little changed.'

The three dismounted, and Davis, taking the pick, struck the cap of the reef with the head of it, knocking off some lumps of stone. As he did so a wild 'Holloa!' rang up the gully. All started and looked at each other with faces suddenly white and hearts quickly beating. There was something uncanny in such a cry rising out of the surrounding solitude.

'Blacks?' said Bennett, doubtfully. Davis shook his head. Once more the loud shout was raised, apparently coming from the direction of the inscribed rock.

'Let's go and see what it is, anyway,' said Davis – and they mounted and rode down the gully again, Bennett, who had picked up a bit of the quartz, putting it into his saddle-pouch as they rode along.

Maxwell had not spoken since the cry had been heard, his face was pale and occasionally he muttered to himself, 'Go back, go back!' The packhorses were quietly cropping what scanty grass there was; all seemed peaceful and quiet.

'I believe it was a bird after all; there's a kind of toucan makes a devil of a row – have a look round old man,' said Davis to Bennett, and they both rode up and down the bank of the river, leaving Maxwell standing near the rock where he had dismounted. Nothing could be seen, and the two returned and proposed going up the gully again.

'You fellows go and come back again, I want to get out of this – I'm upset,' said Maxwell, speaking for the first time in a constrained voice.

Davis glanced at his friend. 'Right you are, old man, no wonder you don't feel well; we'll just make sure of the reef and come back. If you want us, fire your pistol; we shan't be far off.'

The two rode back to their disturbed work and hastily commenced their examination of the stone. There was no doubt about the richness of the find, and the reef could be traced a good distance without much trouble. They had collected a small heap of specimens to take back, when suddenly the loud 'Holloa!' once more came pealing up the gully followed instantly by a fainter cry and two revolver-shots.

Hastily mounting, the two galloped back.

The packhorses, as if startled, were walking along their tracks towards home, followed by Maxwell's horse with the bridle trailing; its rider was stretched on the ground; nothing else was visible.

Jumping from their horses they approached the prostrate man. Both started and stared at each other with terror-stricken eyes. Before them lay a skeleton clad in Maxwell's clothes.

'Are we mad?' cried Davis, aghast with horror.

The fierce sun was above them, the bare mountains around, they could hear the horses clattering up the range as if anxious to leave the accursed place, and before them lay a skeleton with the shrunken skin still adhering to it in places, a corpse that had been rotting for years; that had relapsed into the state it would have been had the former trance been death. Blind terror seized them both, and they mounted to follow the horses when an awful voice came from the fleshless lips: 'Stay with me, stop! I may come back; I may – '

Bennett could hear no more, he stuck the spurs in his horse and galloped off. Davis would have followed but he was transfixed with terror at what he saw. The awful object was moving, the outcast spirit was striving desperately to reanimate the body that had suddenly fallen into decay. The watcher was chained to the spot. Once it seemed that the horrible thing was really going to rise, but the struggle was unavailing, with a loud moan of keenest agony and despair that thrilled the listener's brain with terror it fell back silent and motionless. Davis remembered nothing more till he found himself urging his horse up the range. The place has never been revisited.

*   *   *

In an asylum for the insane in a southern town there is a patient named Bennett, who is always talking of the wonderful reef he has up North. He has a specimen of quartz, very rich, which he never parts with day or night. He is often visited by a man named Davis, who nursed him through a severe attack of fever out on the Nicholson. The doctors think he may yet recover.

A Haunt of the Jinkarras

ERNEST FAVENC

In May, 1889, the dead body of a man was found on one of the tributaries of the Finke River, in the extreme North of South Australia. The body, by all appearances, had been lying there some months and was accidentally discovered by explorers making a flying survey with camels. Amongst the few effects was a Letts Diary containing the following narration, which although in many places almost illegible and much weather-stained, has been since, with some trouble, deciphered and transcribed by the surveyor in charge of the party, and forwarded to *The Bulletin* for publication.

[*transcribed from the dead man's diary*]

March 10, 1888 – Started out this morning with Jackson, the only survivor of a party of three who lost their horses on a dry stage when looking for country – he was found and cared for by the blacks, and finally made his way into the line where I picked him up when out with a repairing-party. Since then I got him a job on the station, and in return he has told me about the ruby-field of which we are now in search; and thanks to the late thunder-storms we have as yet met with no obstacles to our progress. I have great faith in him, but he being a man without any education and naturally taciturn, is not very lively company, and I find myself thrown on to the resource of a diary for amusement.

March 17 – Seven days since we left Charlotte Waters, and we are now approaching the country familiar to Jackson during his sojourn with the natives two years ago. He is confident that we shall gain the gorge in the Macdonnell Ranges tomorrow, early.

March 18 – Amongst the ranges, plenty of water, and Jackson has recognised several peaks in the near neighbourhood of the gorge, where he saw the rubies.

March 19 – Camped in Ruby Gorge, as I have named this pass, for we have come straight to the place and found the rubies without any hindrance at all. I have about twenty magnificent stones and hundreds of small ones; one of the stones in particular is almost living fire, and must be of great value. Jackson has no idea of the value of the find, except that it may be worth a few pounds, with which he will be quite satisfied. As there is good feed and water, and we have plenty of rations, will camp here for a day or two and spell the horses before returning.

March 20 – Been examining some caves in the ranges. One of them seems to penetrate a great distance – will go tomorrow with Jackson and take candles and examine it.

March 25 – Had a terrible experience the last four days. Why on earth did I not go back at once with the rubies? Now I may never get back. Jackson and I started to explore this cave early in the morning. We found nothing extraordinary about it for some time. As usual, there were numbers of bats, and here and there were marks of fire on the rocks, as though the natives had camped there at times. After some searching about, Jackson discovered a passage which we followed down a steep incline for a long distance. As we got on we encountered a strong draught of air and had to be very careful of our candles. Suddenly the passage opened out and we found ourselves in a low chamber in which we could not stand upright. I looked hastily around, and saw a dark figure like a large monkey suddenly spring from a rock and disappear with what sounded like a splash. 'What on earth was that?' I said to Jackson. 'A jinkarra,' he replied, in his slow, stolid way. 'I heard about them from the blacks; they live underground.' 'What are they?' I asked. 'I couldn't make out,' he replied; 'the blacks talked about jinkarras, and made signs that they were underground, so I suppose that was one.'

We went over to the place where I had seen the figure and, as the air was now comparatively still and fresh, our candles burnt well and we could see plainly. The splash was no illusion, for an underground stream of some size ran through the chamber, and on looking closer, in the sand on the floor of the cavern, were tracks like a human foot.

We sat down and had something to eat. The water was beautifully fresh and icily cold, and I tried to obtain from Jackson all he knew about the jinkarras. It was very little beyond what he had already told me. The natives spoke of them as something, animals or men, he could not make out which, living in the ranges underground. They used to frighten the children by crying out 'jinkarra!' to them at night.

The stream that flowed through the cavern was very sluggish and apparently not deep, as I could see the white sand at a distance under the rays of the candle; it disappeared under a rocky arch about two feet above its surface. Strange to say when near this arch I could smell a peculiar pungent smell like something burning, and this odour appeared to come through the arch. I drew Jackson's attention to it and proposed wading down the channel of the stream if not too deep, but he suggested going back to camp first and getting more rations, which, being very reasonable, I agreed to.

It took us too long to get back to camp to think of starting that day, but next morning we got away early and were soon beside the subterranean stream. The water was bitterly cold but not very deep, and we had provided ourselves with stout saplings as poles and had our revolvers and some rations strapped on our shoulders. It was an awful wade through the chill water, our heads nearly touching the slimy top of the arch, our candles throwing a faint, flickering gleam on the surface of the stream; fortunately the bottom was splendid – hard, smooth sand – and after wading for about 20 minutes we suddenly emerged into another cavern, but its extent we could not discern at first for our attention was taken up with other matters.

The air was laden with pungent smoke, the place illuminated with a score of smouldering fires, and tenanted by a crowd of the most hideous beings I ever saw. They espied us in an instant, and flew wildly about, jabbering frantically, until we were nearly deafened. Recovering ourselves we waded out of the water, and tried to approach some of these creatures, but they hid away in the darker corners, and we couldn't lay hands on any of them. As well as we could make out in the murky light they were human beings, but savages of the most degraded type, far below the ordinary Australian blackfellow. They had long arms, shaggy heads of hair, small twinkling eyes, and were very low of stature. They kept up a confused jabber, half whistling, half chattering, and were utterly without clothes, paint, or any ornaments. I approached one of their fires, and found it to consist of a kind of peat or turf; some small bones of vermin were lying around, and a rude club or two. While gazing at these things I suddenly heard a piercing shriek, and, looking up, found that Jackson, by a sudden spring, had succeeded in capturing one of these creatures, who was struggling and uttering terrible yells. I went to his assistance, and together we succeeded in holding him still while we examined him by the light of our candles. The others, meanwhile dropped their clamour and watched us curiously.

Never did I see such a repulsive wretch as our prisoner. Apparently he was a young man about two or three and twenty, only five feet high at the outside, lean, with thin legs and long arms. He was trembling all over, and the perspiration dripped from him. He had scarcely any forehead, and a shaggy mass of hair crowned his head, and grew a long way down his spine. His eyes were small, red and bloodshot; I have often experienced the strong odour emitted by the ordinary blackfellow when heated or excited, but never did I smell anything so offensive as the rank smell emanating from this creature. Suddenly Jackson exclaimed: 'Look! look! he's got a tail!' I looked and nearly relaxed my grasp of the brute in surprise. There was no doubt about it, this strange being had about three inches of a monkey-like tail.

'Let's catch another,' I said to Jackson after the first emotion of surprise had passed. We looked around after putting our candles upright in the sand. 'There's one in that corner,' muttered Jackson to me, and as soon as I spotted the one he meant we released our prisoner and made a simultaneous rush at the cowering form. We were successful, and when we dragged our captive to the light we found it to be a woman. Our curiosity was soon satisfied – the tail was the badge of the whole tribe, and we let our second captive go.

My first impulse was to go and rinse my hands in the stream, for the contact had been repulsive to me. Jackson did the same, saying as he did so – 'Those fellows I lived with were bad enough, but I never smelt anything like these brutes.' I pondered what I should do. I had a great desire to take one of these singular beings back with me, and I thought with pride of the reputation I should gain as their discoverer. Then I reflected that I could always find them again, and it would be better to come back with a larger party after safely disposing of the rubies and securing the ground.

'There's no way out of this place,' I said to Jackson.

'Think not?' he replied.

'No,' I said, 'or these things would have cleared out; they must know every nook and cranny.'

'Umph!' he said, as though satisfied; 'shall we go back now?'

I was on the point of saying yes, and had I done so all would have been well; but, unfortunately, some motive of infernal curiosity prompted me to say – 'No! let us have a look round first.' Lighting another candle each, so that we had plenty of light, we wandered round the cave, which was of considerable extent, the unclean inhabitants flitting before us with beast-like cries. Presently we had made a half-circuit of the cave and were approaching the stream, for we could hear a rushing sound as though it plunged over a fall. This noise grew louder, and now I noticed that all the natives had disappeared, and it struck me that they had retreated through the passage we had penetrated, which was now unguarded. Suddenly Jackson, who was ahead, exclaimed that there was a large opening. As he spoke he turned to enter it; I called out to him to be careful but my voice was lost in a cry of alarm as he slipped, stumbled, and with a shriek of horror disappeared from my view. So sudden was the shock, and so awful my surroundings, that I sank down utterly unnerved comprehending but one thing: that I was alone in this gruesome cavern inhabited by strange, unnatural creations.

After a while I pulled myself together and began to look around. Holding my candle aloft I crawled on my stomach to where my companion had disappeared. My hand touched a slippery decline; peering cautiously down I saw that the rocks sloped abruptly downwards and were covered with slime as though under water at times. One step on the treacherous surface and a man's doom was sealed – headlong into the unknown abyss below he was bound to go, and this had been the fate of the unhappy Jackson. As I lay trembling on the edge of this fatal chasm listening for the faintest sound from below, it struck me that the noise of the rushing water was both louder and nearer. I lay and listened. There was no doubt about it – the waters were rising. With a thrill of deadly horror it flashed across me that if the stream rose it would prevent my return as I could not thread the subterranean passage under water. Rising hastily I hurried back to the upper end of the cavern following the edge of the water. A glance assured me I was a prisoner, the water was up to the top of the arch, and the stream much broader than when we entered. The rations and candles we had left carelessly on the sand had disappeared, covered by the rising water. I was alone, with nothing but about a candle and a half between me and darkness and death.

I blew out the candle, threw myself on the sand and thought. I brought all my courage to bear not to let the prospect daunt me. First, the natives had evidently retreated before the water rose too high, their fires were all out and a dead silence reigned. I had the cavern to myself, this was better than their horrid company. Next, the rising was periodical, and evidently was the cause of the slimy, slippery rock which had robbed me of my only companion. I remembered instances in the interior where lagoons rose and fell at certain times without any visible cause. Then came the thought, for how long would the overflow continue. I had fresh air and plenty of water, I could live days; probably the flood only lasted twelve or twenty-four hours. But an awful fear seized on me. Could I maintain my reason in this worse than Egyptian darkness – a darkness so thick, definite and overpowering that I cannot describe it, truly a darkness that could be felt? I had heard of men who could not stand twenty-four hours in a dark cell, but had clamoured to be taken out. Supposing my reason deserted me, and during some delirious interlude the stream fell and rose again.

These thoughts were too agonising. I rose and paced a step or two on the sand. I made a resolution during that short walk. I had matches – fortunately, with a bushman's instinct, I had put a box in my pouch when we started to investigate the cavern. I had a candle and a-half, and I had, thank Heaven! my watch. I would calculate four hours as nearly as possible, and every four hours I would light my candle and enjoy the luxury of a little light. I stuck to this, and by doing so left that devilish pit with reason. It was sixty hours before the stream fell, and what I suffered during that time no tongue could tell, no brain imagine.

That awful darkness was at times peopled by forms that, for hideous horror, no nightmare could surpass. Invisible, but still palpably present, they surrounded and sought to drive me down the chasm wherein my companion had fallen. The loathsome inhabitants of that cavern came back in fancy and gibbered and whistled around me. I could smell them, feel their sickening touch. If I slept I awoke from, perhaps, a pleasant dream to the stern fact that I was alone in darkness in the depth of the earth. When first I found that the water was receding was perhaps the hardest time of all, for my anxiety to leave the chamber tenanted by such phantoms, was overpowering. But I resisted. I held to my will until I knew I could safely venture, and then waded slowly and determinedly up the stream; up the sloping passage, through the outer-cave, and emerged into the light of day – the blessed glorious light, with a wild shout of joy.

I must have fainted; when I came to myself I was still at the mouth of the cave, but now it was night, the bright, starlit, lonely, silent night of the Australian desert. I felt no hunger nor fear of the future; one delicious sense of rest and relief thrilled my whole being. I lay there watching the dearly-loved Austral constellations in simple, peaceful ecstasy. And then I slept, slept till the sun aroused me, and I arose and took my way to our deserted camp. A few crows arose and cawed defiantly at me, and the leather straps bore the marks of a dingo's teeth, otherwise the camp was untouched. I lit a fire, cooked a meal, ate and rested once more. The reaction had set in after the intense strain I had endured, and I felt myself incapable of thinking or purposing anything.

This state lasted for four and twenty hours – then I awoke to the fact that I had to find the horses, and make my way home alone – for, alas, as I bitterly thought, I was now, through my curiosity, alone, and, worst of all, the cause of my companion's death. Had I come away when he proposed, he would be alive, and I should have escaped the awful experience I have endured.

I have written this down while it is fresh in my memory; tomorrow I start to look for the horses. If I reach the telegraph-line safely I will come back and follow up the discovery of this unknown race, the connecting and long-sought-for link; if not, somebody else may find this and follow up the clue. I have plotted out the course from Charlotte Waters here by dead-reckoning.

March 26th: No sign of the horses. They have evidently made back. I will make up a light pack and follow them. If I do not overtake them I may be able to get on to the line on foot.

[end of the diary]

Note – The surveyor, who is well-known in South Australia, adds the following postscript –

The unfortunate man was identified as an operator on the overland line. He had been in the service a long time, and was very much liked. The facts about picking up Jackson when out with a repairing party have also been verified. The dead man had obtained six months' leave of absence, and it was supposed he had gone down to Adelaide. The tradition of the jinkarras is common among the natives of the Macdonnell Range. I have often heard it. No rubies or anything of value were found on the body. I, of course, made an attempt to get out, but was turned back by the terrible drought then raging. As it is now broken, I am off, and by the time this reaches you shall perhaps be on the spot.

The Mystery of Major Molineux

Marcus Clarke

Marcus Clarke (1846–1881) was born in England and educated at Cholmely Grammar School, Highgate. Following his father's death in 1863, he emigrated to Australia where he settled in Melbourne. In his early days he was heavily involved in the Bohemian life of Melbourne. He became a sub-librarian at the State Library of Victoria and wrote extensively for the Australian press. He was editor of some Melbourne magazines and wrote his novels for them as serials as well as many short stories; one of these novels was *His Natural Life*, which was serialised in the *Australian Journal* in 1870 and published, substantially revised, in book form in 1874. A tale of wrongful imprisonment, rape, murder and cannibalism, *His Natural Life* has become an Australian classic. Clarke was also heavily involved in the theatre and he married the actress Marian Dunn in 1869. His hectic lifestyle led to bouts of anxiety and illness, which were exacerbated by insolvency in 1874 and 1881. Nevertheless, some of his best work was done in the few years before his early death in 1881 of erysipelas, including 'The Mystery of Major Molineux' which was published posthumously in *The Mystery of Major Molineux, and Human Repetends* (Melbourne, 1881).

Prologue
[*extracted from the Diary of an Army-Surgeon*]

HOBART TOWN, 6th August, 1839

I have come to the conclusion today that the strange behaviour of Major Molineux has something in it which is quite beyond ordinary eccentricity. I think that I have found in him a case worth studying.

When I arrived here, ten weeks ago, from Calcutta, I was insufferably bored with the place, and cursed Grosscot for inducing me to visit it. An officer of Irregular Horse may find some enjoyment in playing billiards at the Ship, or in drinking brandy and water at the barracks, but for a man of forty, compelled to take compulsory leave of a profession in which he delights, Hobart Town possesses few charms. When I prescribed a dose of quietness and pure air for myself, I did not intend to live utterly without intellectual society; but the old Major has given me something to think about.

Let me first describe him. He is a tall, thin, muscular man, of commanding presence and military bearing. He has white hair, a white moustache, and a very red face. He is always tightly buttoned and braced. He carries a thick stick, and wears buff gloves – a common sort of fashion enough for retired officers. But with all this there is something more. His blue eyes are always withdrawing themselves from you to furtively glance behind you. I have turned round a dozen times, when playing whist with him, to see if anybody was overlooking my hand. His large, long, white fingers are perpetually twitching and working, and he has a habit of drawing one hand through the other, as though to disencumber himself of a glove. His voice is singularly low and soft for so large a man. You expect, from his manner of walking and sitting, that he will presently roar out at you, but he speaks in a singularly apologetic sort of way, in an undertone, and without any assertion of authority.

The most curious idiosyncracy of Major Molineux, however, is this: he ceases to be on each Thursday in the week.

A constant visitor to the Union Club, I have observed that the Major never makes his appearance on that day. Suggesting to McBride (manager of the Derwent Bank) that perhaps the old gentleman was unwell, I was told that he never appears on Thursdays. Debating with Johnstone (of the — 1st) if it would be well to ride over and visit the invalid, I was told that the Major never receives visitors on Thursdays, and being anxious to send a small cheque for a night's losings at whist, on Wednesday, I was told by the postmaster that I might as well wait until Friday, as no letters were taken in at Castle Stuart on Thursday morning.

Castle Stuart is a huge, colonial-built, red-brick house on the road to New Norfolk. It is sunk in a spacious bush-park, not unadorned with shrubs and trees planted at some expense. The stables are unusually large, and the out-houses almost like barracks. In former days the Major kept a large household, but since the sudden death of an orphan niece, to whom he was much attached, he has persistently refused to entertain company, and contented himself with the humblest retinue. An old man, and a woman still older who acts as cook, are, with their master, the sole inmates of Castle Stuart.

It can readily be understood that this condition of affairs has given rise to some comment. Hobart Town is not a large place, and, as the society consists almost entirely of military officers and the civil service, the strange conduct of the Major has been food for scandal during many a day. He, however, appears to busy himself but little with the conjectures concerning him. He rides into town twice a week for his rubber of whist, and, apart from his day of seclusion, comports himself like every other half-pay officer in similar circumstances. Bagally, the man, and Mary Pennithorne, the maid, are deaf to all hints and persuasions. Indeed, the old woman is almost imbecile, and the man, a queer, wizened old rascal – a manumitted convict – who walks lame and has a trick of talking to himself – professes to know nothing whatever concerning his master's eccentricity.

Now, there is nothing very remarkable in an old bachelor, who has lost the only person for whom he may be presumed to care, keeping a sparse table and living an inexpensive life. But this weekly seclusion is a puzzle to the whole community. No one seems to think that the Major has had any event of importance happen to him on a Thursday, nor that it is necessary or proper for him to shut out, at that particular time, the world and its surroundings. The death of Miss Tremayne occurred on a Monday, and, moreover, it was noticed – so they tell me – that the Major had begun to avoid society on Thursdays before that sad event took place.

The first time that this remarkable dislike to be seen abroad on the fifth day of the week openly manifested itself was – I am informed at the club – at a levee given by Governor Arthur on the occasion of his arrival. Everybody in the city who had any pretensions to social rank attended as a matter of course, and no military or naval officer could have absented himself without causing the gravest scandal. Major Molineux attended, but his behaviour was said to be most extraordinary.

His carriage drove up to Government House with the blinds closely drawn. After some seconds, the door was opened and the Major, dressed in full uniform, and leaning on the arm of Miss Tremayne, appeared. His face was, in strong contrast to its customary hue, of a death-like paleness, and a clammy perspiration beaded his brow. On stepping out into the light he placed his hand before his eyes, as though to shade them from the sun, and then drew himself up with an effort, as though nerving himself for some dreadful task. He pressed his niece's hand with the air of one who might take an eternal farewell, and then tottered, rather than walked, through the corridor. He passed through the special door set apart for those having official cards of entry, and, making his way straight for the dais, attempted to tender his respects to the representative of his Sovereign. His Excellency, who had heard of Major Molineux's services, would have detained him with some words of kindly recognition, but, at the moment he stretched out his hand, the Major paused, and fixing his eyes on the group behind the Governor, seemed as though about to utter some startling announcement. His mouth remained open, but no sound issued from it, while the convulsive working of his features betrayed some powerful emotion. One of Colonel Arthur's staff stepped forward and took the unfortunate gentleman by the arm. The contact seemed to recall him to himself, and, stammering some incoherent excuse, he allowed himself to be led to his carriage, where his niece waited for him in an evident condition of anxiety.

The next morning he called on the Governor and explained that a sudden indisposition, for which he could not account, had prostrated for the moment his physical powers. His excuses were, of course, accepted, with many expressions of regret for his illness, but since that day he has never quitted his house on a Thursday. Some months afterwards Miss Tremayne died, and the Major then dismissed his servants and commenced to lead the solitary and strange existence in which I found him.

Chapter 1

I have just read the above, which was written nearly forty years ago, when I was on a visit to Hobart Town to recruit my health, which a long residence in India with the regiment to which I had been attached as surgeon had considerably impaired. For reasons which will, in the course of this narrative, be apparent to the reader, I found it inconvenient to continue any daily record of one of the most remarkable cases which ever came under my experience. Indeed, it became – as will be seen – advisable that there should be no written statement extant of Major Molineux's misfortune, and for half a lifetime I have put away my knowledge of the facts as one puts away some family secret. But the sight of the faded ink of my diary, and the certainty that, ere long, I shall be incapable of narrating the occurrences which influenced the whole of my subsequent career in life, have induced me to briefly state as much as I may of one of the saddest and most terrible histories ever confided to a professional ear.

JULIUS FAYRE, M.D.
Late Surgeon-Major

Apart from the peculiarity which I have recorded in my diary, no man could be more courteous than Major Molineux, and few more entertaining. He did not ask me to Castle Stuart, it is true, but he was good enough to devote many mornings to making me acquainted with the beauties of the country more immediately surrounding Hobart Town, and entertained me by many amusing anecdotes of early colonial days. He, too, had been in India in early manhood, and we passed many a pleasant hour in comparing notes as to our travels and experiences in that wonderful country. Entering the army at an age when most men are fagging in the cricket field, or spelling out their daily modicum of Horace, Major Molineux had seen much service in many countries. His genial manner, soft voice, and digni-fied bearing added much to the charm of his narratives.

Though for the most part self-educated, as must necessarily be the case when a man enters early on the business of life, he had accumulated more than considerable information on many topics not generally touched upon save by very active minds. In addition to his fund of anecdote, and his acquaintance with what may not inaptly be called the personal history of our more celebrated military campaigns, he was a naturalist of no mean attainments, an accom-plished taxidermist, well read in the literature of natural science, and possessed of by no means a contemptible knowledge of physiology. I was agreeably surprised one day, shortly after our first acquaintance, to find that his response to some casual remark of mine, upon an experiment recorded in a medical journal which I had received from England, betrayed an acquaintance with the subject which would have been notable even in a professional man, but which, coming from a layman, was quite remarkable.

'Yes,' said he, in reply to my query, 'I take a great interest in matters of that nature – a very great interest.'

He seemed about to say more, but turned the conversation abruptly, nor could he be afterwards brought to resume the discussion.

One other subject was, as a matter of course, taboo between us – the existence of such a day of the week as Thursday. I once purposely mentioned the day, affecting not to be aware of his antipathy to it, but the result forbade me to repeat the experiment. Major Molineux became visibly disturbed. The colour left his face, and he trembled violently. His appearance, in fact, was that of a man who had just received some nervous shock, or who had unexpectedly swallowed some nauseous and poisonous substance. He recovered himself with difficulty, and took occasion to make a hasty departure. He did not wholly resume his friendly relations with me for some days, being apparently fearful lest, by inadvertence, I should again offend, and though my curiosity was piqued almost beyond endurance, I took care not to risk the loss of so polished an acquaintance by impertinent intrusion into that which, after all, was no business of mine.

The time passed pleasantly. Our bi-weekly 'rubbers' and our almost daily conversations continued, to our common content. My leave had nearly expired, and I had already begun to make preparations for carrying my reinvigorated liver back to the land of hepatalgia, when one of those accidents which are the providences of romance occurred.

The next neighbour of Major Molineux was a gentleman named Rochford. He too had been in the King's service, and like my friend had sold out, in order to settle down upon the fine estate which he had acquired under the operation of the colonial land laws. Captain Rochford – for he assumed brevet rank on the sale of his lieutenant's commission – owned a somewhat similar house to that of Major Molineux, for all the houses in that colonial day were built on the same plan, and after the same pattern. But the cheerful residence of Captain Rochford was in marked contrast to the gloomy mansion and overgrown garden of the owner of Castle Stuart. Not only were the grounds of Ashmead Park kept in the completest horticultural condition, but the house was enlivened by a constant gaiety, in which the good magistrate's charming daughter took a conspicuous part.

Miss Beatrice Rochford was, when I first knew her, a beautiful young girl of sixteen, having at once that exquisite complexion and that nobly rounded figure the possession of which makes the native-born of the most delightful of the Australasian colonies a sort of commingling of Devonshire loveliness of face with Spanish splendour of form. She was the only child, and both her father and her mother spoiled her. Allowed to have her own way in everything, she would have grown up without culture, and almost without education, had it not been for the more than sisterly friendship displayed by Miss Tremayne. While Miss Tremayne lived she exercised over the excitable and impetuous nature of Beatrice an influence greater than that of any other person.

From all that I could gather, Agnes Tremayne had been a girl of rare promise. Miss Rochford told me that all she knew of music – and she played brilliantly – had been taught her by her dead friend, and her mother confidentially informed me that, had it not been for the Major's niece insisting that Beatrice should share her studies, the water-colour drawings which decorated the breakfast-room at Ashmead would never have been executed.

One day Miss Rochford showed me a portrait of Agnes Tremayne. It was a miniature, very beautifully painted on ivory by the celebrated Wainwright, and represented a fair girl with lofty forehead and large grey eyes.

'A refined and delicate face,' was my comment as I handed back the picture.

'And a good face,' said the impetuous Beatrice, kissing the miniature 'No one knows what she endured in that dreadful house.'

'You rouse my curiosity,' I said. 'What is this mystery concerning Major Molineux?'

'I don't know,' said Miss Rochford. 'I think poor Agnes knew, and the knowledge killed her. You are aware that they say the house is haunted.'

'They say that of all houses which are shut up. Pray what shape does the familiar spirit take?'

'You laugh, of course, Dr Fayre, but, nevertheless, there is something horrible to me about Castle Stuart. The closed windows, the desolate garden, that horrible old cripple, and Mary Pennithorne, with her toothless mouth – ugh! the thought of it makes me shudder.'

'But, my dear young lady, there is nothing horrible in lameness, and though the absence of teeth may render Mrs Pennithorne unsightly, the poor woman is to be pitied rather than shuddered at.'

'Of course. But I cannot help shuddering at ugly things. Even the Major, for all his soft voice and smooth ways, is sometimes repulsive to me. I think of him shut up in that lonely place every Thursday in the week, and wonder what horrible act of wickedness he is committing, or what dreadful penance he is inflicting on himself for some past crime.'

'You have never been to the house, then?'

'Never since poor Agnes's death. Nor would I go even if I was asked. I rode up once to escape a thunderstorm, and went round to the back of the stables. They were empty; the windows of the rooms were boarded up, and not a creature was about the place, not even a dog. When I turned the corner, I could see the room which had once been Agnes's bedroom. The curtains had been taken down, and the window was wide open, like a great blankly-staring Eye. It was horrible, and I turned Sultan round, and never drew rein until I was at our own park gates.'

'But this is mere fancy, Miss Rochford. There is no reason to suppose that Major Molineux is anything but the best and kindest of men. I have felt nearly as much interest as you do in the matter, and all my inquiries but serve to show me that your father's old friend is most honourably esteemed.'

'Then why does he shut himself up for twenty-four hours every week?' persisted the laughing beauty, with that carelessness as to the motives of others, and that inability to understand the unconventional, which is peculiar to the young and happy. 'I should dearly like to discover his secret. Would not you, Dr Fayre?'

'I confess that I should be glad if he would reveal it to me,' I replied, 'for, as you say, it is a most puzzling business.'

'Then we will penetrate the mystery together,' said she, flashing a dazzling smile on me from between her red lips. 'Here is my hand upon it!' but, ere I could imprison the tiny fingers, she was gone.

I did not dream how sadly and how soon her jest would be realised.

Chapter 2

I have said that Miss Rochford was allowed to have her own way by her parents. She did, in fact, as she pleased; stayed at home to paint and read for the best part of one week, and during the next would close the piano, put away her unfinished watercolours, fling her books into a corner, and go scampering over the country upon her Arab horse, Sultan.

I have heard my Indian friends say that, if an Arab horse is not docile, he is more difficult to manage than any other. Sultan was certainly a proof, in some sort, of the truth of this statement. He was awkward in the stable, and even his own groom was not without some little dread of him. When mounted by a stranger, he seemed to lose all control over himself, and though Beatrice Rochford was absolutely without fear, and rejoiced in sitting her plunging and rearing steed her father, was always threatening to exchange the beautiful but unruly creature for a more placid, if less showy, animal.

But the wilful girl pouted and coaxed by turns, until the good Captain pressed his grizzled moustache upon her smooth, young brow and withdrew his determination for that time. He had, indeed, a well-merited admiration for his daughter's skill as a horsewoman and, during some of our many pleasant riding parties, I have often reined my steed alongside his more mettlesome hunter to watch Beatrice, as, sitting well back in the saddle with her hands low on her horse's wither, her veil blown like a streamer from her hat, and her dainty figure swaying like a willow to every bound of the snorting horse, she allowed the delighted beast to take his own course through bush and brake, until, with heightened colour and ringing laugh, she flung him on his haunches not five lengths from where we stood.

She was a feather-weight, and her hand was light as gossamer, but Sultan had been perfectly bitted, and dropped his head to the curb like a colt. So long as his temper was not crossed he was perfection.

'You shall never sell him, papa!' the lovely girl would cry after one of these daring flights, and the noble horse arched his muscular neck to the caress of the stroking whip-handle, as though to ask pardon for his occasional outbreaks of ill-humour.

One day we were returning from a long ride to New Norfolk, a charming village situated on the banks of the Derwent, which in some places assumes the aspect of an English trout-stream. The day had been chilly, for we were approaching winter, and fires had already made their appearance in the hospitable rooms of Ashmead. The road lay by the side of the stream, which brawled and foamed, some distance below us, over its rocky boulders, and the unwonted coldness of the air, together with the peculiar aspect of the swiftly-flowing brook, brought distant England vividly to my thoughts.

'How like this is to a scene in one of the mountain counties of England, Rochford!' I said.

'It is,' he returned. 'I wonder if either of us will see them again?'

The question was a pertinent one, and I fell into a reverie of recollection in which all but the existence of home and friends was for the moment forgotten. I was aroused by an exclamation from Captain Rochford, and, raising my head, became conscious that Beatrice was no longer with us. My companion's horse fretted under the restraint of the bridle, and I guessed that, finding us both wrapped in thought, she had, with her customary impulsiveness, galloped off down the rocky road alone.

'Let us push on,' I said. 'It is getting dark. We shall overtake her soon.'

'It is not that,' said Rochford. 'Look there!' and he pointed to a turn of the road which, visible to us on account of our elevated position, could not be seen by anyone in the gap through which Beatrice was evidently riding.

A bullock team attached to a wagon loaded with timber, apparently cut from the land of Major Molineux, had 'camped' in the track. The driver was asleep by the side of the road, and the animals had taken advantage of the absence of his formidable whip to snatch a moments' respite from their toil. There were eight in all, and they were disposed right across the road, one of the polers and the two leading bullocks lying down.

Rochford shouted at the full strength of his voice, but the man did not stir. He was evidently drunk. I could distinguish or thought I could distinguish, the rapid ring of Sultan's hoofs in the pass, as he was being urged at the top of his speed to the collision which awaited him. I, too, called out, but the word that rose to my lips was 'Beatrice!' I knew in that moment that the liking I – the middle-aged army surgeon – had for this beautiful and wayward girl, who was almost young enough to be my daughter, was a feeling warmer than mere friendship.

Breathless we awaited that which we knew must come. It was useless, worse than useless, to follow down the gap. We should only encourage the horse to greater speed, and should see nothing of the catastrophe. It came at last. Round the rock at full speed wheeled the flying horse, and simultaneously his rider saw the danger. There was but one chance, and that was balked. Just as she reined Sultan for the desperate leap, the drunkard tried to rise.

A less uncertain-tempered horse might even then have escaped. But the Arab saw the uncouth figure with the hated whip, swerved, fell on the great horns, recovered himself, with a scream of pain, and rolled backwards over his rider twenty feet sheer into the river.

How we reached the spot I never knew. There are some actions which, under great excitement, one performs automatically. I was told afterwards that I had fastened my bridle swiftly to a branch, and, leaping down from crag to crag, had gained a jutting point below the spot where the unhappy girl had fallen, had plunged into the stream, and, dragging her from the dead horse, had drawn her to the bank. I only remember standing, in my wet clothes, beside her, watching some faint colour of life gradually creep back to her white lips, while her father, like a man beside himself, galloped off to Castle Stuart for assistance.

When he returned with old Bagally, I had regained my composure. Nothing steadies the nerves of a surgeon – if he loves his profession – like an immediate necessity for the display of his utmost skill. Beatrice was cold and almost pulseless, her left arm was broken, and, when I raised the eyelids from the once lovely eyes, nothing remained of those large and liquid pupils but two scarcely perceptible specks.

'I have bad news for you,' I said; 'I cannot, of course, speak definitely yet as to the full extent of her injuries, but Miss Rochford has broken her arm, and has received severe concussion of the brain.'

'I will borrow Molineux's carriage,' said Rochford.

'No,' said I; 'I am not prepared to risk the journey. Miss Rochford must be taken to the house at once.'

The lame servitor looked askance, but Captain Rochford made light of all objections. 'Molineux would never be so absurdly fanatical as to refuse us his hospitality in such an emergency,' he said; 'I will answer for him.' So, making a litter with saplings and blankets brought from the house, we carried the still unconscious girl through the open door and placed her in a room to which Mrs Pennithorne directed us.

I set the broken arm at once, and apprehended no danger on that score; but, on examination, I found a comminuted fracture of the skull with displacement of the external table, and dreaded the result upon so highly sensitive and delicate an organisation as that possessed by my patient. It was clear that she must remain where she was for some days, perhaps for weeks, and I recommended my friend to continue his journey home with all speed and send out Mrs Rochford to act as nurse.

'I will remain here until you return; and, indeed, if Major Molineux will permit it,' I added, 'I will stop for the next twenty-four hours, at all events.'

Rochford departed, and, in obedience to my summons, Mrs Pennithorne appeared. She was a pale woman, with a strangely frightened air, and furtive, light-blue eyes. The misfortune of which poor Beatrice Rochford had spoken was very apparent, and certainly very repulsive.

'Let me have candles and a fire,' I said to her. 'I must stop here tonight. When do you expect Major Molineux home?'

'He is at home now, sir,' replied the old woman, in a low voice, which her imperfect articulation rendered almost unintelligible; 'but he cannot see anyone.'

For the first time I remembered that it was Thursday evening.

Chapter 3

A bright fire, and homely but plentiful preparations for supper, exercised on me their cheering influence, and I succeeded in shaking off a certain depression of spirits which had seized me so soon as the imperative necessity for attending to my patient left me leisure for reflection.

The old housekeeper had, according to my directions, contrived accommodation for Mrs Rochford in the same room with her daughter, while I was given a bedroom in the next corridor. Supper was served in a spacious apartment downstairs, which seemed to be used by the master of the house as dining-room and library combined. A portrait of the deceased Miss Tremayne, painted by the same hand which had executed the miniature in the possession of Beatrice Rochford, hung on the wall over the chimney, and beneath it was placed the Major's dress-sword and some withered branches of cypress. A heavy writing-table of solid fashioning occupied the embrasure of one of the windows, and, lying upon it, were some three or four volumes, evidently freshly imported from London.

A new book has always an irresistible attraction for me, and, moreover, on this occasion I was anxious to see what sort of literature my eccentric friend affected. Judge of my surprise to find that three of the works treated of the higher mathematics, and the fourth was the last speculation of a physician, whose name had a European fame, upon insanity!

Taking up the lamp, I examined the shelves. I expected to find there works which a military man of culture would naturally purchase, and I was not mistaken. *The Life of Sir David Baird*, Orme's *Hindostan*, and Southey's *Peninsular War*, elbowed Dubose's *History of the Prince Eugene* and Mackenzie's *Tippoo Sultan*, while Churchhill and Harris's *Voyages* sat pleasantly alongside Barclay's *Universal Traveller*, and the early volumes of the *Despatches* of the Duke of Wellington. Oliver's *Entomology*, and Labillardiere's *Plants of New Holland*, together with some fragments of Bewick, filled in the spaces between Shaw's *Lectures on Zoology*, while Audubon's *Birds of America*, with some few volumes of fiction, enlivened the higher shelves. The best of the collection, however, was almost entirely composed of treatises on mathematics and the latest works on mental disease. Not only were Bayle, Boyle, and La Place in their due place of honour, but the Norwegian Abel sat up beside them, and the latest volume of the *Philosophical Transactions* had between its leaves a paper covered with calculations made in dispute of Hopkins' statements anent luni-solar precession and nutation.

A row of folios, in sheepskin, bore the honoured names of Galen, Hippocrates, and Avicenna. The best editions of Harvey, Bichat, and Fothergill lay, with the last number of the *Medical and Surgical Transactions*, near them, while I could see that the Swiss edition of Tissot bristled with page-markers. But on the table were piled books which seemed strangely out of place in the house of a military officer however cultured. Boehave de Goster, Didier, Cabanis, and Schenck are not authors which one would expect to meet out of the library of a physician, nor are the *Opuscula* of Van Helmont, *La science de l'homme* of Bartletz, *or Lehrsätze* of Prochascha, works with which a retired major of the line would be likely to soothe his leisure hours.

I was interrupted at once in my researches and in my reflections by the arrival of the carriage containing Captain Rochford and his wife.

As may be readily imagined, the poor mother was in a condition of great anxiety. Nor was her trouble much alleviated by a visit to the sick-room. Miss Rochford was still unconscious, and though, by the application of wet cloths to the head, I was enabled to keep the inflammation in check, I could as yet offer no decided opinion as to the result of the case. It might, indeed, be even yet necessary to use the trephine, but I did not desire to alarm either of the parents, and I made the best assurances I could of their daughter's ultimate recovery.

'One thing,' I said, 'is absolutely necessary – perfect quiet. If you move Miss Rochford from this house until I am fully satisfied that she can bear the journey, I will not be responsible for the consequences. Tomorrow we will, if you choose, call in the family doctor. Tonight the case is under my care.'

Captain Rochford was good enough to express his perfect confidence in my skill, and took leave of us in terms which seemed to indicate that his mind was at ease. I pressed him to stop, but he declined.

'I learn from the old man, Bagally,' he said, 'that Major Molineux has been informed of our presence in the house, and that nothing but the extreme urgency of the case induces him to allow us to remain. I will come back again in the morning.'

Although I defended our involuntary host from the grave charge of discourtesy, I felt that, perhaps, it was well to intrude upon his strangely enforced privacy as little as possible. Having paid a last visit to my patient, and given directions for my immediate recall in case of need, I returned to the dining-room, determined to enjoy myself for a few hours by browsing among the scientific pasturage so curiously and so liberally provided.

I found it impossible to fix my attention on the page. Speculations which, at another time, would have enchained me, vaguely glimmered into my consciousness and disappeared again before I could grasp them. Insignificant and forgotten events of my past life suddenly sprang into my memory with startling distinctness, and an apparent importance wholly disproportioned to their true value as factors in the sum of my existence. I recalled faces of my boyhood, and seemed to hear voices, long ago silent, whispering about me. The wind had risen with the moon, and the night foreboded tempest. The rushing of the swollen stream mingled with the lashing of the rain, as it beat faster and faster upon the panes, while the distant flapping of some unhinged shutter gave querulous and doleful token of the desolation which reigned around the mysterious and ill-omened house.

I more than half repented that I had insisted upon the establishment of Miss Rochford in a place so dismal and so fraught with gloomy recollections. But her removal would have been attended with graver danger, and my better sense informed me that my fears were merely fancies engendered by shaken nerves and mental strain. Resolving to get the poor girl into the more cheerful society of her own domestic circle without delay, I adjusted another log on the fire, and endeavoured to rally my faculties into some more pleasant mood.

Alas! I but succeeded in making myself more uneasy than before. The chink of the falling embers sounded like low, warning cries, the roar of the river became a threatening voice, the scream of the blast was like the last appeal of some wildly parting soul, the indistinctly-heard rustling of the trees seemed to urge flight.

Through this medley of sounds and sensations the intermittent flap of the loose shutter recurred at irregular intervals, like the sound made by one who, with failing strength and yet passionate persistence, would gain shelter from some pursuing terror. I felt horribly alone. From above me looked down the sad, wild eyes of the dead girl, and about me were only the tokens of the strange, perhaps hideous, speculations of the mysterious recluse.

At that moment I heard a stealthy footfall in the passage.

Without pausing to think, I flung wide the door, and confronted the intruder.

At first I felt inclined to burst into laughter. Old Bagally was creeping towards the staircase with a tray, upon which was spread meat and wine.

'Bringing me something to eat?' I said, ashamed of my abrupt outbursting from the door, and yet glad of this momentary companionship with humanity.

'It is for the Major, sir,' said he, endeavouring to pass, and seeming unaccountably agitated.

'But the Major doesn't want two forks and two knives, and all that meat,' said I. 'Perhaps someone sups with him?'

'What is that to you?' said the old man, with a sudden, savage snarl, making as though, having both hands engaged, he would have bit me sideways in his wolf-like fury. 'You have had all you want; if not,

I'll bring you more. Leave us alone. We have our own ways,' and, vouchsafing no further parley, he climbed the stairs which led to his master's apartments.

More puzzled than ever, I returned to the gloomy dining-room. Had I stumbled into a house of madmen? Was the unreasoning terror of the toothless beldame but a form of idiocy? Was the old convict, with his ape-like skull and his canine rabidity, a maniac?

And the master of this desolated and death-haunted ruin, who shut himself up for one day in the week, and enshrouded that day with such precautions against being taken unawares, that his very food must be conveyed to him at night, and by stealth – what was he? Was he, too, insane? Had he brooded upon madness until he had become mad himself? Was he doing penance, as Beatrice had suggested, for some frightful crime? Did those doors, behind which he lived his forlorn life, conceal some poor relative whose sad calamity was held a misfortune, to be bolted in and barred away from men?

Or – most horrible thought of all – did he keep concealed above, and watched by the crazy pair, some poor wretch upon whose dazed brain and diseased body he might practise devilish experimental arts, if haply he might work out one or other of the wild theories propounded in some of the more speculative of his philosophers? Even as the thought shaped itself there rang through the house a series of piercing shrieks.

Chapter 4

In another instant I was at the head of the stairs, but paused in my onward flight, for the sounds issued from the room occupied by Beatrice and her mother.

Mrs Rochford was lying on the floor senseless. Ringing the bell furiously, I raised her to her bed, and, with the assistance of the old woman, whom the cries of the unhappy lady, not less than my importunate summons, had brought to the spot, I succeeded in restoring her to consciousness. Her first words were –

'Is it gone?'

'What?' I asked.

'The white face at the window!' said Mrs Rochford. 'That imploring, maddened face!'

'What can she mean?' I asked Mary Pennithorne, but the old woman, moping and mowing, made no reply.

'I see, madam,' I said, flinging wide the lattice, 'the storm has passed, and with it the cause of your alarm. Some leafy branchlet carried by the wind, perhaps even some more wrathful gust than usual, has, while rousing you from sleep, given form to a passing dream. Look, the sky is almost cloudless.'

And in truth, the tempest had, during the time we had been occupying ourselves with the frightened woman, quite passed away. The scene was one of exquisite peacefulness. The clouds had almost withdrawn, and the wet trees sparkled in the beams of a glorious moon, which rode high in a serene heaven. All felt the influence of the scene. Beatrice, sunk in her stupor, alone was ignorant alike of sounds and sights; but her mother composed herself with a smile at her former fears, and as I sought my comfortable couch, I felt that science and sentiment alike bid me laugh at the ungrateful fancies which an atmosphere surcharged with electricity could breed in a brain usually so cool as mine.

The excitement of the day caused me to sleep longer than my wont, and it was nearly eight o'clock when I awoke. I discovered by the hot water jug, with its carefully placed towel, that the rude valetage of Bagally had already been exercised in my chamber, and, before I had completed my *toilette*, the old servant introduced himself with the compliments of his master, and information that breakfast would be ready for us in half-an-hour.

Captain Rochford had already arrived, and with him I visited the sick room. Beatrice was still insensible, but Mrs Rochford was up and dressed. Rochford laughed at her story of the ghost, and, gathering courage from my assurance that the patient was progressing favourably, we went down to breakfast in something like good spirits.

Major Molineux received us with more than courtesy. He lamented the accident, but trusted that the skill of a surgeon so well known as myself, and the careful attention of a mother so devoted as Mrs Rochford, would soon restore his fair guest to her wonted health.

'I'm afraid,' he said, as he assisted us to the dish before him, 'that my poor house is but a gloomy place for a convalescent, and I trust that Miss Rochford's convalescence may be early. Such as are the resources of the place, however – command them. I regret that I was unable to render you any personal assistance yesterday, but I must compensate for my enforced neglect by devoting myself to all your services during the next few days.'

The language was of the politest, but there was no mistaking its meaning. Rochford and I looked at each other. It was quite evident that Major Molineux did not desire that we should pass another Thursday under his roof.

I trust that Miss Rochford may be able to travel to her own home before this day week,' said I, somewhat pointedly. 'In the meantime, let me thank you for the courtesy with which we were received, and especially for the hospitality of last night."

The hand with which the Major was lifting the teacup to his lips trembled slightly, but he said, merely, 'It was a wild night – a night of storms. I trust you were not disturbed.'

'I was most terribly disturbed,' said Mrs Rochford – I think I have said that she was not a woman of much force of character, or quickness of apprehension – 'I had the most shocking dreams. A white face at the window – '

'Nonsense, Mary,' interrupted Rochford; 'you were nervous.'

'There is no one in the house but myself and the two servants,' said the Major, who had completely regained his composure, 'and I am sure neither of them would have the temerity to disturb your slumbers. Pray,' he added, turning in stiff condescension to old Bagally, 'have you been amusing yourself by terrifying my guests?'

The old man seemed dumb-stricken. He tried to speak, but words failed him. Lifting up his hands with a gesture of terror, he made for the door, and, turning as he went, displayed again that wolf-like savagery of aspect, the which I had observed on the previous night.

'A curious fellow,' said Major Molineux, cracking the shell of his egg, 'but faithful. An old convict, of course, I have touched some tender chord, perhaps.'

Perhaps he had, for Dame Pennithorne waited upon us during the rest of the meal, and even brought the Major his cigar-case, when we found ourselves in the dilapidated but spacious verandah, prepared to seek the solace which, in those days, was supposed to lie in Manilla tobacco.

The conversation, of course, was of the accident and its results. The prospects of the patient's recovery, the punishment to be meted out to the self-indulgent bullock-driver, the quality of Sultan's temper, and the equestrian skill of Miss Rochford, were all debated in turn. A learned discussion was held upon fracture of the skull, and I was compelled to illustrate as best I might the operation of the trephine. At last, exhausted with surgery, and convinced that he was thoroughly competent to treat a similar case, should he ever meet with one, Rochford betook himself to visit the scene of the accident, and left me alone with our host.

Major Molineux seemed uneasy. He got up and paced the broken tiles of the piazza floor, talked of twenty things in a breath, and flung away his half-consumed cigar, only to light another an instant after.

'You are restless this morning,' I said, willing to gain, if I could, some information concerning the mysterious seclusion of yesterday. 'Did you not sleep well?'

'Oh, yes,' returned the Major, indifferently, 'I slept well enough,' and then he fixed his eyes on the wall behind me with that strange stare of which I have already spoken, and wiped from his brow some large beads of sweat which had suddenly appeared there. 'I seldom sleep very soundly.'

'Indigestion, I suspect,' I continued, in a careless tone. 'A man who eats enough for two people at about midnight can scarcely wonder if he suffers from nightmare.'

With a visible effort my interlocutor withdrew his gaze from space, and looked me in the eyes.

'Then you saw Bagally with the tray,' said he. 'I am ashamed of my voracious appetite,' he added, with an attempt at a smile, 'and try to laugh myself out of my gluttony by demonstrating to my actual vision that I do, in fact, partake of a double portion of food.'

'Your notion is ingenious, but I fear that you will never effect a cure by its means. Let me feel your pulse.' He gave me his wrist. The hand was hot and dry, the pulse full and bounding. 'I will write you a little prescription which may do you good. Give me a sheet of paper,' and I led the way to the library. 'There,' said I, folding the sheet; 'though I saw Woodville and Sowerby on your shelves, I doubt if you are fully acquainted with the virtues of the lily tribe.'

'You have been among my books, then,' said the Major, looking round.

'I have, and am surprised to find so excellent a collection of works in – pardon me for saying it – so unexpected a place.'

'Books are my only companions,' said Major Molineux, and, as he spoke, he scanned the table a little nervously, as though to see which of the volumes had attracted my attention.

Determined to penetrate the secret which I was now convinced existed, I pressed my advantage. 'I see that you study the higher mathematics. This calculation on the variation of parameters is not made by a school-boy, while here' – and I lifted from the table a sheet of paper – 'is something headed. "*Probability that an event observed several times in succession depends upon a cause which facilitates its reproduction"*, in which the calculation is made by finding the equation of the logarithmic curve.'

Major Molineux changed colour, and took the paper from my hands. 'I did not know that I had left the records of my folly thus carelessly exposed,' said he. 'The fact is that I have always been a lover of anything which approaches an exact science, and the calculation of probabilities is a fascinating subject. I am foolishly fond of it,' and, as he spoke, he tore the paper into pieces and flung them into the basket at his feet.

'Some men say that mathematicians are mad,' I said. 'If this be so, you have the antidote as well as the bane, for seldom have I seen, even in the libraries of my professional brethren, so fine a collection of works on mental disease as that which I examined last night.'

I had gone too far for his patience.

'Doctor Fayre,' said he, 'you are my guest, and my house is at your disposal so long as the illness of my old friend's daughter compels you to remain in it; but let me remind you that an old man who lives by choice a recluse, may have sought such seclusion in order that he might be spared these very comments upon his private tastes which you have just been pleased to make,' and, bowing stiffly, he left the room.

Chapter 5

He did not appear that day, nor at breakfast the next morning. I felt that I deserved the reproach which his absence conveyed, and was angry with myself for having so far permitted my curiosity to outrun my discretion. But the more I reflected upon the circumstances of the case, the more convinced did I become that Castle Stuart held within its walls some mystery of mind or body, upon the like of which it was not given to man to frequently look; and, despite the Major's rebuff and my own self-consciousness, I resolved not to abandon my quest. In pursuance of this resolution I sauntered out into the garden the next afternoon, thinking to fall in with the old servant. I was not disappointed. I found him standing in a little glade, or opening in the brushwood, staring with all his might at the upper windows of the house.

'What interests you?' I cried, taking a guinea from my pocket. Can you not spare time for a little friendly chat?'

He looked nervously about him, pocketed the gold piece, and, pointing to a coarse patch of verdure at his feet, whispered: 'It was here he did it.'

'Did what?' I asked.

'Cut his throat,' said the old man, 'and they buried him here, with a stake through his heart. But that can't hold him.'

'What do you mean, man?' I asked, experiencing a fresh access of horror at this hideous and unexpected story. 'Who is buried here?'

'Savary, the forger; him as found his wife gone as well as his liberty. This was where he saw them walking. The Captain was a handsome man, and Mrs Savary had been a beauty, they say. She died mad for all that,' and he laughed the discordant laugh of one whose experience of life has been of the sort to make him rejoice in others' woe.

'What was the Captain's name?'

'Tremaine. He was the Major's brother-in-law. *He*'s dead too, and Savary will soon see them all out.'

'Does his ghost walk, then?' I asked, attempting a laugh; but the day was cloudy, and a cold wind seemed on a sudden to chill me.

'Ask Mrs Rochford. She saw him last night. Listen. Two years ago I was sitting up with the old hag in the kitchen, when I heard the door-bell. It was blowing a storm like it was last night, and the wind went shrieking round the house as if it wanted to get in and tear us. It was the Major's Thursday, and I daren't go near him for my soul. I crept to the door, thinking some traveller had got out of his track, for no one who knew us would come to Castle Stuart; but before I could open it there was an awful screech and something went whirling round the house like a pack of dogs. I heard them bellowing and grunting at the back, and ran upstairs to look. I looked out of that window' – he pointed to the room where Mrs Rochford had slept the night before – 'and I saw something like a herd of huge swine on Savary's grave, rooting, and snarling, and slavering in it, and then I slammed to the window, for some awful thing with a white face was there trying to save itself from those hellish beasts. The noise continued for five or six minutes, and then the sky cleared like it did last night, and I saw no more!'

'You have a cheerful imagination, my friend,' said I; 'but, pray, do you couple this delectable story with your master's day of seclusion?'

Once more the ugly look came into his face. 'Nay, I know nothing of that; and it's no business of yours either, though you are a doctor. Doctors cannot cure Major Molineux's complaint.'

'Then you think that he is ill?'

'Not I; he's well enough.'

'Look ye, Bagally,' I said, determined to try a last chance, 'you are too sensible a man to believe this nonsense about ghosts, and suicides, and hunted souls. I am a doctor; I shall be here some days. I may be able to do your master good. Tell me' – and I exhibited another guinea – 'what is the mystery in connection with Major Molineux?'

'He is possessed by a devil,' said Bagally; and then, as if he had said too much, made for the house with grotesque, uneven strides, and left me standing on the coarse grass that sprung from the dishonoured grave where the suicide lay with a stake through his heart.

A voice roused me from my reverie. Major Molineux himself was at my side.

'Fayre,' said he, 'I have overheard the last words of your conversation. I do not expect you to pay attention to the vulgar fancies of an ignorant hind. The story of the wretched being who lies buried at your feet is neither part of my history nor does it concern my family. The romance which was sought to be woven around his name and that of my dear sister's husband has been long ago proved false, and it was perhaps the gratification of a desire to preserve from derision the last resting-place of a man more sinned against than sinning which caused the report to first obtain circulation. When my niece came to live with me I caused the fence, which formerly surrounded Arthur Savary's grave, to be removed, and, unless some chattering imbecile like old Bagally had informed her of the story, this portion of the park possessed for her no more interest than any other. The fantasies of women are innumerable.' He spoke rapidly, and with some heat. It was quite evident that he expected a reply, and a direct one.

'No one, Major Molineux,' said I, is less superstitious than myself, but I have seen so much of what is termed superstition resolve itself into fact, that I am not prepared to pronounce any fantasy of the imagination as wholly baseless. But before we proceed further, let me feel sure of my ground. I came here only in my character as a physician in attendance upon a patient who has been made unavoidably your guest. I find myself face to face with an extraordinary enigma, yourself. Your peculiar studies, your secluded life, above all, your strange disappearance from all society on one day in the week, have combined to raise in me a curiosity which I cannot stifle. What is the mystery which darkens your life?'

Major Molineux planted himself firmly on his feet, and took both my hands in his own. His face was deadly pale, and he seemed to be nerving himself for a great effort. 'Do not turn from me. Do not shun me,' he said. 'Had it not been for your persistence, I had never spoken. Bagally is right. One day in each week I am possessed by a devil.'

'Come, come,' said I, a little shaken, despite my self-control, as the powerful old man searched my eyes with his, 'there are many sorts of devils – devils of wrath, and devils of discontent, and we all are now and then, at the mercy of such.'

'Ay,' said Major Molineux, 'but to be possessed, as I am, by – no, I cannot speak it, I could not repeat, nor could you listen to the tale. Forget what I have said, and' – he pressed my arm with painful violence – 'swear to mention to no living soul that which I have unguardedly betrayed.'

'A physician's lips are sealed without an oath,' said I. 'You may rely on me. And now I must see Miss Rochford. Let us go in.'

He regained his self-possession before we reached the house, and not during the day was the subject again mentioned between us. I thought it better for the development of the case to permit my patient – for so I now considered him – to begin a confidence which I feared might be withdrawn if I pressed him too closely. Seeing that I touched only on indifferent matters, he presided at dinner with his customary composure, and entertained us all with the stores of a mind acquisitive of information and fastidious in the imparting of it.

'The old gentleman was never more amusing,' said Rochford, as I parted from him in the hall. 'When we move Beatrice, I'll ask him to come to Ashmead; the change would do him good.'

'Ask him, by all means,' said I, 'and I will second your entreaties. If we can once break the chain of recurring events in his life we may give him another lease of it. Our intrusion, unwelcome though it was at first, has already roused him into something like gaiety. Miss Rochford should be well enough in a fortnight to be moved, for her case looks in every way favourable.'

'How can I ever repay you for your kindness?' said Rochford.

I knew a method by which he could repay me a thousandfold, but I did not think it wise to mention it at that moment. Alas! events soon occurred which rendered it impossible for me to ever ask that favour which I prized so highly.

On Wednesday afternoon, Major Molineux begged to see me alone. He led the way to his library, carefully closed the door, and, after much prelude, began to talk about his malady.

'I wish to ask you,' said he, 'if it is possible for a man to be mad and know that he is mad?'

'There are different kinds of madness,' said I, feeling that I must speak with caution. 'An insane man may have lucid intervals during which he reviews acts done during the period of his insanity, and condemns them. A man may have an uncontrollable impulse to commit a certain act – as to jump out of a window, for instance – and yet be quite conscious of the folly and even wickedness, of his morbid promptings. I knew a case in India of a soldier who was seized with just such a morbid desire. He felt compelled to murder someone very near and dear to him, and at last deserted in order to do it. Arrived in the town where the intended victim lived, he absolutely had himself tied up by the people of the inn, until the proper authorities could be sent for to secure him. Some months afterwards the object of his morbid lust for blood died, and the man at once recovered. He described his sufferings while resisting his impulse as terrible. Surely no devil worse than this could possess a man. And yet he could hardly be called mad.'

'You give me a few grains of comfort,' said Major Molineux, 'though I have no such fearful impulse as that which you describe. Every week, from ten o'clock on Wednesday night until ten o'clock on Friday morning, I am the prey to the most bestial and awful delusion which it has entered into the mind of man to conceive. I know that the fault is in my own brain, and that I am but the dupe of imagination. But where that fault lies I have sought in vain to find. Science brings me no solace, and, though my sense laughs at my imagination, I dare not confront the hideous thing which my imagination has created to mock my sense.'

'You are not alone in your misfortune, dear sir,' said I. 'There have been many men, haunted by phantoms, who have lived to make them but a source of amusement. The operation of ghost-seeing is simple enough. We recall a landscape, which we have seen. We will it to return, and it is instantly present. That is to say that we project from us that which we wish to recall, and look at it, and listen to it, as if it were again external to us. An artist draws a dead face from memory, while a musician plays an air forgotten by his hearers – the same effort too, of will, which recalled the lineaments of a corpse, and the notes of the opera, could people a house with ghosts, and fill the darkness with the voices of the dead.'

'Ah,' said the Major, with a sigh, 'mine is no such illusion as those which you have mentioned. No voices of angel or of demon speak to me. No faces, grotesque or enchanting, present themselves to my gaze. My delusion, and delusion it is, though I am half persuaded of its truth, is so horrible, so damning, so fearful in its naked insistence of the beast in our fallen natures that I have been tempted not once, but a hundred times, to set my spirit free from the soul-destroying bands which enwrap it.'

He spoke with sober vehemence, and appalling earnestness.

'That this feeling is part of the delusion I know, but that does not make it more bearable. For nine years I have endured a weekly agony, compared with which, the keenest torments of man's devising are as naught. In body and in soul I have suffered more than tongue can tell. Save that my reason did not desert me, I should have speedily qualified myself for a place beside the poor wretch over whose grave I confessed my secret; and yet I ask you, can I lay claim to the possession of reason, when I am the sport of an imagining so foul as that which torments me?'

'But,' said I, gently, 'you have not yet told me the nature of this delusion.'

'I dare not,' said Major Molineux. 'You would quit the house. To no human ear can I speak the history of my unspeakable degradation.' He rose suddenly.

'Tomorrow is Thursday,' he said, 'come into my room tonight, and see what I dare not speak,' and he left me.

Miss Rochford had regained consciousness, and I hoped that the next few days would see her in a fair way of recovery. Mrs Rochford had laughed off her fears, and attributed, as I did, the visitant's face to a more mortal source than that of the wandering soul of a suicide. Rochford was in high spirits at the approaching departure, and even Mrs Pennithorne seemed less terrified than usual. I could not have had a more propitious hour for the investigation of the mystery which bad baffled me, and I waited with much anxiety for midnight, which – being about the time I had seen Bagally on the previous week – was, I thought, a customary hour with the Major for taking his oddly-timed meal.

I was not amiss in my calculations. As the timepiece in the hall rang out the hour, the old convict appeared with the tray.

'Your master has desired me to see him,' I said, 'and I will go up with you.'

'As you please,' said Bagally, roughly; 'but take care.'

He led the way along the great corridor until he came to a double door.

'If he is not waiting on the other side,' said he, 'you'll be lucky,' and, opening a slide in the panel, he pushed in the tray with its burthen, bolting the panel quickly.

I stood uncertain how to act. Bagally turned to descend the stairs.

'Will you not go in?' I asked.

'Not for all the money in Hobart,' said the man, his very hair bristling. 'Listen.' I bent my ear to the door, and could distinguish the confused sounds of voices.

'Who is with him?' I asked. But the old servitor had left me. I was alone, and from the other side of the oak panel came a sound which caused my blood to curdle in my veins. In another instant I should have fled.

'Molineux! Major Molineux!' I cried, and rapped at the panel. The door shot back, and I entered. The passage was pitch dark; but in the distance I could see a lighted candle in what appeared to be a bedroom. I advanced towards it. The door shut behind me, and I felt someone place what seemed to be a hand on my shoulder.

Major Molineux was right. Words refuse to lend themselves to the depiction of that which the horror-fixed eye saw in that lonely chamber.

Chapter 6

Mrs Rochford was the only person whom I met at the breakfast-table the morning after my visit to Major Molineux's room. The Major himself, for reasons which I could readily appreciate, desired to postpone, as long as possible, an interview with one who had become possessed of his unhappy secret, and Rochford had intimated his intention of arriving later in the day. Now that his daughter was out of danger, there was really no real reason for his presence, which, indeed, was a daily element of disturbance in the sick room.

'When do you think that Beatrice can be moved?' asked Mrs Rochford. 'I long to have her at home again under my own roof; for, though Major Molineux is most kind and attentive, I experience a sense of depression in this house which I cannot shake off.'

'I quite agree with you that the sooner Miss Rochford is got home the better,' I replied, 'though the feeling of which you speak is attributable only to your own anxiety, and perhaps in some measure to the unwonted quietude of Castle Stuart after the bustle of Ashmead. Nevertheless, we must be cautious. I never like to disturb a case of fracture, however slight, for at least twenty days, and we have been here but barely seven.'

'True,' she said; 'this is Friday. I had forgotten,' and her glance at the vacant place at the foot of the table noted to me the circumstance which had escaped her memory.

Some slight confusion in my manner must have betrayed me, for, with a woman's quickness, she said suddenly, 'Doctor Fayre, you look worn and ill this morning. Tell me, do you know anything about this mystery of Major Molineux?'

'My dear madam,' I said, 'I am a doctor, and I cannot speak even indirectly of matters which have come to my knowledge in the exercise of my profession. Major Molineux has been complimentary enough to ask my advice upon certain points connected with his health, but I am as yet but very partially informed as to his case.'

'Nay,' said she, 'I did not mean to put an impertinent query; but it has occurred to me that, in return for the Major's kindness to my daughter, Beatrice might, by-and-bye, rouse him from his melancholy, and even win his confidence as to the secret cause of his malady.'

If you have ever chanced, when in conversation, to hear a phrase innocently uttered which conveys to your private ear a world of esoteric meaning, you will comprehend the quick pang I felt at this sudden approximation of two ideas. Beatrice and my patient of last night! That pure girl and that most unhappy being, whose hideous hallucination made him doubtful of his humanity! When a student in Paris, I had seen the body of a beautiful girl exposed on a dissecting-table for some needful demonstrations in anatomy. The sight shocked me then, and as, obedient to the law of association, the picture of that nerveless figure, so passive under the searching knife and exploring eye, rose again before me, I almost saw the pallid features shape themselves into a likeness of those of Beatrice.

'Do not think of such a thing, madam,' I cried. 'It is quite imposs- ible. Miss Beatrice must never know aught of the – ' and I stopped abruptly. Was I not already committing myself?

Poor Mrs Rochford quite failed to appreciate my fervour, but I was glad to see that she attributed it more to zeal for her daughter's welfare than to any serious illness affecting Major Molineux.

'I had no intention, of course,' she said, 'of urging the project now, but by-and-bye, when change of air and scene might be tried on both – '

'Let us defer the consideration until then,' I said; and with some difficulty succeeded in retaining my composure sufficiently to sit out the untasted meal.

Left to myself, I began to reflect. Upon what a hideous thing had I stumbled! Far from being, as I had suspected, the melancholic craze of a hypochondriac – who might believe himself a teapot or a wash-hand basin, Tiberius Caesar, or Alexander the Great – the hallucination of Major Molineux was one which blended itself so inextricably with the affairs of his daily life that he could no more escape from it than he could stay his pulse at will. Bound as I was by the most solemn pledges of personal and professional honour, I had taken upon myself the burden of a frightful secret which I must lock for ever in my own heart, or share, and sicken in the sharing, with the unhappy man whose choking breast was its only other repository. And, having acquired the knowledge of this polluting horror, I must bear it with me for ever; for, did my skill haply succeed in removing from my companion's mind his belief in the absolute entity of it, still the image of it was there stamped upon the brain, and ready to start into grisly life again at any instant.

Nor was it possible to fix the idea in words. Even now, after thirty years, I can recall the agony of mind with which, pacing in the deserted park by the lonely grave of the suicide, I strove to bring the abstract horror of the thing into some shape, that I might grapple with it and defy it. In vain. It eluded my mental grasp as a jelly-fish slips through the fingers. Formless and void, it yet was there – a foul and filthy thought, profaning the shrine of sense.

And he – the wretched man in whose brain-cells this more than chimaeric growth of shame and horror had been fed and fostered – what was my suffering to his? I saw clearly the line which separated the delusion of the one day from the comparative sanity of the other six. I could trace, far down in the beginnings of mental being, the first growth of the appalling thought which now mounted reason's throne and shook the sceptre of judgment. *I* was no believer in the damning mystery. Mine was, after all, but the experience of one who, meeting a leper uncovered in the by-way, has to wash in many waters ere he can return to forget that loathsome sight, among men of sound flesh and healthy limb. But the leper – poor ruin – knowing his own bitter fate – cut off for ever from the intimacy of the honest, put away from the sight of the noble, the very manhood which, supporting him in his trial, urges him to retain what semblance to his fellow-men the cankering corruption may have left him, and make an exit from life while he is yet a step removed from rabid putrescence – what far-reaching depths of anguish and of shame has not his soul plumbed in the swift descent of its despair?

One thing was certain. Having thus possessed myself of the knowledge of Major Molineux's terrible story, I was bound, by every tie of honour and humanity, to alleviate his sufferings. Such of my brethren who are read in the literature of insanity will understand me when I say that I shuddered at the task. I am not what the world terms a religious man, and in those days I was perhaps less so than the experience of a long life has taught me since to be; but, in reviewing the case of this unfortunate gentleman, I found myself involuntarily offering up a petition to a Higher Power on his behalf. I had – during the long vigil of the dread night – mastered all physical symptoms, and arrived at the conclusion that, though science might palliate the tortures of the sufferer, she could not restore him 'whole and in his right mind'. 'I am possessed by a devil,' the poor man had said to me; and I did not profess to have the power of exorcism. Still, much might be done. The relief to his burdened mind must be already great, and if I could but prevail on him to discuss the theme – and my flesh crept with disgust as the thought thrilled my nerves – in calmness, haply some break in the continuity of the hallucination would be discovered whereby I could prevent the recurrence of the phenomena, or at least destroy the regularity of their appearance. The trial, distasteful as it was, should be made, and I sought the house, to give directions to Bagally to send to Hobart for some drugs with which I had resolved to begin the treatment.

I found the old servant in something of an anxious mood. He was evidently desirous of knowing how I had sped with his master, and I thought it a good opportunity to ascertain how much or how little he himself had learned.

'I had a long conversation with Major Molineux last night, Bagally,' said I; 'and I have every hope that I may do him some good. Pray, when did you first observe the symptoms of his illness?'

'I have lived with him for seventeen years,' said the convict, with something approaching to tenderness in his voice, 'and for the first eight years he was the same as the rest of us. Then he began to keep to the house and avoid company, then to his room, and so by degrees to what you know him.'

'Have you ever seen him during one of his attacks?' I asked.

'Never, thank God! but I have seen them as have – God help 'em!'

'Whom do you mean?'

'Miss Agnes. She saw him; and she never held up her head after. 'Twas one of them windy nights, like the one I was telling you about. When the screeching began, it seems that Miss Agnes got frightened, and ran out, calling for her uncle. The old woman there slept next Miss Agnes, and she says she heard the Major's door open, and him come out to her. Then Miss Agnes cried out upon God to save her; and when Pennithorne got to her she was lying, fainted, in the passage. She was took with shivering that night, crying out on names we didn't know for someone to help her. The doctor – 'twas old Murchison – said 'twas a cold she took in running out from her warm bed to the passage. We knew better, Pennithorne and I. 'Twas fright she died of.'

'I am afraid that Mrs Pennithorne is as much a romancer as you are,' said I, with a most unsuccessful attempt at a smile. 'Dr Murchison was, no doubt, quite correct in his diagnosis. However, I want you to go into the town for these few matters,' and I handed him the paper. 'The Major has consented to submit to my treatment; but you know how sensitive he is, and I trust to your discretion to make no remarks either to him personally or to others.'

'You needn't fear,' returned he, unhitching the bridle from its peg. 'I've lived too long here not to know how to hold my tongue.' He hobbled to the door, and then came quickly back with an awkward gesture, meant to indicate self-possession. 'Cure him,' he said, and thrust something into my hand. It was one of the guineas I had given him over the suicide's grave.

Pondering over the confirmation of my worst fears, which the manner of the death of poor Miss Tremayne gave me, I resolved to see if I could obtain any information from Dame Pennithorne. The kitchen was a large one, and amply furnished with necessary utensils of all sorts. Our visit had compelled an almost entire change in the domestic policy of the household, and evidences of plenty, and even luxury, abounded. A fat-faced wench, employed in assisting a boy scullion to scour a huge fish-kettle, destined to contain our Friday fare, directed me to a door which led into a sort of stillroom or housekeeper's closet – the private apartments of the woman to whom Miss Rochford had taken so strong a dislike.

Mrs Pennithorne was seated before the empty grate, staring, with all her dazed might, into the fuelless fireplace. She did not hear me approach, and, coming close behind her, I tapped her lightly on the shoulder. The effect was curious. She did not start nor scream; she simply trembled violently, turning, as she did so, her head slowly round, until her glassy eyes – round and unspeculative as those of a fish – met mine. Her toothless mouth, open in the curve of expectation, seemed not unlike that of a cod. Had I taken her hand I should have almost expected to find it cold.

Slowly her senses undazzled, and she recognised me. 'I was thinking of you, sir,' she mumbled, her wrinkled cheeks flapping together like bellows. 'But I daren't speak to you.'

'Why not? What mystery can you have to conceal?'

She looked round her again with that frightened air of which I have before spoken, and then suddenly clutching my arm, with all her choppy fingers distended like the claws of a bird, she whispered to me –

'Take her away, doctor. For God's sake, take her away.'

'You mean Miss Rochford,' said I. 'Now, listen, Mrs Pennithorne; I want you to tell me what you know of Miss Tremayne's death. It took place in that very room, did it not? Answer me.'

She stared wildly, gaping and goggling after her unpleasant manner. From the adjacent kitchen came the laughter of the scullion and the cook-maid.

'Come, Mrs Pennithorne,' I repeated, 'recollect yourself. What took place before Miss Tremayne's death?'

'She met him,' said the old woman, nodding at the wall nearest the house. 'I know nothing more. But there is a curse upon this house, which brings agony and woe to all who live in it.'

I looked at the crone with aroused curiosity. Was my conjecture right, and was she, too, a victim to some form of mental aberration? It was likely enough. There is contagion in insanity, and it might be that the lonely life led by a woman of her age, whose constant employment was speculation upon a mystery in another's life, had rendered her also a monomaniac. I felt a sudden repulsion to the house and its belongings. The old woman had no coherent tale to tell; and if she had? The atmosphere seemed hot with the breath of madmen. I paid a hurried visit to Beatrice, saddled my horse myself, and galloped into the town. I felt that I must have a few hours of commonplace life, or I, too, might become the sport of those unseen agencies which take up their abodes in pampered bodies and neglected minds.

Chapter 7

Soothed and sustained by a night's rest in the unromantic precincts of the Club, I returned to Castle Stuart with all the cobwebs swept out of my brain, and with a positive professional delight at the prospect of the cure of Major Molineux.

I found my poor friend anxiously awaiting my arrival, and, so soon as lunch was disposed of, he drew me aside.

'I have felt an inexpressible relief,' he said, 'since I revealed to you my fearful trouble, and something like hope begins to light up the darkness within.'

'That is a good symptom,' said I; 'and now we will have a little physical history to follow upon the mental one.'

I asked him a series of questions upon his general health, and found, as I expected, that he had been for years a stranger to anything like regularity of life. He ate when he pleased and what he fancied, walked but little, and would often sit for a day together without moving from the table where he pursued his physiological studies. He was emaciated in body, but of late, and as his malady had progressed, he had become more and more addicted to the use of large quantities of animal food, with which he drank weak brandy and water.

'I find,' said he, 'that I grow less and less able to eat vegetables or bread without experiencing serious inconvenience, not merely as regards indigestion, but as concerns the extent and pressure of that which I know to be a delusion of the brain.'

'Of course,' I replied, with that wisdom which doctors affect when they are at fault for a diagnosis; 'the normal condition of things in the body is changed when certain substances are taken into it; and, in certain other conditions of it, moreover, there are produced within it organic products which affect the organs of the senses and interfere with their functions. Indian hemp, opium, and a thousand other substances, have the power to set to sleep some senses and open others, while – and this I suspect is at the bottom of your sorrows – some abnormal condition of things within has set you astray as to your relations to things without.'

'Then you think,' cried the poor man, almost joyfully, 'that I am not necessarily diseased in brain?'

'Necessarily? No. The body of a man is a mere bundle of organs for condensing external facts, as says a writer with whom I hope by-and-bye to make you acquainted. The man has a hearing organ, a seeing organ, and so on. In each organ there is a receiving nervous surface; from this surface, leading into the man, is a communicating nervous cord; while, at the end of this cord, is a nervous centre, which takes up the impression conveyed and makes it part of the individual's experience.'

'And mischief may be present anywhere and in any of these parts?'

'Exactly. But to lay the finger of science on the particular part is often impossible. The surface, the cord, or the centre may be to blame, and we thus pass, at a bound, from the merest physical invest-igation into a psychological speculation of the most intricate and uncertain nature.'

Major Molineux cast a wistful glance at Val Helmont and the rest.

'But is it not possible for science to reason with something like certainty in such matters? The universe is governed by fixed laws. Fixed laws rule the bodily and mental health of man. I have twenty times calculated the chances of the periodical return of my malady. An astronomer can as accurately calculate the return of a passing world. Anatomy has laid open to us all the secrets of the human machine. Is there none, then, who can penetrate into this poor body and pluck forth the heart of its mystery?'

He spoke with eagerness, but without passion; and as I saw him there, and recalled his awful doom, I felt my heart throb with a pity which swallowed up, once and for ever, all other feelings.

'Dear Major Molineux, dear friend,' I said, 'science cannot do what you ask. See, here,' and I drew down a chart of the nervous system, which was affixed in its box to the wall. 'Here are the nerves which emanate from the brain, and which are under the control of the will. Here are the ganglionic nerves, which are not under the control of the will. See how all the great vital organs depend upon these last for the performance of their functions. And these ganglionic organs tell us nothing. The heart beats, the lungs breathe, the stomach digests, but we take no note of their motions. It is only when these organs are *diseased* that we become conscious of their existence. A reflex action now begins. Sense on soul and soul on sense, discussing, arguing, disputing. The body is slowly informed of the capacities of the mind: the mind gradually takes upon itself the functions of the body. See here, here, here – these myriads of glands, each working under the influence of the nerves distributed to them. Each filament, each follicle participates in the general disorder and a chain of morbid association between mental and corporeal organs, binds mind to body – a chain the woven links of which are intertwisted beyond human skill to loose. You ask me to show you the heart of your mystery; as well ask me to show you Thought made visible.'

'And yet these men,' said the Major, glancing at his shelves, 'more than half believed that among the many forces of great nature was one – supreme, eternal – which, in its varying shape, was health, air, gold, love, jealousy and death.'

'Others besides your mystics,' said I, 'have recognised such a force, but they have given it a name. So far as man is concerned, there are in him two distinct manifestations of this force – the Will and the Intellect. Will is instinctive and unwearied; Intellect is reflective and fatigable. But the Intellect is as a bridle to the Will, and sometimes it happens that Will takes the bit in its teeth and runs away. Then takes place something like that of which you complain, and the mere instinctive and animal part of the man assumes sole control of his personality. Is this Madness? If the deliberative faculties cannot regain the mastery over the executive faculties – yes!'

'No,' said Major Molineux; 'if such a force exists, Madness and Sanity are but terms. We are all parts of one great whole, and discord is impossible. Nay, that which seems discord may be harmony, and my awful sufferings a necessary part of the universal joy. Yet why should I bear this burden? I am not a wicked man. Heaven is my witness that I have lived uprightly according to my lights. Why am I singled out from all my fellow-men to be the subject of so fearful an outrage? If my body has sinned, let it be punished; but why make sport of my intellect, and leave God-like reason at the mercy of the basest part of Man?'

He walked up and down as he spoke, and I watched him with increased interest. He had evidently thrown off the mask, and was speaking in his real character. The genial *militaire*, the entertaining host, the learned mathematician, the well-read physiologist – these were mere characters assumed by him as garments of disguise. The real man was before me – no longer calm, courteous, and self-restrained, but fevered with suffering, and wild with undefined anxiety. This man interested in the speculations of Holland or Van Holst, the discoveries of Laplace, and the philosophy of Newton! The wide world held for him but one subject – the maddening speculation on his own madness.

'We have talked long enough this evening,' said I, 'and Rochford will be here to bid us goodbye directly. Calm yourself, and receive him with your wonted ease.'

He grasped my hand convulsively, and after a few moments' silence, resumed, in a less high-strung tone, 'I will be calm, Doctor. I always try to be so. But is it not terrible, this fight between a strong Will and a flagging Intellect? And each mysteriously helps the other, for I feel that if for an instant I relax my determination to be sane, at that instant I shall become a raging madman. Did we live in olden times one would say that an angel and a devil were fighting for my soul.

He fell back on the sofa with a faint laugh, and, at the same moment, Rochford entered hurriedly. 'Major,' he said, 'forgive me for disturbing your chat, but Beatrice has given signs of consciousness.'

The young girl's name recalled us both to present surroundings.

'Go to her at once, Fayre,' said Major Molineux; 'I am tired, and shall seek rest. Remember, the house is as your own, Rochford, and do not scruple to use it.'

'When did it happen?' I asked, as we ascended the stairs.

'About ten minutes since. Her mother was watching her, when suddenly the child opened her eyes and said, "Agnes".'

'The name of Miss Tremayne. I confess you somewhat surprise me. I should have expected that any remark she might have made would have been in reference to the accident. I wonder if she regained consciousness earlier, and unknown to you?'

'I was asleep,' said Mrs Rochford, 'nearly all last night, and I certainly fancied when I awoke that Beatrice had slightly changed her position, but there was no other sign of increased vitality, and I dismissed the matter from my mind.'

I raised Miss Rochford on her pillows, and took her hand. The fingers closed on mine, and a faint smile passed over her lips.

'You are right,' I said; she is conscious. The greatest care is now required. No noise, no conversation; above all, no sudden excitement. This is the most critical period in a case like hers.

I remained for some time in the apartment, and persuaded Rochford to stop the night. We passed an agreeable *tête-à-tête*, and on the next day had the satisfaction to find that the invalid was growing steadily convalescent. In the afternoon Major Molineux made his appearance. He was in unusually good spirits, and told me that he had felt better than he had done for many a day.

'Whether it is your medicine or your society, doctor, which has so benefited me, I don't know, but I feel a new man.'

We expressed our congratulation, and the Major surprised us both by stating that he had determined to visit the village of Green Ponds, where he had an estate.

'Do you know,' said he, 'that I have been going through my banker's book and looking up some land valuations, and I find that I am worth more than ninety thousand pounds.'

'And what do you intend to do with it?' asked Rochford, lighting his cigar. 'Some fortunate relative in England, I suppose.'

'By no means,' said Major Molineux. 'I have left it to your daughter.'

There could be, of course, no further discussion after so startling a statement, and I hastened to change the subject by suggesting that a sojourn of two or three days at Green Ponds would assist the cure which had been so happily begun.

'You have lived too long here,' I said. 'This house is gloomy, and you know every tree and shrub by heart. There is nothing like change of scene. Each object brings with it new associations, and opens up new trains of thought. Take my advice.'

'I will,' said Major Molineux, cheerily. 'I feel benefited already by the mere thoughts of the journey. May I see Miss Beatrice before I go?'

Rochford looked at me for a reply. I had rather that she had not been disturbed, but, after the magnificent avowal of the legacy, it would seem churlish to have refused.

'You may, but for a moment only,' I said. 'You will forgive me, but it is important that her newly recovered intelligence should be allowed healthy sleep after its enforced fainting fit.'

Together we mounted to the room. Beatrice was breathing regularly, and her eyes were closed in peaceful slumber.

'Poor girl,' said Major Molineux. 'She was a great favourite with my little Agnes,' and, leaning over the bed, he touched the forehead of the sleeper with his lips.

An astonishing, and to me unaccountable, change took place in the features and conduct of the invalid. Her face flushed crimson red, she opened her eyes, and, raising herself to a sitting posture, stared wildly about her. At sight of Major Molineux, she fell back as though life had suddenly left her.

'Some ugly dream, perhaps, has disturbed her,' said I, 'and the touch of your lips brought about the imagined catastrophe. She will soon recover.'

In effect, so soon as Rochford and our host had withdrawn from the room, Beatrice revived; tears rolled from beneath her eyelids and she feebly sought for my hand, holding it fast in hers, as though clinging to some saving stay.

'I was wrong to have admitted him,' I said to Mrs Rochford. 'I should have remembered that your daughter had always a dislike to him.' Low as were the tones in which I spoke, Beatrice must have heard and understood them, for she increased the pressure of her slender fingers on mine. 'He visits Green Ponds today,' I continued, 'and, at my persuasion, will stay a day or two there; so that he is not likely to alarm us again, however foolish we may be.' As I concluded, my sentence, Beatrice released my hand with a sigh of relief.

That sigh betokened much that was unpleasant to my self-love. From the moment when I had seen her life in danger I had confessed to myself that I had loved her. It is true that I was almost old enough to be her father, but love is a passion which takes no thought of years, and my affection had sensibly increased with my prolonged attendance on her. I had saved her life, and it would seem as if that life belonged to me, and I might hope, in the future, to bend it to my will. The glance of her eyes, the smile on her lip, the pressure of her hand, seemed, I thought, to indicate that she, in her inmost heart, owned a feeling for me warmer than friendship. But the instant relaxation of the muscles at the mention of the Major's absence showed me that she had besought my attention merely to shield her against some threatened danger. Her unreasoning dislike to Major Molineux had returned at the sight of him, and she wanted me near her only because she imagined that I would prevent a repetition of his visit.

Nevertheless, I did not despair of winning her, and, taking my hat, went in search of Rochford. He knew my position and my prospects. The island in which he lived, lovely though its climate and scenery might be, was not a place where he would be likely to meet with a better match than myself for his daughter, despite the difference in our ages. Captain Rochford was not rich. He had often told me that his yearly income never amounted to more than £700 a year, and – I suddenly stopped. I had forgotten the statement made by Major Molineux concerning the disposition of his fortune. Beatrice Rochford, with £90,000 dowry, might choose, even in London, among men of rank and estate. It was impossible, moreover, that I should, after hearing the promise concerning the legacy, go to the father of the heiress and ask for her hand. I should appear a mercenary adventurer, whose unblushing conduct was dictated by the meanest motives.

The position was embarrassing. Now that I clearly perceived that Beatrice Rochford was beyond my reach, my love for her grew more intense. I could put away the thought of her so long as I knew that she was near me, and that there was, at least, a possibility of my being able to win her for closer companionship. But now I realised that I must think of her no more. I began to suffer the pangs of sudden remorseful jealousy. 'Why had I not spoken earlier? Why had I not, at least, allowed Rochford to have guessed at my feelings?' And this misfortune had come upon me by the act of the man upon whose behalf I had assumed a responsibility that darkened my waking hours, and bid fair to cause me profound mental disturbance. What could have induced Major Molineux to become generous so abruptly? Angry with myself and circumstances, I resolved to put an end to this state of suspense. I would return at once to India, and, in the meantime, would see Beatrice as little as possible.

'Rochford,' I said, after dinner, 'I have received letters from Calcutta which I have too long neglected. I must return forthwith.'

'You are sudden in your determination,' said Rochford, with a slightly wounded air.

'I should have mentioned it before, but the precarious condition of Miss Rochford forbade my inflicting on you any inconvenience. She has now recovered consciousness, and, with careful nursing, needs small medical attendance.'

'Well,' said Rochford, 'we shall be all sorry to lose you – Beatrice, especially, I know – but a man of talent cannot be expected to spend his days in an out-of-the-way nook like this.'

It was on the tip of my tongue to say that I should ask nothing better than such a fate under certain conditions; but I thought of the £90,000, and was silent.

The next day I went to Hobart to make preparations for departure, and found that it would be impossible for me to leave for at least three weeks. I resolved, however, that I would not spend that time in the society of the Rochfords, but make one of a fishing party to the south-west coast of the island.

I was prevented from going by the following circumstance, which I simply record here without any speculation as to how it came about or what induced it.

On Thursday evening, the second day after I had left Castle Stuart, I was playing a rubber of whist in the card-room of the Club, when I felt someone touch me on the left shoulder. I turned round, and saw no one. Somewhat puzzled, I commenced to deal, when I heard a sharp sound, as if produced by the swish of a descending whip, and the cards were – so it seemed – struck from my hands. I raised my eyes, and, over my partner's head, I saw the face of Beatrice Rochford, floating as though in air. The lips were almost blue, and the wildly-sweeping hair framed a face of waxen pallor. The eyes – those wonderful eyes into which I had so often gazed – were alone alive, and they were fixed on me with an expression of imploring agony. Muttering some incoherent excuse, I hurried from the table, ordered out my horse, and galloped down the road to New Norfolk.

I had no doubt whatever then, and I have none now – I have already said that I do not intend to speculate upon the peculiarity of the case – that I was summoned to witness a catastrophe of some kind. I was not prepared for that which awaited me at Castle Stuart. The house was lit in the whole of the upper front, and there were lights moving about the lower rooms. Rochford himself took my horse.

'I had some instinct that you would come. Go upstairs.'

I went straight to Beatrice's room, and found her dead.

But death, in its mercy, usually leaves, for the last look of the sorrowing survivors, composed features and restful eyelids. Miss Rochford's body was rigid. Her hands were clenched and her eyes wide open, while that once lovely face was deformed with an expression of such supernatural horror that I could not glance at it again.

'How did this happen?' said I, to the mumbling and shivering Pennithorne, who had been set by Rochford on guard at the door, with strict orders not to let the bereaved mother see the fearful sight within.

'Why didn't you take her away?' she said, mopping and mowing in her usual fashion. 'I told you what would happen. She has seen him.'

My blood ran cold.

'Has the Major returned?'

'He returned last night, and kept his room all day as usual. We left Miss Rochford for a few minutes, and when we came back she was like you saw her, and *this* was on the table.'

She gave me an unopened letter, addressed to myself, in Major Molineux's handwriting. Without waiting to inspect its contents, I crossed the corridor and made my way direct to the Major's bedroom. He was lying on his face on the floor – dead, and standing on the table was an empty two-ounce phial, and an empty wine-glass.

Hastily I tore open the letter. It was written in a firm, bold hand, and evidently intended to be read by other eyes than mine. It was, in fact, Major Molineux's last effort to keep from the world's knowledge the fact that his mental life had in it anything to conceal.

Castle Stuart
24th Nov, 1835
MY DEAR DOCTOR FAYRE – My mind is so unhinged by long suffering, that I have at length determined on committing suicide. I have left the whole of my property, save some small legacies, to Miss Beatrice Rochford. Turner and Thompson have the will, and I have written to them to come to Castle Stuart so soon as my letter is received. Keep my keys in your possession until their arrival, and then deliver to them my effects. They will settle all my accounts. I wish you health and happiness.

I am, yours truly,

J. MOLINEUX

Chapter 8

An inquest was held the following day and I stated as much of the foregoing history as I thought desirable.

It was clear that, if a verdict of *felo de se* was returned, the will would be set aside and the immense fortune forfeited to the Crown.

I repeated in brief the account of the late Major's malady, saying that he was subject to a delusion of a nature which I could not reveal, which seized him on every Thursday, and that during that time I did not consider him responsible for his actions. The whole city was aware of his peculiar conduct in secluding himself on that day, and the jury returned, by direction, a verdict of 'temporary insanity'.

Twenty-seven hours after death an examination was held by the doctor of the regiment, a resident surgeon, and myself, the result of which I carefully preserved.

The emaciation was considerable. The deceased having fallen on his face, there were marks of contusion on his left temple. The body exhaled an odour of prussic acid. The eye did not present any particular appearance. The stomach was remarkably capacious, and the contents were set aside for analysis. In some parts of the mucous membrane of this organ, especially near the upper and inferior orifices, there were marks of recent inflammation, particularly in stellated patches, where slight marks of extravasation were visible. In several portions of the small intestines the external hue was dark, almost approaching to livid, and the mucous membrane of these portions was vividly or darkly red, but without extravasation or perceptible injection of the vessels. The large intestines exhibited no marks of disease of any kind, and the liver, spleen, elementary, kidneys, and abdominal viscera were all perfectly sound.

Before a knife was laid on the body, I expressed a wish that the ganglionic centres might be carefully examined, as I conceived that perhaps some irritation of the nerves of organic life played an important part in the phenomena exhibited by the patient. The solar plexus was therefore minutely investigated, but nothing abnormal was perceptible.

In the thorax there was great and varied disease. The lungs were studded with tubercles, especially the superior lobes, and extensive adhesions existed between the pleurae costales and the pleurae pulmonales. None of the tubercles had broken down so as to discharge their contents through the bronchial tubes.

The heart was not larger than usual, but the pericardium was universally adherent. The organ itself presented one of the finest specimens of 'simple hypertrophy' which I have ever seen. The parietes of the left ventricle were an inch and a quarter in thickness, and the cavity was with difficulty discovered. It could not have contained four drachms of blood, if so much, scarcely a third of that which a healthy left ventricle would be capable of throwing off at each contraction. There was nothing abnormal in the arteries, and the blood in every part of the body was perfectly fluid.

The brain was large and remarkably firm, the vessels rather congested, but there was no visible trace of disease in the head. The skull was of unusual thickness and density.

And now comes the most remarkable part of the pathology. Upon the pneumo-gastric, or *vagus* nerve of the left side, just before the recurrent is given off, there was affixed a hard, jagged body, the size of a kidney bean, composed of calcareous matter, and probably, a diseased bronchial gland, converted into this substance. The union of the nerve and the ragged mass was so intimate that no dissection, without cutting the nerve or the calcareous matter itself, could separate them. The foreign body had, in fact, penetrated, or at least invaded, the nerve, which was thickened at this part. Lower down, and involving the cardiac, pulmonic and oesophageal plexuses in a labyrinth of perplexity, were several diseased bronchial glands, rendering the dissection a tedious and difficult operation.

When we consider that the *vagus* nerve rises in the medulla oblongata, and is distributed chiefly to the great organs not under our control, and that it communicates with almost all the ganglionic nerves, we can form some idea of the disturbance produced in the system by a jagged calcareous mass implanted, as it were, in one of the most important nerves of the great vital viscera. It will be noticed that the majority of the organs to which the pueumo-gastric nerve distributes its functions were found changed in structure or disordered in function. The state of the heart probably accounted for the great emaciation, combined with the incessant craving for animal food, while the fact that it could not circulate more than one-third the usual quantity of blood through the lungs, must have produced deficient sanguification in the pulmonary apparatus whatever was the amount of digestion. Diseases of the heart are very apt to affect the brain, and my colleagues and myself agreed that dissection showed that the mental functions were disturbed by physical changes, and that the monomania in this instance, as probably in many others, was dependent on corporeal rather than moral causes.

I followed to the grave the remains of the lovely girl I had once thought to make my wife, and a few weeks afterwards quitted Hobart Town, and I have never revisited it.

The mystery of Major Molineux has now been told – at least as much as can be told without violating a confidence which I even now hold sacred. There are many points in this strange and dreadful history which I cannot attempt to explain. The periodicity of the attack is one of these; the exact relation which the injury to the nervous system bore to the peculiarly horrible form which the delusion assumed is another. The *par vagum* are the agents of communication between the mind and matter of a man, between his soul and his body, and their derangement would affect both spirit and flesh. How, I cannot say. Nor dare I speculate on the dread question why Providence permitted a poor wretch to endure tortures incomparable even among the torments of the heathen's fabled hell, and that without a particle of moral guilt.

The Bunyip

ROSA CAMPBELL PRAED

The bunyip occupies the same place in Australian folklore as the Wendigo in that of North America. It haunts lonely billabongs where it claims unwary travellers who stumble into its lair. While the Bunyip hasn't attracted the same quality of writing as the Wendigo, the following story, first published in *Coo-ee: Tales of Australian Life by Australian Ladies* (1891), conveys something of its mystery and terror. Its author, Rosa Praed (1851-1935), was well-qualified to write about the Bunyip – she was born in Queensland and grew up on remote stations in the Burnett River District where she would have heard many folk tales about such things; subsequently, her marriage to Arthur Campbell Praed in 1872 saw her endure three lonely years on an isolated station at Port Curtis. In 1875 they moved to England where she became a prolific and popular writer. She had a great interest in the occult, and many of her novels have a supernatural element, including *The Soul of Countess Adrian* (1891) and *The Brother of the Shadow* (1886). After separating from her husband, she lived with Nancy Harwood (1899–1927) whom she believed to be the reincarnation of a Roman slave girl, and based the novels *Nyria* (1904) and *Soul of Nyria* (1931) on the experience. 'The Bunyip' was first published in *Coo-ee: Tales of Australian Life by Australian Ladies*.

Everyone who has lived in Australia has heard of the Bunyip. It is the one respectable flesh-curdling horror of which Australia can boast. The old world has her tales of ghoul and vampire, of Lorelei, spook, and pixie, but Australia has nothing but her Bunyip. There never were any fauns in the eucalyptus forests, nor any naiads in the running creeks. No mythological hero left behind him stories of wonder and enchantment. No white man's hand has carved records of a poetic past on the grey volcanic-looking boulders that overshadow some lonely gullies which I know. There are no sepulchres hewn in the mountain rampart surrounding a certain dried-up lake – probably the crater of an extinct volcano – familiar to my childhood, and which in truth suggests possibilities of a forgotten city of Kör. Nature and civilisation have been very niggard here in all that makes romance.

No Australian traveller ever saw the Bunyip with his own eyes; and though there are many stockman's yarns and black's *patters* which have to do with this wonderful monster, they have all the hazy uncertainty which usually envelops information of the legendary kind. Some night, perhaps, when you are sitting over a camp fire brewing quart-pot tea and smoking store tobacco, with the spectral white gums rising like an army of ghosts around you, and the horses' hobbles clanking cheerfully in the distance, you will ask one of the overlanding hands to tell you what he knows about the Bunyip. The bushman will warm to his subject as readily as an Irishman to his banshee. He will indignantly repel your insinuation that the Bunyip may be after all as mythical as Alice's Jabberwock; and he will forthwith proceed to relate how a friend of his had a mate, who knew another chap, who had once in his life had a narrow escape from the Bunyip, and had actually beheld it - and in a certain lagoon not a hundred miles from where you are squatting. He himself has never set eyes upon the Bunyip, nor has his mate, but there is not the smallest doubt that the other chap has seen it.

When facts come to be boiled down, however, 'the other chap's' statements will seem curiously vague and contradictory; and if the details are to be accepted as they stand, a remarkable contribution to natural history must be the result.

The Bunyip is the Australian sea-serpent, only it differs from that much-disputed fact or fiction in that it does not inhabit the ocean, but makes its home in lagoons and still deep water-holes. For rivers and running creeks it appears to have an aversion. No blackfellow will object to bathe in a river because of the Bunyip, but he will shake his woolly head mysteriously over many an innocent-looking water-hole, and decline to dive for water-lily roots or some such delicacy dear to the aboriginal stomach, on the plea that 'Debil-debil sit down there.'

Debil-debil and Bunyip are synonymous terms with the blackfellow while he is on the bank of a lagoon, though 'Debil-debil' in the abstract represents a much more indefinite source of danger, and has a far wider scope of action than most mythological deities. 'Debil-debil' is a convenient way of accounting, not only for plague, sickness, and disaster, but also for peace, plenty, and good fortune. According to the religious code of the Australian aboriginal, Ormuzd and Ahriman do not work at opposite poles, but combine and concentrate themselves under one symbol. The supremacy of Debil-debil is uncontested, and he deals out promiscuously benefits and calamities from the same

hand. A medicine-man professing to be in confidential communication with Debil-debil, may kill or cure a blackfellow according to his
pleasure. The natives have a superstition, in common with many
primitive nations, that if an enemy possesses himself of a lock of hair
from the head of one to whom he wishes ill, and buries it in the
ground beneath a gum tree, the despoiled person will sicken and die
as the hair rots away. In that case Debil-debil must be 'pialla-ed'
(entreated) by the sick person to unbury the hair and cast it in the fire,
when the charm will be dissolved. The medicine-man, therefore, has
but to assure his patient that Debil-debil has refused or acceded to his
request, and death or speedy recovery will be the consequence.

The blacks have an impish drollery and love of mischief, and they
delight in imposing on the credulity of their white auditors. Thus the
stories of their superstitions must not be accepted too literally. But it
is certain that when they show a distinct reticence in regard to any
reputed article of faith, it may safely be looked upon as genuine. The
blacks never will volunteer information about the Bunyip; it has
always to be dragged out of them. When a blackfellow disappears,
it is generally understood that the Bunyip has got hold of him, and
the particular water-hole in which the monster is supposed to live
becomes more than ever an object of terror, and a place to be
avoided. The water-hole may have been hitherto uncondemned by
tradition, and the blacks may choose to disport themselves in it; but
if one of them, seized with cramp or enmeshed in weeds, sinks to rise
no more, the terrible cry of 'Bunyip' goes forth, and those waters are
from henceforth shunned.

The Bunyip is said to be an amphibious animal, and is variously
described: sometimes as a gigantic snake; sometimes as a species of
rhinoceros, with a smooth pulpy skin and a head like that of a calf,
sometimes as a huge pig, its body yellow, crossed with black stripes.
But it is also said to be something more than animal, and among its
supernatural attributes is the cold, awesome, uncanny feeling which
creeps over a company at night when the Bunyip becomes the subject
of conversation; and a certain magnetic atmosphere supposed to
envelop the creature, and to spread a deadly influence for some space
around, rendering even its vicinity dangerous, is particularly dwelt
upon. According to legend, it attracts its prey by means of this
mysterious emanation, and when sufficiently near, will draw man or
beast down to the water and suck the body under, and without sound
or struggle the victim disappears, to be seen no more. It is silent and
stealthy, and only very rarely, they say, and always at night, has been

seen to rise partially from the black water which it loves, and utter a strange moaning cry like that of a child or a woman in pain. There is a theory that water is a powerful conductor for the kind of electricity it gives out, and that a pool with dry abrupt banks and no outlying morass is tolerably safe to drink from or to camp by; but a lagoon lying amid swamp has always an evil reputation, and in some districts it is very difficult to persuade a blackfellow to venture into such a place.

One of the most famous haunts of the Bunyip, round which all sorts of stories gathered, though I never could really authenticate one of them, is a lagoon that we all knew well, and which used to furnish my brothers with many a brace of wild-fowl for our bush larder.

This lagoon is about four miles long, in some parts very deep, in others nothing but marsh, with swamp-oaks and ti-trees and ghostly white-barked she-oaks growing thickly in the shallow water. The wild-duck is so numerous in places that a gun fired makes the air black, and it is impossible to hear oneself speak, so deafening are the shrill cries of the birds which brood over the swamp.

We were none of us very much afraid of the Bunyip, though I confess to many an anxious shudder, and to having stopped and switched a stick behind me in order to make sure that all was right, when I found myself at dusk walking by the banks of the lagoon. A curious fascination, which was assuredly not the magnetic attraction of the Bunyip, used to draw me there; the place was so wild and eerie and solitary, and appealed so strongly to my imagination. I liked nothing better than to go with my brother on moonlight nights when he went down there with his gun over his shoulder to get a shot at wild-duck; the creepy feeling which would come over us as we trod along by the black water with dark slimy logs slanting into it, and reeds and moist twigs and fat marsh plants giving way under our footsteps, was quite a luxurious terror. There were such strange noises, the faint shivering sound made by the spiky leaves of the swamp-oak, the flapping of the she-oaks' scaly bark, the queer gurgling 'grrur-urr-r' of an opossum up a gum tree, the swishing of the ducks' wings when they rose suddenly in the distance, the melancholy call of the curlews – all these, breaking the silence and loneliness of the night, were indescribably uncanny and fascinating; but I am bound to say that during these expeditions we never saw a sign of the Bunyip.

We were travelling once up country – my brother Jo and I – and had arranged to camp out one night, there being no station or house of accommodation on the stage at which we could put up. The dray, loaded with stores and furniture for the new home to which we were bound, had been started some days previously, and we had agreed to meet the drivers at a certain small lagoon, known as the One-eyed Water-hole, and camp there under the dray tarpaulin. We were riding, my brother driving a pair of pack-horses with our swags, and we were unable to carry any convenience for spending a night in the bush.

It was the month of November, and the heat was overpowering. The red gum oozed from the iron-bark trees and fell in great drops like blood. The deafening noise of the forest was in strange contrast to the night silence and loneliness of the lagoon I have described. All the sounds were harsh and grating – the whirring of grasshoppers and locusts, the chattering of parrots and laughing-jackasses, the cawing of cockatoos and scuttling of iguanas through the coarse dry blady grass. It was a relief to the heat and monotony, when, as the sun set, we left the timbered ridges and came down upon a plain, across which a faint breeze blew, and where we could see, at the foot of a distant ridge, the One-eyed Water-hole and our dray beside it, loaded high, and covered with a huge tarpaulin that hung all round it like a tent.

The men were busy making a fire and watering the bullocks. They had got down their blankets and the rations and tin billys and quart pots from the dray, and Mick, who had been hut-keeper to a party of shearers, was mixing Johnny-cakes on a piece of newly-cut bark, ready for baking when the logs had burnt down into ashes and embers. Some of the others had cut tufts from the grass trees on the ridge, and strewn them on the earth under the dray for us to lie upon. Very soon we were all comfortably camped, and as night closed in and the stars shone out, the scene became more and more picturesque. Our fire had been lighted a few yards away from the lagoon, which, deep and black where the banks were high, widened out at the lower end into a swamp of she-oaks, their white lanky stems standing out against the darker background of ridge, densely covered with jungle-like scrub.

We had eaten our meal of beef and hot Johnny-cakes all together by the dray, and there was something striking about the appearance of the men, in their bright Crimean shirts and rough moleskin trousers and broad-brimmed cabbage-tree hats, as they lounged in easy attitudes, smoking their pipes and drinking quart-pot tea, while they waxed communicative under the influence of a nip of grog, which had been served out to them apiece.

They were telling shearing stories – how Paddy Mack and Long Charlie had had a bet as to which could shear a sheep the fastest; how

Father Flaherty, the priest from the township, who had come over to see the shearing in full swing, timed them by his watch; how at the word 'off' the shears slashed down through the wool, and how the quickest man sheared his sheep in less than a minute, and the other a second and a half later. Then Mick had to tell of a man who used to shear his hundred and twenty sheep in the day, and on his way from the wool-shed to the hut jump over a four-foot-six post and rail fence, which after having been bent double all day was a feat he might be proud of.

Then somehow – perhaps it was the wilderness and loneliness of the place, or the wind across the plain, or the sighing of the she-oaks, or the weird 'poomp' of the bullock bells – the talk got on to eerie things, and from the authentic story of Fisher's Ghost it was an easy transition to the Bunyip and all its supernatural horrors. Most of the men had some Bunyip tale to relate; and as we talked a sort of chill seemed to creep over us, and one could almost fancy that the horrible monster was casting its magnetic spell upon us from the dark swamp close by. After a bit, when it was discovered that the billys were empty, and that we wanted more water to make some fresh tea, no one seemed inclined to go down to the lagoon to fetch it, and Mick, taking a firestick to light his pipe, said slowly –

'Begorra, Charlie, we must look out here for the Bunyip. You ask old Darby Magrath if he'd like to camp down by the swamp of the One-eyed Water-hole all night by himself. I remember Darby telling me that when he was riding across this plain one night after shearing, his horse stopped of a sudden and trembled all over under him – just like a bullock in the killing yard when you drop the spear into his neck. Darby says he felt cold all through his bones; and then a queer sort of noise came up from the water – a kind of sound like a baby moaning – and he just clapped spurs into his old yarraman (horse), and never pulled up out of a gallop till he had got over the range and was at the 'Coffin Lid' public, five miles on. The horse was all dripping with sweat, and poor old Darby as white as a corpse.'

'Well, I don't know much about the thing myself – never had no Bunyip experiences myself; but unless Gemmel Dick is *the* most almighty liar' – began Long Charlie, taking out his pipe in preparation for a blood-curdling yarn and then stopping suddenly, for at that moment there came a curious sound from the lagoon, or the swamp, or the plains to our left, we could not tell whence – a wild, thrilling sound, which at first seemed scarcely human, but which, when repeated after the interval of a moment or two, struck my heart as if it were the cry of some dying animal, or of a child in dire distress and agony.

We all started and looked anxiously at each other, waiting until it came again, and not quite liking to confess our tremors, when one of the men exclaimed nervously – 'Say, what's that?'

'Wallabi bogged,' pronounced Long Charlie oracularly, and was beginning once more –

'Well, as I was telling you, if Gemmel Dick ain't *the* most – '

But that strange, horrible cry from the lagoon – yes, it must come from the swamp end of the lagoon – broke the night silence again, and stopped Long Charlie a second time. It was more prolonged, more certain, than it had been before. Beginning low, a sort of hoarse muffled groan, it swelled into a louder, shriller note, which we at once imagined might be the strained broken coo-ee of a child in pain or terror.

Every one of us rose.

'By Jove! I'll tell you what I believe it is,' said my brother Jo excitedly. 'That's some free-selector's kid lost in the bush. Come along, you fellows. Don't be funky of the Bunyip.'

He darted down towards the swamp, which lay some little distance from our camp, the dark heads of the she-oaks rising above a thick veil of white mist, that shrouded completely the less lofty and more straggling branches of the ti-trees. The rest of us followed him closely. It must be said that we were not deterred at that moment by any thought of the Bunyip and its supernatural atmosphere. Long Charlie, the most practical of the party, waited to detach a rough lantern which hung from one of the staples of the dray, and caught us up as we reached the borders of the swamp. The sound had ceased now. Coo-eeing loudly, we peered through the cold clinging mist among the brown twisted branches of the ti-trees, which shook their scented bottle-brush blossoms in our faces. Under our feet, the ground, which had been trodden into deep odd-shaped ruts by the cattle coming down to drink, gave way at every step. We could hear the soft 'k-sssh' of the displaced water, and we shivered as the slimy ooze mounted over our insteps and trickled down through our boots, while the pulpy rushes sprang back as we forced ourselves through, and struck our hands with clammy touch.

It was a dreary, uncanny place, and even through our coo-ees the night that had seemed so silent on the plain was here full of ghostly noises, stifled hissings, and unexpected gurglings and rustlings, and husky croaks, and stealthy glidings and swishings.

'Look out for snakes,' said Long Charlie, flourishing his lantern. 'And don't all of us be coo-eeing all the time, or when the little chap sings out we shan't be able to hear him.'

We stopped coo-eeing, and presently the wail sounded again, fainter and more despairing, we fancied, and urging us to greater energy. Though we tried to move in the direction of the voice, it was impossible to determine whence it came, so misleading and fitful and will-o'-the-wisp-like was the sound. Now it seemed to come from our right, now from our left, now from the very depths of the lagoon, and now from the scrub on the ridge beyond.

I don't know how we got through the deeper part of the swamp without getting bogged; but we did at last, and reached the scrub that straggled down to the water's edge. Here was dense, and in places impenetrable foliage; rough boulders were lying pell-mell at the foot of the ridge, and creepers hung in withes from the trees, with great thorns that tore our hands and our clothes. We did not know which way to turn, for the cry had ceased, and the dead silence of the scrub was like that of the grave. We waited for a minute or two, but it did not come again.

'I believe it was the Bunyip after all,' said Mick, with a shudder. 'And look here, I shall head the lagoon, I ain't going to cross that swamp again. It's all nonsense about the little 'un, not a child nor a grown man or beast could have forced theirselves down here.'

Long Charlie flashed his lantern along the wall of green, and, stumbling over stones and logs, we walked as well as we could, skirting the scrub and making for the head of the lagoon. We paused every now and then, straining our ears for the voice that had led us hither, and once it sounded faint but thrillingly plaintive, and guided us on.

At last there came a break in the jungle, a narrow track piercing the heart of the scrub, and then a wider break, and a warning cry from Long Charlie in advance –

'Hello! Look out! It's a gully – pretty deep. You might break a leg before you knew it. Keep along up the track.'

We kept along up the track, waiting to let Long Charlie go first with his lantern. Suddenly the moon, which had risen while we were in the swamp, sent a shaft of light down through the opening, and showed us, a little way ahead, where the track widened out and then stopped altogether, a tiny plateau, in the centre of which stood a great white bottle tree, its trunk perfectly bare, bulging out in the centre like a garment swelled by the wind, and looking in its fantastic shape like a sentinel spectre.

It gave one a strange creepy feeling to see this huge white thing rising up so solemnly in the midst of the gloom and the solitude. There was something else white on the grass – something almost the same shape as the bottle tree lying across at its foot. The moon was dim for a moment or two. Nobody spoke, we pressed up the ridge side, then a hoarse smothered ejaculation burst from Long Charlie's lips, and as he spoke the moon shone forth again, and he shifted his lantern so that its gleam fell athwart the white prostrate form and upon a snake, brown and shiny and scaly and horrible, which uncoiled itself, and with a swift, wavy motion disappeared into the depths of the scrub.

It seemed to us, we said afterwards, as though we could hear each other's hearts beating. The men were too horrified to utter a sound. At last Long Charlie said, in a deep, awe-stricken voice –

'By God! that beats me.'

And then Mick, moving a little nearer, cried, with a sob in his brawny throat –

'It's Nancy – little Nancy – Sam Duffy's girl from the "Coffin Lid", and it was only the other day she came out and served me with a nobbler.'

Paddy Mack was sobbing too, they all seemed to know and love the child.

'She wur so fond of looking for chuckie-chuckies in the scrub, and quantongs and things. And she might have knowed, poor little Nancy! that if she wanted quantongs, I'd have got 'em for her; and didn't I string her a necklace only last shearing! But she was always a child for roaming – she wasn't afraid of snakes, nor blacks, nor nothing – she said she liked to hear the bell-bird call, and that it seemed to be always calling *her*. I've heard her say that – poor little Nancy! – always smiling when she carried a chap out a nobbler. And now the bell-bird has rung her home.'

Long Charlie only said again, 'That beats me.'

They couldn't account for it; the child had been dead some hours, they said. They couldn't believe it was that snake which had bitten her, and they declared that the cry we heard must have been the Bunyip, or little Nancy's ghost.

Lupton's Guest
A Memory of the Eastern Pacific

LOUIS BECKE

In his day Louis Becke (1855–1913) was compared with Rudyard Kipling and Robert Louis Stevenson. He was born in Port Macquarie, New South Wales, and educated in Sydney, but left school at fourteen to sail for America. For most of the next twenty-five years he worked as a trader in the Pacific, and his experiences formed the basis of many of his novels and short stories. A chance meeting with Ernest Favenc sparked his writing career; Favenc introduced him to J. F. Archibald the founder of the important Australian literary journal, *The Bulletin*, and Becke began submitting stories set in Australia and the Pacific. He moved to England in 1896, and subsequently lived in a variety of different countries before returning to Sydney in 1909. He died forgotten and in poverty four years later. Becke wrote several fine supernatural tales, and this, from *The Ebbing of the Tide: South Sea Stories* (1895), is the pick of them.

A long sweeping curve of coast, fringed with tall plumed palms casting wavering shadows on the yellow sand as they sway and swish softly to the breath of the brave trade-wind that whistles through the thickly-verdured hummocks on the weather side of the island, to die away into a soft breath as, after passing through the belt of coconuts, it faintly ripples the transparent depths of the lagoon – a broad sheet of blue and silver stretching away from the far distant western line of reef to the smooth, yellow beach at the foot of the palms on the easternmost islet. And here, beneath their lofty crowns, are the brown thatched huts of the people and the home of Lupton the trader.

This is Mururea. And, if it be possible, Mururea surpasses in beauty any other of the 'cloud of islands' which, lying on the blue bosom of the Eastern Pacific like the islands of a dream, are called by their people the Paumotu. And these people – it is not of very long ago I speak – are a people unto themselves. Shy and suspicious of strangers, white or brown, and endued with that quick instinct of fear which impels untutored minds to slay, and which we, in our civilised ignorance, call savage treachery, they are yet kind-hearted and hospitable to those who learn their ways and regard their customs. A tall, light-skinned, muscular people, the men with long, straight, black hair, coiled up in a knot at the back, and the women – the descendants of those who sailed with broken Fletcher Christian and his comrades of the *Bounty* in quest of a place where to die – soft-voiced, and with big, timorous eyes.

* * *

'Twas here that Ben Peese, the handsome, savagely humorous, and voluble colleague of Captain 'Bully' Hayes, the modern rover of the South Seas, one day appeared. Lupton, with his son and two natives, were out searching the beach of a little islet for turtles' eggs, when the boy, who had been sent to obtain a few young drinking coconuts from a tree some little distance away, called out, '*Te Pah*!' (a ship). A few minutes passed, and then, outlined against the narrow strip of coconuts that grew on the north end of the main islet of the lagoon, Lupton saw the sails of a schooner making for the only opening – a narrow passage on the eastern side.

Now vessels came but rarely to Mururea, for Du Petit Thouars, the French Admiral of the Pacific fleet, had long since closed the group to the Sydney trading ships that once came there for pearl-shell, and Lupton felt uneasy. The vessel belonging to the Tahitian firm for whom he traded was not due for many months. Could the stranger be that wandering Ishmael of the sea – Peese? Only he, or his equally daring and dreaded colleague, Bully Hayes – would dare to sail a vessel of any size in among the coral 'mushrooms' that studded the current-swept waters of the dangerous passage.

What did he want? And honest Frank Lupton, a quiet and industrious trader, thought of his store of pearl-shell and felt still more doubtful. And he knew Peese so well, the dapper, handsome little Englishman with the pleasant voice that had in it always a ripple of laughter – the voice and laugh that concealed his tigerish heart and savage vindictiveness. Lupton had children too – sons and daughters – and Peese, who looked upon women as mere articles of merchandise, would have thought no more of carrying off the trader's two pretty daughters than he would of 'taking' a cask of oil or a basket of pearl-shell.

* * *

His anxious face, paling beneath the tropic bronze of twenty years'
ocean wanderings, betrayed his feelings to the two natives who were
now pulling the boat with all their strength to gain the village, and
one – Maora, his wife's brother, a big, light-skinned man, with that
keen, hawk-like visage peculiar to the people of the eastern islands of
Polynesia, said –

''Tis an evil day, Farani! No ship but that of the Little Man with
the Beard hath ever passed into the lagoon since the great English
fighting ship came inside,' (he spoke of 1863) 'for the reef hath
grown and spread out and nearly closed it. Only the Little Bearded
Devil would dare it, for he hath been here twice with the Man of the
Strong Hand' (Hayes). 'And, Farani, listen! "The hand to the club!"'

They ceased pulling. From the village came the sound of an almost
forgotten cry – a signal of danger to the dwellers under the palms –
'The hand to the club!' – meaning for the men to arm.

* * *

Lupton hesitated. The natives would, he knew, stand to him to a man
if violence to or robbery of him were attempted. But to gain the
village he must needs pass close the vessel, and to pass on and not
board her would savour of cowardice – and Lupton was an Englishman, and his twenty years' wanderings among the dangerous people
of some of the islands of the Paumotu Group had steeled his nerves
to meet any danger or emergency. So, without altering the course of
the boat, he ran alongside of the vessel – which was a brigantine –
just as she was bringing to, and looking up, he saw the face he
expected.

'How are you, Lupton, my dear fellow?' said Peese, as the trader
gained the deck, wringing his hand effusively, as if he were a long-
lost brother. 'By Heavens! I'm glad to meet a countryman again, and
that countryman Frank Lupton. Don't like letting your hand go.'
And still grasping the trader's rough hand in his, delicate and smooth
as a woman's, he beamed upon him with an air of infantile pleasure.

* * *

This was one of Peese's peculiarities – an affectation of absolute
affection for any Englishman he met, from the captain of a man-of-
war (these, however, he avoided as much as possible), to a poor
beachcomber with but a grass girdle round his loins.

'What brings you here, Captain Peese?' said Lupton, bluntly, as
his eye sought the village, and saw the half-naked figures of his native

following leaving his house in pairs, each carrying between them a square box, and disappearing into the puka scrub. It was his pearl-shell. Màmeri, his wife, had scented danger, and the shell at least was safe, however it befell. Peese's glance followed his, and the handsome little captain laughed, and slapped the gloomy-faced and suspicious trader on the back with an air of *camaraderie*.

'My dear fellow, what an excessively suspicious woman your good Màmeri is! But do not be alarmed. I have not come here to do any business this time, but to land a passenger, and as soon as his traps are on the beach I'm off again to Maga Reva. Such are the exigencies, my dear Lupton, of a trading captain's life in the South Seas, I cannot even spare the time to go on shore with you and enjoy the hospitality of the good Màmeri and your two fair daughters. But come below with me and see my passenger.' And he led the way to his cabin.

*   *   *

The passenger's appearance, so Lupton told me, 'twas enough to make a man's blood curdle, so ghastly pale and emaciated was he. He rose as Lupton entered and extended his hand.

'My friend here,' said the worthy little Ishmael, bowing and caressing his long silky beard, 'is, ah, hum, Mr Brown. He is, as you will observe, my dear Lupton, in a somewhat weak state of health, and is in search of some retired spot where he may recuperate sufficiently – '

'Don't lie unnecessarily, sir.'

Peese bowed affably and smiled, and the stranger addressed Lupton.

'My name is not Brown – 'tis of no consequence what it is; but I am, indeed, as you see, in a bad way, with but a few months at most to live. Captain Peese, at my request, put into this lagoon. He has told me that the place is seldom visited by ships, and that the people do not care about strangers. Yet, have you, Mr Lupton, any objections to my coming ashore here, and living out the rest of my life? I have trade goods sufficient for all requirements, and will in no way inter-fere with or become a charge upon you.'

Lupton considered. His influence with the people of Mururea was such that he could easily overcome their objections to another white man landing; but he had lived so long apart from all white associations that he did not care about having the even monotony of his life disturbed. And then, he thought, it might be some queer game con-cocted between the sick man and the chattering little sea-hawk that sat beside him stroking and fondling his flowing beard. He was about to refuse when the sunken, eager eyes of 'Mr Brown' met his in an almost appealing look that disarmed him of all further suspicion.

'Very well, sir. The island is as free to you as to me. But, still, I could stop anyone else from living here if I wished to do so. But you do look very ill, no mistake about that. And, then, you ain't going to trade against me! And I suppose you'll pass me your word that there isn't any dodge between you and the captain here to bone my shell and clear out?'

For answer the sick man opened a despatch-box that lay on the cabin table, and took from it a bag of money.

'This,' he said, 'is the sum I agreed to pay Captain Peese to land me on any island of my choice in the Paumotu Archipelago, and this unsigned order here is in his favour on the Maison Brander of Tahiti for a similar sum.'

Signing the paper he pushed it with the money over to Peese, and then went on –

'I assure you, Mr Lupton, that this is the only transaction I have ever had with Captain Peese. I came to him in Tahiti, hearing he was bound to the Paumotu Group. I had never heard of him before, and after today I will not, in all human probability, see him again.'

'Perfectly correct, my dear sir,' said Peese. 'And now, as our business is finished, perhaps our dear friend, Lupton, will save me the trouble of lowering a boat by taking you ashore in his own, which is alongside.'

Five minutes later and Lupton and the stranger were seated in the boat.

'Good-bye, my dear Lupton, and *adios* my dear Mr Brown. I shall ever remember our pleasant relations on board my humble little trading vessel,' cried the renowned Peese, who, from former associations, had a way of drifting into the Spanish tongue – and prisons and fetters – which latter he once wore for many a weary day on the cruiser *Hernandez Pizarro* on his way to the gloomy prison of Manilla.

The boat had barely traversed half the distance to the shore ere the brigantine's anchor was hove-up and at her bows, and then Peese, with his usual cool assurance, beat her through the intricate passage and stood out into the long roll of the Pacific.

* * *

When Lupton, with his 'walking bone bag', as he mentally called the stranger, entered his house, Màmeri, his bulky native wife, uttered an exclamation of pity, and placing a chair before him uttered the simple word of welcome *Iorana*! and the daughters, with wonder-lit star-like eyes, knelt beside their father's chair and whispered, 'Who is he, Farani?'

And Lupton could only answer, 'I don't know, and won't ask. Look to him well.'

He never did ask. One afternoon nearly a year afterwards, as Lupton and Trenton, the supercargo of the *Marama*, sat on an old native *marae* at Arilpahi, the Village of Four Houses, he told the strange story of his sick guest.

*　　*　　*

The stranger had at first wished to have a house built for himself, but Lupton's quiet place and the shy and reserved natures of his children made him change his intention and ask Lupton for a part of his house. It was given freely – where are there more generous-hearted men than these world-forgotten, isolated traders? – and here the Silent Man, as the people of Mururea called him, lived out the few months of his life. That last deceptive stage of his insidious disease had given him a fictitious strength. On many occasions, accompanied by the trader's children, he would walk to the north point of the low-lying island, where the cloudy spume of the surge was thickest and where the hollow and resonant crust of the black reef was perforated with countless air-holes, through which the water hissed and roared, and shot high in air, to fall again in misty spray.

And here, with dreamy eyes, he would sit under the shade of a clump of young coconuts, and watch the boil and tumble of the surf, whilst the children played with and chased each other about the clinking sand. Sometimes he would call them to him – Farani the boy, and Teremai and Lorani, the sweet-voiced and tender-eyed girls – and ask them to sing to him; and in their soft semi-Tahitian dialect they would sing the old songs that echoed in the ears of the desperate men of the *Bounty* that fatal dawn when, with bare-headed, defiant Bligh drifting astern in his boat, they headed back for Tahiti and death.

*　　*　　*

Four months had passed when one day the strange white man, with Lupton's children, returned to the village. As they passed in through the doorway with some merry chant upon their lips, they saw a native seated on the matted floor. He was a young man, with straight, handsome features, such as one may see any day in Eastern Polynesia, but the children, with terrified faces, shrank aside as they passed him and went to their father.

The pale face of the Silent Man turned inquiringly to Lupton, who smiled.

''Tis Màmeri's teaching, you know. She is a Catholic from Magareva, and prays and tells her beads enough to work a whaleship's crew into heaven. But this man is a "Soul Catcher", and if any one of us here got sick, Màmeri would let the faith she was reared in go to the wall and send for the "Soul Catcher". He's a kind of an all-round prophet, wizard, and general wisdom merchant. Took over the soul-catching business from his father – runs in the family, you know.'

'Ah!' said the Silent Man in his low, languid tones, looking at the native, who, the moment he had entered, had bent his eyes to the ground, 'and in which of his manifold capacities has he come to see you, Lupton?'

Lupton hesitated a moment, then laughed.

'Well, sir, he says he wants to speak to you. Wants to *pahihi* (talk rot), I suppose. It's his trade, you know. I'd sling him out only that he isn't a bad sort of a fellow – and a bit mad – and Màmeri says he'll quit as soon as he has had his say.'

'Let him talk,' said the calm, quiet voice; 'I like these people, and like to hear them talk – better than I would most white men.'

* * *

Then with his dark, dilated eyes moving from the pale face of the white man to that of Lupton, the native wizard and Seer of Unseen Things spoke. Then again his eyes sought the ground.

'What does he say?' queried Lupton's guest.

'D— rot,' replied the trader, angrily.

'Tell me exactly, if you please. I feel interested.'

'Well, he says that he was asleep in his house when his "spirit voice" awoke him and said' – here Lupton paused and looked at his guest, and then, seeing the faint smile of amused interest on his melancholy features, resumed, in his rough, jocular way – 'and said – the "spirit voice", you know – that your soul was struggling to get loose, and is going away from you tonight. And the long and short of it is that this young fellow here wants to know if you'll let him save it – keep you from dying, you know. Says he'll do the job for nothing, because you're a good man, and a friend to all the people of Mururea.'

'Mr Brown' put his thin hand across his mouth, and his eyes smiled at Lupton. Then some sudden, violent emotion stirred him, and he spoke with such quick and bitter energy that Lupton half rose from his scat in vague alarm.

'Tell him,' he said – 'that is, if the language expresses it – that my soul has been in hell these ten years, and its place filled with ruined hopes and black despair,' and then he sank back on his couch of mats, and turned his face to the wall.

The Seer of Unseen Things, at a sign from the now angry Lupton, rose to his feet. As he passed the trader he whispered – 'Be not angry with me, Farani; art not thou and all thy house dear to me, the Snarer of Souls and Keeper Away of Evil Things? And I can truly make a snare to save the soul of the Silent Man, if he so wishes it.' The low, impassioned tones of the wizard's voice showed him to be under strong emotion, and Lupton, with smoothened brow, placed his hand on the native's chest in token of amity.

'Farani,' said the wizard, 'see'st thou these?' and he pointed to where, in the open doorway, two large white butterflies hovered and fluttered. They were a species but rarely seen in Mururea, and the natives had many curious superstitions regarding them.

'Aye,' said the trader, 'what of them?'

'Lo, they are the spirits that await the soul of him who sitteth in thy house. One is the soul of a woman, the other of a man; and their bodies are long ago dust in a far-off land. See, Farani, they hover and wait, wait, wait. Tomorrow they will be gone, but then another may be with them.'

Stopping at the doorway the tall native turned, and again his strange, full black eyes fixed upon the figure of Lupton's guest. Then slowly he untied from a circlet of polished pieces of pearl-shell strung together round his sinewy neck a little round leaf-wrapped bundle. And with quiet assured step he came and stood before the strange white man and extended his hand.

'Take it, O man, with the swift hand and the strong heart, for it is thine.'

And then he passed slowly out.

Lupton could only see that as the outside wrappings of fala leaves fell off they revealed a black substance, when Mr Brown quickly placed it in the bosom of his shirt.

*   *   *

'And sure enough,' continued Lupton, knocking the ashes from his pipe out upon the crumbling stones of the old marae, and speaking in, for him, strangely softened tones, 'the poor chap did die that night, leastways at *kalaga moa* [cockcrow],' and then he refilled his pipe in silence, gazing the while away out to the North-West Point.

* * *

'What a curious story,' began the supercargo, after an interval of some minutes, when he saw that Lupton, usually one of the merriest-hearted wanderers that rove to and fro in Polynesia, seemed strangely silent and affected, and had turned his face from him.

He waited in silence till the trader chose to speak again.

Away to the westward, made purple by the sunset haze of the tropics, lay the ever-hovering spume-cloud of the reef of North-West Point – the loved haunt of Lupton's guest – and the muffled boom of the ceaseless surf deepened now and then as some mighty roller tumbled and crashed upon the flat ledges of blackened reef.

* * *

At last the trader turned again to the supercargo, almost restored to his usual equanimity. 'I'm a pretty rough case, Mr, and not much given to any kind of sentiment or squirming, but I would give half I'm worth to have him back again. He sort of got a pull on my feelin's the first time he ever spoke to me, and as the days went on, I took to him that much that if he'd a wanted to marry my little Teremai I'd have given her to him cheerful. Not that we ever done much talkin', but he'd sit night after night and make me talk, and when I'd spun a good hour's yarn he'd only say, "Thank you, Lupton, good-night", and give a smile all round to us, from old Màmeri to the youngest *tama*, and go to bed. And yet he did a thing that'll go hard agin' him, I fear.'

'Ah,' said Trenton, 'and so he told you at the last – I mean his reason for coming to die at Mururea.'

'No, he didn't. He only told me something; Peese told me the rest. And he laughed when he told me,' and the dark-faced trader struck his hand on his knee. 'Peese would laugh if he saw his mother crucified.'

'Was Peese back here again, then?' inquired Trenton.

'Yes, two months ago. He hove-to outside, and came ashore in a canoe. Said he wanted to hear how his dear friend Brown was. He only stayed an hour, and then cleared out again.'

'Did he die suddenly?' the supercargo asked, his mind still bent on Lupton's strange visitor.

'No. Just before daylight he called me to him – with my boy. He took the boy's hand and said he'd have been glad to have lived after all. He had been happy in a way with me and the children here in Mururea. Then he asked to see Teremai and Lorani. They both cried when they saw he was a goin' – all native-blooded people do that if they cares anything at all about a white man, and sees him dyin'.

' "Have you any message, or anything to say in writin', sir?" I says to him.

'He didn't answer at once, only took the girls' hands in his, and kisses each of 'em on the face, then he says, "No, Lupton, neither. But send the children away now. I want you to stay with me to the last – which will be soon."

'Then he put his hand under his pillow, and took out a tiny little parcel, and held it in his closed hand.'

* * *

'Mr Lupton, I ask you before God to speak honestly. Have you, or have you not, ever heard of me, and why I came here to die, away from the eyes of men?'

'No, sir,' I said. 'Before God I know no more of you now than the day I first saw you!'

'Can you, then, tell me if the native soul-doctor who came here last night is a friend of Captain Peese? Did he see Peese when I landed here? Has he talked with him?'

'No. When you came here with Peese, the soul-seer was away at another island. And as for talking with him, how could he? Peese can't speak two words of Paumotu.'

He closed his eyes a minute. Then he reached out his hand to me and said. 'Look at that; what is it?'

It was the little black thing that the Man Who Sees Beyond gave him, and was a curious affair altogether. 'You know what an *aitu taliga* is?' asked Lupton.

'Yes a "devil's ear" – that's what the natives call fungus.'

* * *

'Well,' continued Lupton, 'this was a piece of dried fungus, and yet it wasn't a piece of fungus. It was the exact shape of a human heart – just as I've seen a model of it made of wax. That hadn't been its natural shape, but the sides had been brought together and stitched with human hair -- by the soul-doctor, of course. I looked at it curiously enough, and gave it back to him. His fingers closed round it again.

' "What is it?" he says again.

' "It's a model of a human heart," says I, "made of fungus."

' "My God," he says, "how could he know?"

Then he didn't say any more, and in another half-hour or so he dies, quiet and gentlemanly like. I looked for the heart with Màmeri in the morning – it was gone.

*   *   *

'Well, we buried him. And now look here, Mr —, as sure as I believe there's a God over us, I believe that that native soul-catcher bas dealings with the Devil. I had just stowed the poor chap in his coffin and was going to nail it down when the *kanaka* wizard came in, walks up to me, and says he wants to see the dead man's hand. Just to humour him I lifted off the sheet. The soul-catcher lifted the dead man's hands carefully, and then I'm d—d if he didn't lay that dried heart on his chest and press the hands down over it.

' "What's that for?" says I.

' " 'Tis is the heart of the woman he slew in her sleep. Let it lie with him, so that there may be peace between them at last," and then he glides away without another word.'

*   *   *

'I let it stay, not thinking much of it at the time. Well, as I was tellin' you, Peese came again. Seeing that I had all my people armed, I treated him well and we had a chat, and then I told him all about "Mr Brown's" death and the soul-saver and the dried heart. And then Peese laughs and gives me this newspaper cutting. I brought it with me to show you.'

Trenton took the piece of paper and read.

*   *   *

'Lester Mornington made his escape from the State prison at San Quentin (Cal.) last week, and is stated to be now on his way either to Honolulu or Tahiti. It has been ascertained that a vast sum of money has been disbursed in a very systematic manner during the last few weeks to effect his release. Although nearly eight years have elapsed since he committed his terrible crime, the atrocious nature of it will long be remembered. Young, wealthy, respected, and talented, he had been married but half a year when the whole of the Pacific Slope was startled with the intelligence that he had murdered his beautiful young wife, who had, he found, been disloyal to him.

'Entering the bedroom he shot his sleeping wife through the temples, and then with a keen-edged knife had cut out her still-beating heart. This, enclosed in a small box, he took to the house of the man who had wronged him, and desired him to open it and look at the contents. He did so, and Mornington, barely giving him time to realise the tragedy, and that his perfidy was known, shot him twice, the wounds proving fatal next day. The murderer made good his escape to Mexico, only returning to California a month ago, when he was recognised (although disguised) and captured, and at the time of his escape was within two days of the time of his trial before Judge Crittenden.'

*   *   *

'There's always a woman in these things,' said Lupton, as the super-cargo gave him back the slip. 'Come on.'

And he got down from his seat on the wall. 'There's Màmeri calling us to *kaikai* – stewed pigeons. She's a bully old cook! Worth her weight in Chile dollars.'

The Haunted Pool
A Tale of the Blue Mountains

EDWARD WHEATLEY

The following story appeared in *The Sydney Mail* on 8th November 1879. I have been unable to find any information on Edward Wheatley at all. He does not appear in any bibliography, catalogue or history of Australian literature that I can find, and the name may be a pseudonym. 'The Haunted Pool' is an evocative tale of the Australian bush, linking Australian and classical mythology, and is worth reviving here.

The sun was high in the heavens as we reached the edge of the valley, towards which we had all morning been walking.

For hours we had plodded through sand among monotonous gum trees, and now, all of a sudden, stood upon the brink of a vast precipice which seemed to have been rent out of the tableland over which we had been travelling, by some mighty convulsion of nature. Below us lay an almost inaccessible valley, sheer down beneath us some 1500 feet, while the gums which clustered thick within it were dwarfed into the semblance of tiny ferns by the distance. The head becomes giddy as one gazes into such vast depths, and I clung to a tree which stood close by, while I was lost in indescribable awe at the spectacle before me. A waterfall rushed over a rock close to us, dissolving into thin spray long before it reached the bottom of the gulf, and away in the distance a stream wound its tortuous way through the valley, looking like a thread of silver thrown into relief by the dark background of the gum-tree scrub through which it forced its way.

'Well, old boy, what do you think of that? Beats anything you've ever seen in the old country, doesn't it?' said Bob Smith, one of my companions. 'It is indeed very different,' replied I; 'but it is more impressive, more awful than beautiful, I think. I should have been sorry to have missed seeing it before returning to England, but I should dread having to live here. The place looks as if it might be haunted, and I wouldn't spend a night in that gloomy valley alone for all the wealth of the Indies.' ' "Haunted!" ' said Jack Smith, brother to the former speaker, for these two were my old college friends, showing me the lions of their adopted home. ' "Haunted!" You may well say that. It is, too, as I can tell to my cost.' 'Indeed,' returned I, 'you interest me, do tell me about it.' 'Oh, hang it,' said Bob, 'don't bother us with that old story of yours. Let's get lunch ready, for I'm as hungry as a hunter, and after we've attended to the wants of the inner man I don't mind smoking a cigar while you bore Harry with your story of the Haunted Pool.'

Half an hour later, lunch having been duly disposed of, while we three puffed the fragrant weed, reclining on a knoll which gave us an uninterrupted view of the weird valley before us, Jack Smith thus began the tale –

'Do you see that clump of trees away up the valley? Well, a little to the left you will see the river widens out a bit and forms a good-sized pool; this is the spot where some four years ago my adventure befell me. It was in the good old days, when every stream between this and Bathurst was searched for the yellow metal which had sent all New South Wales into a fever, that Bob and I, bitten by the fever like the rest, set off on our "own hook" prospecting. We chose this lonely stream, and, with our swags on our backs, forced our way up from Hawkesbury, until we found ourselves in the deep, dark valley you see below you. We had, of course, been unsuccessful. It was midsummer and the hot sun kept pouring down upon us; while so deep and hidden does the valley lie, so closed up with scrub and gum trees, which, as you know, give no shade, that not a breath of air could reach us. We had toiled up the course of the river, digging and washing in every likely-looking spot; but the work was excessively fatiguing, particularly as we were totally unaccustomed to manual labour; and, besides, we were in perpetual fear of the snake by day, and worried to death by the mosquitoes by night. So, after a week of this sort of thing, you may imagine we were thoroughly knocked up.

'One day, I was a good bit ahead of Bob, who was sulkily engaged in rocking his cradle for the gold which never would show, regularly dead beat, when I suddenly stumbled upon that pool which you see in the distance.

'It was very hot, and the breeze which rustled in the tree-tops did not reach me, parched and perspiring, below. I threw off my swag, and sat down on the margin of the pool. The water was deep, deep enough for a swim, and looked so cool and inviting that I determined to have a dip.

'High rocks, clothed with ferns and creepers, formed the setting of the little bit of water which came tumbling down in a tiny waterfall at the upper end, and, after swirling about into cool little shady nooks and crevices, came brawling out again at the lower end, falling in another miniature cascade into its bed, and thence meandered through the valley. The cool air – for in the vicinity of the pool, in the shade, surrounded by damp ferns and foliage, it was cool – was grateful to me, and I sat for a time on a moss-covered rock dabbling my feet in the water before I made my final plunge. I remember thinking what a beautiful spot it would be for a water-nymph, and wondering whether this Australian streamlet could boast of an Egeria!

'Revolving such fancies, I slipped into the water, and, being a good swimmer, soon made the tour of the rock-bound basin, swim-ming close up to the margin, where the rocks were high above me, revelling in the delightful freedom of the water. Suddenly I heard a splash – a very gentle splash, as of someone slipping, not plunging in. I looked round, fully expecting it was my brother who had arrived, and was coming to join me; but no, it was not he; I could see nothing. "Tush," said I, "it must have been a frog, or something of the sort," and went on. Hush! surely that is someone swimming behind me – gently swish, swish through the water! No, it cannot be; I can see nothing. But still whenever I resumed swimming the gentle splash, splash is audible, and, stopping when I stop, seems to dog my course. Frequently I turn round suddenly to catch my invisible attendant, but always in vain – there is nothing to be seen. "Ho!" laughed I; "it is my Egeria! Ho, ho, what a joke!" And I laughed aloud as I drew myself out of the water and sat myself on the brink again. Somehow my own voice sounded strange and hollow as it was repeated in tiny echoes by the rocks around.

'I sat gazing on the waters below me. I had pulled myself a good bit up from the water, and climbed to a little platform about six feet from the deepest part of the pool, and there I sat gazing and musing. Surely that is something I see below. The water swirled there – I am sure of it. Ha! It is my Egeria! There, there, deep down in the pool I can see her eyes. O! How beautiful they are! There are her lovely arms waving me to come to her; there, her long tresses. O, no! I cannot come; I must not. Surely it must be fancy. But no – there! There again! Slowly she rises to the surface. I can see her all now. O, so lovely a female form – so graceful – I have never seen but in my dreams! Slowly, slowly she swims towards me, gazing at me with her deep, dark, longing eyes. She reaches the bank; gently, she glides towards me – her arms around me – she locks me in her embrace! Firmly she holds me, and tries to pull me gently into the water. "Come, my love!" she whispers softly; "come to my home below! O, I have waiting long for you; it is so lonely here! Come, come, my darling!" Ah, no. I cannot come! She presses herself next to me, her soft breath fans my cheek, she takes me to her heart and tries to kiss me. I struggle to release myself. I feel faint and languid with her sweet breath – my forces are leaving me – I am slipping – slipping. I shriek wildly, and grasp at the trunk of a tree, which stands near me, to prevent my being pulled into the stream below. Suddenly, I hear a shout; it is my brother. "Help, help!" I cry in terror. In an instant her eyes have lost their fond, soft look; a flash of fury gleams in them, which seems to dart into my brain. "Fool!" she hisses, "fool! I will leave you;" and, with a last squeeze of her strong arms, she unwinds them from my neck, and disappears, while I fall fainting on the rock, and remember no more!'

'Aye!' said Bob Smith, chiming in; 'and there I found him with a sun stroke, which culminated in brain fever; and there I had him for a week raving about nymphs and water-sprites until I was nearly driven mad myself.'

'But what was it?' said I, breathless.

'*That*,' rejoined Jack, 'I don't know to this day. Bob says he saw something which looked like a huge white water-snake untwine itself from me as he came up; but, be that as it may, I would not revisit that pool for a thousand pounds!'

A Colonial Banshee

Fergus Hume

Born in England, Fergus Hume's (1859–1932) family emigrated to
New Zealand when he was three. He went to school in Dunedin,
studied law in Otago, and was called to the New Zealand bar in
1885, the same year he moved to Melbourne. Famously, he asked a
Melbourne bookseller what kind of fiction was selling, and being
told that the detective stories of Gaboriau were in vogue, he wrote
The Mystery of a Hansom Cab (1886). Hume was paid £50 for the
outright sale of copyright and subsequently claimed he never received
another cent from the book although it became a great bestseller in
England.

   He returned to England in 1888 where he continued to write prolifically, publishing over 130 books. Several supernatural tales appear in
his rare collection *The Dancer in Red* (1906), including this story, a black
comedy about a banshee with a broad Irish brogue trying to adjust to
life in the colonies.

The average person does not credit the existence of ghosts. He
prides himself on believing nothing but his own eyes, and if these
deceive him into beholding a genuine ghost he excuses their so doing
on the score of hallucination. You cannot convince the average
person that there is anything beyond the actualities of this world.
Certainly he professes a vague belief in immortality, but his conception is so shadowy, that he never faces it with any degree of
confidence. He classes such credulity in the category of 'things
we are not meant to understand', which hazy remark to his mind
accounts for all matters in the way of religion. Take away this
respectable theological view of the supernatural, and he scoffs at
the idea of a phantom world.

   I am an average person, a gross, fleshly, stolid, disbelieving St
Thomas of the present generation, and in accordance with the fit-
ness of things, should subscribe to the comfortable creed above set
forth. I don't. Certainly I was once as materialistic as the average
person could desire, but since I saw and conversed with a *bona fide*
spectre, I have modified my views regarding psychology. She was so

convincing that she left me no option, but to believe. There was no getting round her insistence.

It was a female ghost of the Banshee type, and I met her under the most prosaic circumstances. Priding herself on the verity of her ghostly being she needed neither moated grange, nor blue lights to compass her appearance, in fact she somewhat scornfully dispensed with such old-time accessories, and simply convinced me by a short conversation that she was what she pretended to be. The most sceptical would have attested her authenticity on oath, as I do now, and I was the most sceptical of persons – once.

Her name was Bridget. She was an Irish emigrant. I was always under the impression that ghosts, like fairies, could not cross running water save in an egg-shell, but as I met Bridget in New Zealand she must have been an exception to this rule. She, however, made use of a ship in lieu of an egg-shell, and complained bitterly of having been forced to take such a voyage in the interests of her profession. It had a good deal to do with hatred and revenge – she was Irish, you see. As the interview was not without interest, I hereby set forth a careful report of the same for the benefit of the Psychical Society. Unless Bridget was a liar, her remarks may throw some light on the mysteries of the spiritual world, and those desiring further information had better apply to the nearest ghost-raiser. I don't want to see her again. One such interview is enough for me.

Queenstown was the scene of this remarkable adventure. I am not referring to the Irish town of that name, but indicate thereby the pretty little sanatorium on Lake Wakitipu in New Zealand. It is amusing how very mixed one's geographical ideas become in the colonies. Here for instance you sail up the Maori-christened lake of Wakitipu, stay at Queenstown, the name whereof smacks of Cork, and see from the top of an Antipodean Ben Lomond, the range of the Southern Alps which have nothing to do with Switzerland. It is a trifle confusing at first, but when one gets used to the oddity of the thing it is handy to have spots so widely apart within hailing distance. It is only in Otago that you can go from Queenstown to Ben Lomond in ten minutes.

I was staying in Queenstown for the benefit of my health. Something to do with the lungs I believe, but it is so long ago that I quite forget the exact disease from which I then suffered. Besides, it is not material to this story. It must have been my lungs, however, because the doctor made me climb the lofty peak of Ben

Lomond daily for the benefit of them. There I was accustomed to sit for hours among the ice and snow watching the Earnslaw glacier flashing like a mirror in the sunlight, and the snowy range of the Southern Alps standing like fairy lace-work against the clear blue of the sky.

When not climbing, I wandered about Queenstown and employed my spare time in dodging the goats. There were a great many goats about the place as the unfinished condition of the town rather favoured their existence. You walked down the main street and in two minutes found yourself among the hills – and goats. You surveyed the palatial hotel of the most approved 'Grand' type and turned round to behold a goat-populated section gaping between a red brick chapel and a corrugated iron store. Or you could arrive in five minutes at the outskirts of the town where the goats abounded among the white pebbles and sparse grass. Sometimes in such a place you met a man, more often a goat. I preferred the former myself as he sometimes invited me to have a drink whereas the goats were all distinctly hostile. They are the most distrustful animals I know.

In common with other visitors, I put up at Farmer's Hotel, where I was exceedingly comfortable. Every evening the steamer from Kingston arrived with fresh cargoes of tourists in search of health and scenery. They found both at Queenstown, which is the most romantic and salubrious place I am acquainted with. A trifle wild and lonely, but one must expect that sort of thing in a virgin solitude. I prefer it myself to an overcrowded play-ground like Switzerland. At Queenstown there is no promenade, no band, no theatre, no casino, no bathing. For this latter the waters of the lake are too cold owing to its being fed by glaciers. When I was there, the principal amusements were riding, driving, climbing, and visiting the cemetery. I didn't care about anticipating my funeral myself, but many people went there, and told me they enjoyed it greatly. It was so restful. I did not contradict that statement.

Sometimes we drove to Arrowtown and saw the pack horses in long lines climb the track leading to the Macetown reefs. The sight put me wonderfully in mind of Ali Baba and the forty thieves, for in the distance they looked exactly like mules laden with booty. Leaving Arrowtown there was some excitement in regaining Queenstown by the Shotover Bridge. It was a narrow structure with shallow sides which sprang across a tremendous abyss in the depths of which swirled a rapid stream. The approach was down an incline, and for the moment it seemed doubtful whether the horses would hit the bull's eye of the bridge, or go over into the chasm. Our Jehu was a wonderful driver, and held his team well together, else I am afraid I would not now be writing this story. I never repeated the experiment. It is a mistake tempting Providence twice.

I conscientiously saw all there was to be seen in company with Nora and Michael. These two young scions of the Maguire family were staying at Farmer's with their ancestral Banshee. I don't think the landlord knew of this addition to his list of guests, though Bridget did her best to let him know she was on the premises. She howled, whereon he called the innocent house dog bad names. I am afraid Bridget resented the mistake as a slur on her vocal abilities.

Nora told me all about herself and Michael. They had left Ireland some five years back and taken up their abode in Sydney on account of the brother's health. He, poor fellow, was far gone in consumption, and even the tropical climate of Australia could do but little for his disease. Indeed so much worse did he become, that Nora was advised to try the curative effect of New Zealand air, and for this reason the young couple were staying at Queenstown. When I arrived on the scene they had already been there for some weeks, but Michael did not seem to benefit much by the change. On the contrary, he daily grew weaker and looked more like a shadow than a man.

One day I found her seated by his side in front of the hotel. He had fallen asleep in the warm sunshine, and Nora was dividing her attention between a book and the invalid. When she saw me, however, she softly arose from her seat and joined me in my walk.

'Do you think he looks better today, Mr Durham?' she asked, anxiously.

'Oh, yes!' I replied, trying to comfort the poor girl. 'I see a decided improvement. If anything can cure him, it will be this air.'

'I am afraid the disease has gone too far,' she answered with a sigh, 'poor boy – to think of his coming all these miles only to find a grave.'

'Don't think of such a thing, Miss Maguire.'

'I cannot help thinking, Mr Durham. Since we have been here, twice have I heard the Banshee.'

'The what?'

'The Banshee! Did you not hear it wailing last night?'

'I certainly heard a dog howling at the moon.'

'It was no dog,' said Nora mysteriously, 'it was our Banshee.'

'My dear Miss Maguire, how can you believe in such rubbish?' I remonstrated in a vexed tone, 'there are no such things as ghosts.'

'So many people think, but I know there are ghosts.'

'Have you ever seen one?'

'No! But I have heard the Banshee cry.'

'Nonsense, my dear young lady. Your nerves are out of order with overanxiety. Consult a doctor at once.'

'My nerves are not out of order,' she replied, doggedly, 'I am in perfect health, and thoroughly in earnest. Why, you admit yourself that you heard the cry.'

'I heard a dog howling, Miss Maguire. How can you be so superstitious? This is the nineteenth century. Ghosts went out when gas came in.'

I took no end of trouble to convince that girl. I promised to lend her a copy of Abercrombie's *Intellectual Powers*, where she would find that ghosts are all humbug. I narrated several instances which had come under my notice of supposititious spectres, which had been thoroughly explained away. A logical person would have been convinced by my arguments. But she was a woman, and therefore not logical. All my talk was on this account so much waste of breath.

'Every old woman in Ireland knows the Maguire Banshee,' she said triumphantly; 'for generations the death of one of our family has been predicted by its wailing. My father was killed in the hunting field, and I heard it myself crying round the house on the previous night. When my mother died the Banshee wailed three times, and – '

'I don't believe a word of it,' I interrupted emphatically, 'not one word. The Celtic nature is excitable and prone to superstition. The howling of a dog, the whistling of the wind, the shrieking of a hinge would account for your Banshee. I am a man of sense, Miss Maguire; I laugh at the idea of such folly. Nothing would convince me of the existence of – '

At that moment I swear I felt a cold breath blowing against my cheek. The afternoon was warm and sunny with little or no wind, but for the moment the unexpected chill struck me dumb.

'What is the matter, Mr Durham?' asked Nora, alarmed at the expression of my face, 'are you ill?'

'Ill? No!' I replied, nervously, 'but really you know, ha! ha! I believe you are infecting me with your superstition. I felt a cold breath on my face.'

'It's – '

'Now don't say the Banshee, Miss Maguire, because I can't and won't believe such nonsense. My liver is probably out of order, and our conversation about spectres is apt to tell on the nerves. Let us talk of other things. Your family for instance?'

'There is not much to talk about there,' said Nora, smiling at what she evidently considered a weak explanation, 'my family at one time were rich and numerous. Now we are the only two left, and I don't think Job was poorer than we are!'

'Your estates?'

'Were all sold long ago. My father ran through all that remained of the property, and when he was killed we had nothing but a tumbled-down castle, and a few acres of barren bog. We sold this and with the money came out to Sydney. There, through the influence of an old friend, Michael obtained a good Government appointment. Then his health gave way, and we were advised to come on here.'

'And what do you intend to do when you go back?' I asked, revolving several philanthropic schemes in my mind.

'I don't know! It is questionable if we do go back. I feel certain that Michael will die here, and then I shall be left alone here with but a few shillings.'

'Tut! tut! you must not talk like this,' said I, blowing my nose to conceal some natural emotion evoked by her story; 'the colonial heart is kind! The colonial hand is open. As to your brother, hope for the best!'

'Mr Durham!' said the girl solemnly, 'twice have I heard the Banshee cry – the third time will be fatal.'

It was no use arguing against such obstinacy, so I held my tongue, merely remarking that I hoped the Banshee wouldn't wail. Then as it was growing chilly Nora took her brother inside and left me to my own reflections. They were anything but pleasant, for I felt certain that this foolish belief in the Banshee would aid in killing Michael, as surely as would his disease.

To think of such superstition being prevalent nowadays. Here was a well-educated young lady living among sensible people, yet she believed in such rubbish as ghosts. It has been proved over and over again that there are no such things. A heavy meal, a tired body, a fanciful mind, and lo, a ghost is created. Dyspepsia and hallucination are the parents of all goblins, which exist but in the imagination of their victims. People who see ghosts should write novels and thus work off their superfluous imagination. No wonder we need school boards, when sensible men can tolerate such humbug. Logic and Arithmetic will cure such morbidity. No student of the exact sciences ever saw a ghost.

The breath of cold air? Well I know that puzzled me, but it might be ascribed to the nerves. The cause I am convinced was internal not external. It was a still, sunny day, yet I felt a sensation of cold air on my left cheek. Nerves, or liver only? I am inclined to put it down to the latter, knowing how I suffer from that organ. A liver will make a man believe anything. Perhaps my ghostly interview was the result of a disordered liver, but no – Bridget was too convincing. You can't explain away actualities and though Bridget wasn't exactly an actuality, I certainly can't explain her away.

After that eminently unsatisfactory conversation with Miss Maguire I took a sharp walk to shake the cobwebs out of my brain. Ghost-talk does engender cobwebs in a man's brain, and if you leave them there nobody knows what will happen – but I think Colney Hatch has a good deal to do with the future. Not caring to tend in that direction I walked those ghostly figments out of my memory and sat on a hill top admiring the scenery. The sun was setting and the white peaks were very rosy with his light. It was very beautiful, but very chilly, so not anxious to trouble my lungs with inflammation I returned to the hotel and dinner.

After the meal I went up to my room to put on warmer clothes, and there took place that remarkable visitation of which I speak. The bedroom was quite dark when I entered, and in place of lighting the candle I stood at the window staring at the wonderful white world without. A stream of moonbeams lay across the floor, and beyond the distant peak flashed the moon herself glimmering like a ghost. The comparison put me in mind of Nora's absurd Banshee story, and the memory made me laugh. To my surprise the laugh was repeated in a thin starved echo. I turned round at the sound and saw a woman standing near the door. I am a modest young man, and the intrusion annoyed me.

'Madame,' I said in a dignified tone, 'you have mistaken the room. How did you enter?'

'By the keyhole!'

Heavens! what a voice. It was as thin as a whistle. And then she alluded to an entrance by the keyhole. I began to feel alarmed and passed my hand across my eyes to vanish the hallucination.

'Liver!' said I, seeing the figure still there.

'Divil a bit,' retorted the lady who seemed a cloudy sort of person. 'I'm the Maguire Banshee.'

I don't like practical jokes, and thinking Nora was playing one on me ventured to remonstrate. Before I could say a word the figure glided, or rather floated into the stream of moonlight which lay across the floor. Then I saw it was no joke – it was no liver – it was a ghost!

A merciful baldness prevented my hair standing on end, but my flesh creeped, and I shook as though I had the ague. This apparition upset all my preconceived ideas, and reduced me to a sort of moral pulp. I felt a cowardly inclination to run away. The Banshee was between me and the door, and as the window was twenty feet from the ground. I could hardly leave that way without becoming a ghost myself. I was therefore compelled to remain, and didn't like the idea.

'Why don't ye offer me a sate?' said the Banshee in an irritable tone, 'is it insultin' me ye're afther doin'?'

I pushed forward a seat in great trepidation and she settled on it. I can't say she sat down for she didn't, but simply subsided thereon, like a cloud on a mountain-top. The cold beams of the moon shone full on her face, and the sight did not tend to steady my nerves. I don't want to see another face like it.

It was a grey haggard countenance framed in wild elf locks of tangled red hair. Her mouth was all drawn to one side, and in her eyes dwelt a look of horror. Round her neck hung a fragment of rough rope, and from shoulders to heels streamed a cloudy white robe. The whole appearance of this being was vague and indistinct, the face being the only portion I could see with any degree of clearness. Sitting there in the chilly light, with her filmy dress undulating round her thin form, and her baleful eyes glaring from amid her tangled red hair she was a fearsome object to behold. I shivered and shook and turned away my eyes, but something – I knew not what – ever compelled me to look at her again.

I don't think she was a lady Banshee. Her language was too free, and her manners left much to be desired. Still she behaved in a very affable manner for her, and succeeded to a certain extent in dispelling my fear, though I was anything but comfortable during the interview. She spoke throughout in a hoarse broken voice, alternating with a shrill whistling sound. Constant howling had evidently injured her vocal organs.

'So you don't believe in my existence,' she said, eyeing me in a malevolent manner.

I began to protest, but she cut me short with a whistling sniff and shifted her mouth to the other side of her face.

'No deceit av ye plase. Didn't ye say oi was an hallucination, ye brutal Saxon?"

'You may be now for all I know,' I replied, resenting her rudeness.

She stretched out her arm which elongated itself like a marine telescope, and without moving from her seat clutched me by the wrist with chilly fingers. So cold was her touch that it burnt like fire, and I involuntarily shrieked with pain.

'Whist! ye spalpeen!' she said, contracting her arm again. 'Ye'll athtracht attinshun and me reputashun u'll suffer if oi'm discovered in a jintleman's slapin' room.'

'In that case you had better go away,' I suggested, anxious to rid myself of this nightmare.

'Divil a bit,' she rejoined, composedly. 'Oi've a mind to convarse wid ye about thim Maguires.'

'Why can't you leave them alone? It's impossible for a sick man to get sleep while you howl around the house like an insane hurricane.'

'Wud ye have me neglect me thrade?' said the Banshee, indignantly. ''Tis me juty to wail, worse luck. An' as to slapin', Mick Maguire 'ull slape sound enough one av' these days, nivir fear.'

'Will he die?'

'Av' coorse he'll die. Haven't oi cried the twice an' ut'll be the third toime this night. It's not wastin' me breath oi am.'

'Who are you?'

'Oi'm Bridget.'

I laughed at the unsuitability of the name, whereupon the Banshee looked at me fiercely.

'Fwhat's the matter wid the name?'

'It's like a servant girl's.'

'An' why not? Wasn't oi that same, sorr? Four hundher years ago oi sarved King Patsey Maguire av' Ulster, the ancister av' the prisint family no less.'

'But how did you become a Banshee?'

'Och whirra! whirra! willaloo!' she moaned, rocking herself to and fro, 'wasn't oi the pride av' Ulster an' didn't King Maguire hang me bekaze oi'd nivir give up Taddy Donovan?'

'Did he want to marry you himself?'

'How shuld oi know! Maybe he didn't care about Taddy liftin' thim Kerry cows. An' as Taddy wasn't to be tuk, he hanged me, bad luck to him.'

'Did that hanging turn you into a Banshee?'

'D'y' see this rope, sorr?' she said touching the fragment; 'whin oi died oi tuk the bit wid me as a memory an' swore to haunt thim Maguires for everlastin' till they all died. There's only two now. Whin Mick goes there'ull only be wan. Whin she dies me juty 'ull be ended for ivir.'

'But you can't kill them.'

'Av' coorse not, but I can warn thim of their sorrows. Oi've croied at their wakes for the last four hundher year in Ould Ireland.'

'Why did you come out here?'

'Bekase thim two came. When a Banshee's attached to wan family she has to hould on to thim like the divil. Where they go, she goes, so oi had to imigrate wid the Maguires, bad cess to thim.'

'You don't like the colonies?'

'Divil a bit. Oi've not met a single ghost of any consequence here. There's no ruins to haunt an' hathens like yoursilf don't belave in us.'

'If you find things so unpleasant, why don't you go back to Ireland?'

'How shuld oi know? Whin Nora goes back oi'll go back, but where she is I aim. Mick's dying so me only reckinin' on Nora. Maybe she'll die too though,' added the Banshee, comfortably, 'and thin I can return to me round tower.'

'What Round Tower?'

'County Down no less. Me family sate. Once 'twas King Maguire's, now 'tis mine. Oi sit on it in the cove av' the evenin' an' houl.'

'Pleasant for your neighbours.'

'Iviry one to his juty,' replied the Banshee indifferently; ''tis mine to howl, an' howl I do.'

'Yes! I've heard you!'

'An' sid it was the dog. Oh, oi heard your contimptuous spache.'

'Now look here!'

'Oi want nane av' your bullyin' av' you plase. Respict age. Oi'm four hundher year ould.'

'Yes! you look it!'

'An' so'd you if ye'd to pass nights howlin' in the open air. It's sorry oi am that I let ye see a rale live Banshee.'

'You're hardly alive. However, I apologise for hurting your feelings. I'm not accustomed to entertain Banshees.'

'Maybe that's true. No Saxon has a Banshee.'

'And no colony either.'

'Wait a few hundred years, sorr. Ye want ruins and family sacrats first. Thin the ghosts 'ull come, but not in your toime.'

'I'm not sorry! I don't like ghosts!'

'Maybe ye don't belave in them,' said the Banshee, tauntingly, 'tomorrow ye'll say "oive bin dramin".'

'It's not unlikely!'

'Oi'd like to lave some token av' me visit,' she said in a meditative tone, 'couldn't I lave five black finger marks on your wrist?'

'No thank you,' I replied, shrinking back.

'Or turn your hair white?' she added, persuasively.

'Even you couldn't do that. I'm bald!'

'Ah thin! I'll lave the mark of a gory hand on your cranium.'

'I'm sure you won't. What's the matter?'

For the Banshee had suddenly shot up as high as the roof.

'Whist!' she said shrilly. 'Oi hear his breath failin'.'

'Whose breath?'

'Michael's. The cowld sweat is on his brow an' the rattle is in his throat – it's not long he'll live anyhow. I must wail – an' wail. Whirro!'

'Let the man die in peace,' I urged anxiously.

'Fwhat? wan av' thim Maguires? Sorra a bit. Ye'll hear me wailin' soon.'

'But – '

'Whist oi tell ye! whist. Oi's goin'. 'Tis not Banshees ye'll scoff at agin oi'm thinkin'.'

She spread herself through the room in a cold white mist, and I shrank terrified against the wall. In the white shadow I could see the glare of her fiery eyes like two danger signals. The fog gradually floated out through the open window and the eyes vanished. Then I heard a whistle outside, which I presume was Bridget's way of saying goodbye. After that I went for some brandy.

The Banshee certainly succeeded in curing my scepticism regarding ghosts. I don't want any further proof that they exist after seeing her. She impressed herself too strongly on my memory. Next time I see an Irish ghost, I would like a dozen or so of my friends to be present at the interview. Now when I hear the average person scoffing at the idea of spectres, as I used to do, I tell him my experience. As a rule he doesn't believe me. Perhaps you can read this story and don't believe it either. But it's true for all that.

When I had succeeded in pulling myself together – no easy task – I hurried at once to Michael's bedroom, but was met at the door by Nora who told me he was asleep. Unwilling to alarm her by a description of the Banshee's visit, I held my peace and went out into the open air. Lighting a cigar, for I thought a smoke would soothe my nerves, I strolled up and down in front of the hotel. In a few minutes a young American who was staying there joined me, and though as a rule I found him a nuisance, yet on this occasion I was not ill-pleased with his company.

It was a bright moonlight night, and far in the distance arose the serrated peaks of the mountains. The iron roofs of the houses around glittered like frosted silver in the light, and here and there on the sullen lake glinted a flake of moonfire. All was wonderfully beautiful and absolutely still. Suddenly there sounded a lone, low wail which shivered pitifully through the air, and died away among the mountains. Then a second, closely followed by a third. I knew what that triple cry meant and stopped short in my walk.

'Dog howling, I guess,' said the young American, carelessly.

I heard a whistling sniff near me and turned to see the Banshee glaring at the young man. To him she was invisible, and her speech inaudible.

'A dog howlin',' she said, angrily, 'an' I nivir wailed so iligantly before.'

'Is he dead?' I asked, breathlessly.

'As a door nail,' replied the Banshee and vanished.

'Is who dead?' asked the American thinking I had spoken to him, 'that young Irish fellow? – Hark, what is that?'

Another cry, but this time the utterance of a human throat. I hastened towards the hotel, and arrived at the door to meet Nora on the threshold.

'Did you hear it?' she gasped, throwing herself into my arms.

'Yes, I heard it!'

'I told you the third time. Michael is dead.'

After that she fainted clean away, which action caused me but little surprise. I was pretty near collapsing myself.

* * *

Poor Michael was duly buried in the little cemetery under the shadow of the mighty hill. I attended the funeral, did my best to comfort Nora, and in the end supplied her with money to return to her Sydney friends. I presume the Banshee went with her, but of this I am not certain. Sometimes I heard from Nora in the months which followed her brother's death. When I was at Te Aroha in the North Island last Christmas she wrote and told me she was married and had settled for good in Sydney.

This letter set me thinking about the Banshee. By her own showing she could not leave Nora until she died, so as Nora had decided to stay in Australia, I presume, Bridget would also have to remain. From what I heard, Nora is not likely to die for some time so I am afraid Bridget must be very discontented. Here she has no ghostly friends, no Round Tower, and as yet no reason for wailing, so altogether she must be in a bad way.

One consolation she must have. She is the only Banshee in the colonies. None other is genuine.

The Devil of the Marsh

H. B. Marriott Watson

H.B. Marriott Watson (1863–1921) was born in Melbourne, educated
in New Zealand, and settled in England in 1885 where he took up
journalism. He was assistant editor on *Black and White* and the *Pall
Mall Gazette* and eventually published over fifty books. He collaborated
with James Barrie, of Peter Pan fame, on the play *Richard Savage*. He
also penned several supernatural stories, such as the vampire tale 'The
Stone Chamber'. His short story collections *Diogenes of London and other
Fantasies and Sketches* (1893), *The Heart of Miranda* (1899), *Alarums and
Excursions* (1903), and *Aftermath: A Garner of Tales* (1919) contain the
odd supernatural tale. 'The Devil of the Marsh' is an example of the
1890s English decadence, which is usually associated with Oscar Wilde
and Aubrey Beardsley. It was published in *Diogenes of London and Other
Fantasies and Sketches*.

It was nigh upon dusk when I drew close to the Great Marsh, and
already the white vapours were about, riding across the sunken levels
like ghosts in a churchyard. Though I had set forth in a mood of wild
delight, I had sobered in the lonely ride across the moor and was now
uneasily alert. As my horse jerked down the grassy slopes that fell
away to the jaws of the swamp I could see thin streams of mist rise
slowly, hover like wraiths above the long rushes, and then, turning
gradually more material, go blowing heavily away across the flat.
The appearance of the place at this desolate hour, so remote from
human society and so darkly significant of evil presences, struck me
with a certain wonder that she should have chosen this spot for our
meeting. She was a familiar of the moors, where I had invariably
encountered her; but it was like her arrogant caprice to test my
devotion by some such dreary assignation. The wide and horrid
prospect depressed me beyond reason, but the fact of her neighbourhood drew me on, and my spirits mounted at the thought that
at last she was to put me in possession of herself. Tethering my
horse upon the verge of the swamp, I soon discovered the path that
crossed it, and entering struck out boldly for the heart. The track
could have been little used, for the reeds, which stood high above the

level of my eyes upon either side, straggled everywhere across in low
arches, through which I dodged, and broke my way with some inconvenience and much impatience. A full half hour I was solitary in that
wilderness, and when at last a sound other than my own footsteps
broke the silence the dusk had fallen.

I was moving very slowly at the time, with a mind half disposed to
turn from the melancholy expedition, which it seemed to me now
must surely be a cruel jest she had played upon me. While some such
reluctance held me, I was suddenly arrested by a hoarse croaking
which broke out upon my left, sounding somewhere from the reeds in
the black mire. A little further it came again from close at hand, and
when I had passed on a few more steps in wonder and perplexity, I
heard it for the third time. I stopped and listened, but the marsh was as
a grave, and so taking the noise for the signal of some raucous frog, I
resumed my way. But in a little the croaking was repeated, and coming
quickly to a stand I pushed the reeds aside and peered into the darkness. I could see nothing, but at the immediate moment of my pause
I thought I detected the sound of some body trailing through the
rushes. My distaste for the adventure grew with this suspicion, and
had it not been for my delirious infatuation I had assuredly turned
back and ridden home. The ghastly sound pursued me at intervals
along the track, until at last, irritated beyond endurance by the sense
of this persistent and invisible company, I broke into a sort of run.
This, it seemed, the creature (whatever it was) could not achieve, for
I heard no more of it, and continued my way in peace. My path at
length ran out from among the reeds upon the smooth flat of which
she had spoken, and here my heart quickened, and the gloom of the
dreadful place lifted. The flat lay in the very centre of the marsh, and
here and there in it a gaunt bush or withered tree rose like a spectre
against the white mists. At the further end I fancied some kind of
building loomed up; but the fog which had been gathering ever since
my entrance upon the passage sailed down upon me at that moment
and the prospect went out with suddenness. As I stood waiting for the
clouds to pass, a voice cried to me out of its centre, and I saw her next
second with bands of mist swirling about her body, come rushing to
me from the darkness. She put her long arms about me, and, drawing
her close, I looked into her deep eyes. Far down in them, it seemed to
me, I could discern a mystic laughter dancing in the wells of light, and
I had that ecstatic sense of nearness to some spirit of fire which was
wont to possess me at her contact.

'At last,' she said, 'at last, my beloved!' I caressed her.

'Why,' said I, tingling at the nerves, 'why have you put this dolorous journey between us? And what mad freak is your presence in this swamp?' She uttered her silver laugh, and nestled to me again.

'I am the creature of this place,' she answered. 'This is my home. I have sworn you should behold me in my native sin ere you ravished me away.'

'Come, then,' said I; 'I have seen; let there be an end of this. I know you, what you are. This marsh chokes up my heart. God forbid you should spend more of your days here. Come.'

'You are in haste,' she cried. 'There is yet much to learn. Look, my friend,' she said, 'you who know me, what I am. This is my prison, and I have inherited its properties. Have you no fear?'

For answer I pulled her to me, and her warm lips drove out the horrid humours of the night; but the swift passage of a flickering mockery over her eyes struck me as a flash of lightning, and I grew chill again.

'I have the marsh in my blood,' she whispered; 'the marsh and the fog of it. Think ere you vow to me, for I am the cloud in a starry night.'

A lithe and lovely creature, palpable of warm flesh, she lifted her magic face to mine and besought me plaintively with these words. The dews of the nightfall hung on her lashes, and seemed to plead with me for her forlorn and solitary plight.

'Behold!' I cried, 'witch or devil of the marsh, you shall come with me! I have known you on the moors, a roving apparition of beauty; nothing more I know, nothing more I ask. I care not what this dismal haunt means; not what these strange and mystic eyes. You have powers and senses above me; your sphere and habits are as mysterious and incomprehensible as your beauty. But that,' I said, 'is mine, and the world that is mine shall be yours also.'

She moved her head nearer to me with an antic gesture, and her gleaming eyes glanced up at me with a sudden flash, the similitude (great heavens!) of a hooded snake. Starting, I fell away, but at that moment she turned her face and set it fast towards the fog that came rolling in thick volumes over the flat. Noiselessly the great cloud crept down upon us, and all dazed and troubled I watched her watching it in silence. It was as if she awaited some omen of horror, and I too trembled in the fear of its coming.

Then suddenly out of the night issued the hoarse and hideous croaking I had heard upon my passage. I reached out my arm to take her hand, but in an instant the mists broke over us, and I was groping in the vacancy. Something like panic took hold of me, and, beating through the blind obscurity, I rushed over the flat, calling upon her. In a little the swirl went by, and I perceived her upon the margin of the swamp, her arm raised as in imperious command. I ran to her, but stopped, amazed and shaken by a fearful sight. Low by the dripping reeds crouched a small squat thing, in the likeness of a monstrous frog, coughing and choking in its throat. As I stared, the creature rose upon its legs and disclosed a horrid human resemblance. Its face was white and thin, with long black hair; its body gnarled and twisted as with the ague of a thousand years. Shaking, it whined in a breathless voice, pointing a skeleton finger at the woman by my side.

'Your eyes were my guide,' it quavered. 'Do you think that after all these years I have no knowledge of your eyes? Lo, is there aught of evil in you I am not instructed in? This is the Hell you designed for me, and now you would leave me to a greater.'

The wretch paused, and panting leaned upon a bush, while she stood silent, mocking him with her eyes, and soothing my terror with her soft touch.

'Hear!' he cried, turning to me, 'hear the tale of this woman that you may know her as she is. She is the Presence of the marshes. Woman or Devil I know not, but only that the accursed marsh has crept into her soul and she herself is become its Evil Spirit; she herself, that lives and grows young and beautiful by it, has its full power to blight and chill and slay. I, who was once as you are, have this knowledge. What bones lie deep in this black swamp who can say but she? She has drained of health, she has drained of mind and of soul; what is between her and her desire that she should not drain also of life? She has made me a devil in her Hell, and now she would leave me to my solitary pain, and go search for another victim. But she shall not!' he screamed through his chattering teeth; 'she shall not! My Hell is also hers! She shall not!'

Her smiling untroubled eyes left his face and turned to me; she put out her arms, swaying towards me, and so fervid and so great a light glowed in her face that, as one distraught of superhuman means, I took her into my embrace. And then the madness seized me.

'Woman or devil,' I said, 'I will go with you! Of what account this pitiful past? Blight me even as that wretch, so be only you are with me.'

She laughed, and, disengaging herself, leaned, half-clinging to me, towards the coughing creature by the mire.

'Come,' I cried, catching her by the waist. 'Come!' She laughed again a silver-ringing laugh. She moved with me slowly across the flat to where the track started for the portals of the marsh. She laughed and clung to me.

But at the edge of the track I was startled by a shrill, hoarse screaming; and behold, from my very feet, that loathsome creature rose up and wound his long black arms about her, shrieking and crying in his pain. Stooping I pushed him from her skirts, and with one sweep of my arm drew her across the pathway; as her face passed mine her eyes were wide and smiling. Then of a sudden the still mist enveloped us once more; but ere it descended I had a glimpse of that contorted figure trembling on the margin, the white face drawn and full of desolate pain. At the sight an icy shiver ran through me. And then through the yellow gloom the shadow of her darted past me to the further side. I heard the hoarse cough, the dim noise of a struggle, a swishing sound, a thin cry, and then the sucking of the slime over something in the rushes. I leapt forward and once again the fog thinned, and I beheld her, woman or devil, standing upon the verge, and peering with smiling eyes into the foul and sickly bog. With a sharp cry wrung from my nerveless soul, I turned and fled down the narrow way from that accursed spot; and as I ran the thickening fog closed round me, and I heard far off and lessening still the silver sound of her mocking laughter.

The Accursed Thing

EDWARD DYSON

Edward George Dyson (1865–1931) was born at Morrison near Ballarat
in 1865 and grew up amongst miners and factory workers whom he
brought to life in the short stories and poems he wrote as an adult. He
established his reputation in 1889 when 'A Golden Shanty' appeared
in *The Bulletin*'s Christmas anthology. He subsequently became a
freelance writer, publishing a number of short story collections in
addition to his newspaper work. His goldfield material was published
in *Below and On Top* (1898), *The Gold-Stealers* (1901) and *In the Roaring
Fifties* (1906). He also drew on his work experience in factories, craft-
ing an astute picture of Australian larrikinism, in *Fact'ry 'Ands* (1906),
Benno and Some of the Push (1911) and *Spats' Fact'ry* (1914). Dyson
married Dorothy Boyes in 1914 and looked forward to a successful
literary career, but an attack of encephalitis after the 1919 influenza
outbreak caused a marked decline in his health and creative output.
Dyson died in 1931. 'The Accursed Thing' was published in *The
Bulletin* in August 1922.

Norrid stopped picking for a moment and slapped his knee conclus-
ively. 'It's the damn dam;' he said. Bobbie Norrid had relied upon
the bit of fossicking in Tammil's old claim at Redpepper being a nice
dry job that would last him perhaps right through the present rainy
spell, and here was the pipeclay floor showing little pools and the
wall before him dripping water!

Bobbie had been compelled to build a small platform of slabs
and cover it with a folded sack to have a moderately dry spot to
squat on as he worked at the low roof, chipping down an extra four
or five inches of wash dirt by the original diggers. The latter had
taken only the lowermost strata of gravel, driving in the pipeclay
below and then knocking down about a span's thickness of the
auriferous dirt. What they had taken was, of course, the richest
of the stuff, gold invariably settling on the bottom of the alluvial,
but Bobbie Norrid had discovered that there was sufficient gold
left to justify a fossicker in scraping off a few inches more from the
rood and putting in new 'soldiers', while knocking out the old

timber in order to cut away the small columns of gold-bearing wash above them.

A 'soldier' is one straight log, in this case about 4ft high, with a short, stout slab wedged across the top as a cap to keep the roof up. Norrid substituted a new one for safety, and before removing the original leg; being a very cautious worker in old ground, he allowed no dangerous margin.

'She's as safe as a church,' he had assured the wife, 's'long as I keep her timbered, 'n Bob Norrid ain't sich a Jonnie-come-lately as to go monkeyin' in stale workin's without plenty iv props. Plenty iv props, that's my motter. Plenty iv props lad, 'n there's no 'arm in the world'll come to a man nowhere.'

Norrid was working in a space of about 10ft by 8ft, having a height of 4ft. The walls and floor were nice, soft pipeclay, easily worked and very clean; the roof was of rather tough gravel, matted with cement in places. On the miner's left hand as he knelt at work was the small shaft; behind him, stowed compactly and tight to the roof, the broken reef in that part of the workings he had already been over. Stuck in a spiked holder driven into a 'soldier' on his right, the steady candle burned fully with a yellow radiance.

The shaft was only about 40ft deep, and Bob Norrid was working a long hand, stowing the wash in a pile in one corner nearest the shaft. When he had mined out all the dirt he thought the claim would yield, the missus would come along and haul it with the windlass while he filled the buckets below. Sarah would give a hand, too, with the puddling and cradling. A rare, good, serviceable old mate was Bobbie's missus.

Although it had been raining hard for seven days and as many nights, Bob found the wetness of the old workings inexplicable. He had been down on the previous occasions, and had found the little mine as dry as tinder. Surface rains won't penetrate 40ft of *terra firma*, yet all of a sudden here was the claim leaking like a sieve, with a lively prospect of becoming water-logged if the inflow continued to increase. The solution came in a flash. 'That damn dam!' Bob had been employed with several others during the last month or two in making a big, deep dam for Renbow on a pot within 30 yards of the hole in which he was now working. That dam at the present moment was running a banker, and held a tremendous weight of water. This was the source of the seepage. Bob breathed a sigh of relief.

'No danger from that quarter,' said he, jabbing his pipe-stem in the direction of the dam. 'Jist a little moisture percolatin' through a bit iv drift.'

Norrid resumed his work, picking down the wash. Presently he discarded the pick, struck his pipe stem first in above a content cap-piece, and took up the shovel. He threw one shovelful of gravel towards the shaft, filled the shovel again and turned in the action of throwing. That shovel of dirt was never thrown. In turning the digger had noticed, half-instinctively, something unusual. He paused, dropping the shovel-blade to the floor, staring perplexedly. What was wrong? There was darkness in the shaft. The patch of daylight falling in the shaft was gone. It was as if someone aloft had covered the mouth of the hole.

''Ello, on top there!' cried Norrid. 'What you up to?' The reverb-eration of his voice was strange to him.

Bob went on his knees to the shaft and looked up. The little patch of rain-washed sky that should have been visible was obscured. Above was absolute blackness.

'Hi, on top there! What's the game?'

Again the peculiar effect of the voice returning from a wall. Bob seized the candle and turned to the shaft again. Holding the light well above him he peered upward. A cry of dismay broke from his lips. Terror took him by the heart. Something huge, black, hideous, loomed in the shaft. He seemed to see in its sleek, shining mass a vast, flat, fat face. The candle lent it glittering eyes. As he looked a great, thick chimpanzee-like hand reached down as if to clutch him. With a cry, almost a scream, Norrid fell back, tripped over his shovel and knocked his head against a log. His candle was extinguished. He lay for a moment in utter darkness, stunned, struggling with consciousness. The truth came back to him after he knew not how long, and he cried aloud again, and went sprawling about in the working seeking his matches, horrified at the thought of the grim terror advancing upon him. He felt something like a heavy hand upon his foot, and a shudder of horror went through him. He tugged at his foot but the grip held. Wild with fear he pulled again and his foot came out, leaving his boot in the clutch of the cursed thing.

Bob Norrid found his coat and the matches. He struck a light and looked back. The thing filled the space about the shaft as with the convolutions of a monstrous writhing snake, and was advancing towards him, surging slowly. He lit his candle and retreated the

length of the excavation, whimpering like a child in his horror of
the oncoming force, which he realised as a living, sentient, passion-
less brute-thing bent upon his destruction. A lap of it encroached
with a flopping motion, laying a shapeless hand upon the shovel,
and Norrid sprawled to rescue what was his hope of salvation.
He sought to wrest the shovel away. It would not come. He put all
his strength into the tug, and slowly, reluctantly, the great, flat,
black hand yielded. Norrid threw the shovel and the pick to the far
wall behind him, and forced himself to look more closely, more
rationally, at his enemy.

The oozy mass had now extended well into the excavation. Norrid
had once seen a great hippopotamus issuing from a tank. This
thing, in its blackness and sleekness and formlessness, reminded
him of the animal. There was the same forward heave, the same
vastness, the same suggestion of irresistible force. From the centre
of the mass billowed two bubble-like cheeks. Two highlights in the
greasy surface were pig-eyes blinking at him. Bob turned from it,
sick with a poignant sense of hopelessness. What might a man do
against a fate like this? With a balloon-like movement the thing
moved towards him.

Cold, trembling with round staring eyes, and thin hair that clung in
wet wisps to his scalp and crawled, worm-like, to his cheeks and ears,
Bob Norrid took refuge in the corner that had been the terminus of
the small drive where he was furthest from the foe. He perceived that
quite a third of the space was now filled by the fearful mass, and he
comprehended it was moving for him, seeking only his destruction,
with its smooth, slow but indomitable surge.

Suddenly the old miner cried out for a third time, and, jabbing his
spiked candle into the wall, he seized the pick and began digging.
He dug with furious energy, not looking back, but conscious all the
time of the advancing evil, conscious of the shortness of the time
allowed him. The air compressed into the opening would last him
only a little time, but an almost frantic hope burned in his heart. He
knew that the shaft of the Pioneer, a deserted deep mine, was within
a few feet of where he worked. Perhaps it was nearer than he
imagined. At any rate he must try. He must work as never man
worked before, and with God's help he might win through. Yes,
with God's help.

Norrid prayed. He only knew a prayer of his childhood. 'Gentle
Jesus, meek and mild, look upon a little child.' He repeated it aloud,
and there was more fervour in his soft words than in the mad

clamour of the revivalists. 'Pity my simplicity, suffer me to come to Thee.' Bob's pick flew in his hands, working with the velocity of a steam drill. He shovelled the broken reef behind him. His legs twitched under him. He fancied he felt the cold touch of the ogre upon his ankle, and dug on, gouging his way through the soft, white reef. The air had grown oppressive, perspiration dripped from him, but he heeded neither heat nor weariness – he dug for his life.

Now Bob trusted himself to take another look at the loathsome fate threatening to overwhelm him, and he cried like an animal, turning again to his task. The anaconda-like shape of the thing was accented, it rolled in vast convolutions, any one of which might engulf a man. What a death! What a loathsome end to a man, to be seized in those slimy toils and submerged in the fearful mass, sucked up, lost forever to light and breathing! Norrid worked. He had tunnelled in about two feet. He fancied he detected a hollow, drumming sound from the blows of his pick, and hope swelled in his soul.

But it was slow work. Fortunately the thing behind him was slow, too, but confident and resistless, torturing him with a seeming certitude.

'God bless father and mother, and make Bob a good boy.' It was his mother's appendix to the familiar childish prayer, and it came from Norrid's lips now in perfect faith. 'For Jesus' sake, ahmen!'

Something fell upon his bootless foot, something cold and clammy. He dragged his toes from the heaviness, and yet again he cried aloud, feeling his enemy so near. With passionate force he drove his pick. It went deep in, and stuck on wood. This time Bob's cry was one of exultation. He wrenched the pick free, and a rush of air outward extinguished his candle. The brute thing surged forward and clasped a foot. Bob dug wildly. He beat down the barrier before him. The dirt fell behind the timbers of the Pioneer shaft. Light from the shaft came in to him. He rapidly enlarged the hole, and found himself confronted by a wall of stout, sawn slabs two inches thick, the timbers lining the Pioneer shaft. He beat upon them. They resisted his blows with the solidity of rock. Despair laid its icy talons about his heart. The wretched man screamed again and again his mouth to the inch-wide crack between the slabs.

'Help! Help! Oh, for the love of God, help! Christ have mercy! Jesus have mercy on me!'

He stopped, hearing other voices. No, it was but the reverberation of his own cry, stirring in the deep shaft. Then: 'He's here. He's here. We've got him!'

'Help!' cried Norrid, beating on the slabs.

'All right, Bob. All right, ole man. Arf a minute.'

A slab fell away before a prising bar, and tumbled clamorously into the shaft. Bob dragged himself forward, his head protruded where stood Tim Walsh and Fod Elliott on a staging of rails wedged across the centre of the ladder shaft.

'Help!' wailed Norrid. 'It's got me, Tim. O, God, it's got me!'

The men seized him, and endeavoured to drag him from the small drive he had made. They could not.

'It's all up with me. The thing's got me,' said Bob, livid with terror. 'I knew it 'ud get me.'

'Keep yer pecker up, old lad,' said Walsh. 'It'll be all right, it'll be all right for certain. Don't go and give up now when all the luck's with you.'

The two men hauled at Bob, and slowly he emerged, but the accursed thing did not relax its remorseless grip on him. It was coming too. It had him about the ankles only, but held with such implacable tenacity. Elliott chopped at the stuff as it emerged, sinking his axe into its folds as into black flesh, and literally hewed the prisoner free. Bob stood back into the shaft, supported by his friends, and a terrible nausea was upon him. His enemy, thwarted, surged blackly through the opening, as if reaching for and seeking its prey, then dropped into the shaft of the Pioneer, and a long limb fell into the depth, sinking lower, lower, broke, and recoiled, and sank again.

They got Bob to the surface, and he lay under the open sky in sweet rain, in the arms of his stout old wife, who soothed him as if he had been a babe, while Walsh excitedly explained.

'When the missus came runnin' to me with her tale of the shaft bein' blocked the way it was, I knew what was wrong. I remembered working this ground afore. I remembered how me and Spicer lost a shaft here about 50 yards further up the gully, all through that layer of black pug. If it gets wet it swells and drifts. The new deep dam here must have served to give the pug a thorough soakin', and it began to ooze. It 'ud smash two-inch slabs like wooden matches, and it sticks like glue. There's probably thousands of tons of it behind, swellin' and pushin'. I knew this claim. I knew what you'd do if you wasn't caught in the drift, and got Fod to help, tearin' out the slabs from the Pioneer. Gawd, lad, but the luck's been with you!'

Bobbie Norrid had not heard a word. He was shaking against his wife's breast, his arms were tight about her neck. He was chattering piteously –

'Take me away. For God's sake, take me away – a thousand miles away!'

The Third Murder
A New South Wales Tale

HENRY LAWSON

Henry Lawson (1867–1922) was born born at Grenfell, New South
Wales and had a patchy education as his father sometimes kept him at
home to help with his carpentry. At the age of nine Lawson experienced
problems with his ears and suffered partial deafness for the rest of
his life. Lawson worked for his father until 1883 when he joined his
mother, Louisa, in Sydney. Here he worked as a coach painter and
became interested in the republican movement. He began writing
short stories and verse in the 1880s, but his best literary work appeared
in *The Bulletin* in the 1890s. Although he continued to write, his
decline into alcoholism and mental illness affected the quality of his
work. He was gaoled for failing to pay maintenance and he became a
well-known figure in Sydney as a drunk and beggar. He died of a
cerebral haemorrhage at Abbotsford in 1922. 'The Third Murder: A
New South Wales Tale' was first published in *The Boomerang* in 1890.

The old stone house at Lowther, a deserted two-storey building, in a
lonely valley of the great Dividing Range, seldom fails to attract the
curiosity of strangers. The place was not always lonely – it used to be
a 'thriving' convict settlement, but all the other houses have vanished
like their owners.

This old building had, at the time of my acquaintance with it,
been deserted for over fifteen years. The land on which it was
erected was originally a grant to someone who was an authority in
the dark days of the broad arrow and the triangles, and accordingly
had the house erected by convict labour. The manner of its birth
was prophetic.

The title, at the time of my visit, was in dispute, the principal
claimants being the mortgagees and their heirs; but, according to
popular opinion, no one had a better right to the house than the
ghosts who were alleged to inhabit it.

The building itself was of an oblong shape, unrelieved by gables or
balconies of any kind, and contained eight rooms – four above and

four below, with the ordinary passages and staircase. Immediately under the staircase was a door opening on a flight of stone steps leading down into the cellar below. The cellars, four in number, were each provided with a large brick fireplace, but the whole of the fireplaces in the house, including those of the cellars, had been, for some unaccountable reason, bricked up.

The cellars were supposed to have been the quarters of the convict servants; and the space between the lower floor and the cellar ceilings had been filled with loam, probably for the purpose of deadening sound arising from that quarter.

A large unfinished garret occupied the whole of the space between roof and ceiling, broken only by the wide double chimneys. The garret was only partly floored, and open to the air; and the *débris* left by the birds which inhabited it, filled the spaces between the nine-inch joists and rose in places to the height of six inches above these, testifying to the length of time the place had been deserted.

The doors, set low and wide in the old-fashioned style, were of the best cedar, and all the door jambs were beautifully panelled on the inner side, as also those of the windows; so that altogether the workmanship proves that there were some very capable artisans among the unfortunate convict builders.

From the outside the house looked anything but inviting. The broken and barricaded windows, which, with the exception of those in front, were of diverse sizes and irregularly placed, gave the place, especially at dusk, a sinister and ghost-haunted appearance.

From time to time one or other of the different claimants put a caretaker into Lenton House to hold it in his name, and it was from one of these that I got most of my information. He (my informant) had held the place for several months and then resigned his office. To use his own terms, 'he didn't like it'. He didn't believe in ghosts, mind you, and wasn't afraid as long as he 'didn't see nothing'; but his sleep was disturbed by 'footsteps and things', and he preferred a peaceful night's rest in his own home to the small 'consideration' the claimant allowed him.

He narrated the history of the house from the date of the hewing of the first stone up to the present time. He was an old hand – to use his own words – and had been in the country 'sixty-five years, six months and two days'. He gave me a minute description of a quarrel which took place between the owner and the architect over fifty-five years before when he 'was a mere lad, God bless you', etc., etc. But I steered the old man back to the ghost part of the business, and he became entertaining. He told me that two murders at least had been committed in the house, to say nothing of others that had been 'done right enough'. The legend which related to the first murder ran as follows.

A convict master who occupied the house for a brief period had a dispute with his housekeeper, a young English country girl, an assigned servant of his, because, it was averred, she failed to fall in with his wishes in everything. He killed her with a blow on the temple from a nail hammer, and after carrying the body down into the cellar (conveniently unoccupied at times) he burned it there. The legend further states that he had sufficient influence to have the matter hushed up.

There was no doubt about the second murder, which occurred many years afterwards, when the house was first deserted. A young couple who were out riding one Sunday afternoon took refuge in the building from a thunderstorm. They had a furious quarrel concerning another young man, of whom the lover was jealous, and it ended by the lover stabbing his sweetheart and hiding the body in the cellars. He was hanged.

Added to these murders, tales of convicts being flogged to death and women being murdered formed a harmonious background to the house's history.

I was at this time connected with a party of surveyors at work in the locality; and as I considered that two murders committed in the same house at intervals far apart and almost on the same lines were sufficient to raise a ghost – if such things existed – I determined out of curiosity to pass a night in the Haunted House.

There may be men brave enough to pass a night *alone* in a house of this kind, but I am not of their number. In spite of my aggressive disbelief in the existence of ghosts, I would not sleep alone in a house reputedly haunted for all the money that could be offered me, so I unfolded my project to a mate of mine – a member of the survey party – and one night we took our guns and left camp on a pretended 'possum-shooting expedition. We had a long way to walk before we reached the house, and as it came on to rain shortly after we started our spirits were damped at the outset. However, we arrived at the house shortly after ten o'clock, and took up a position in one of the lower rooms, the door of which commanded the stairway and the top of the flight of steps leading down to the cellars beneath. Both murders were supposed to have taken place in one of the upper rooms, the one immediately above us.

The old caretaker had raised a small crop of maize during his tenure of office, and as he had used this room for a barn the husks which remained made us a good bed.

We took up a position at the far side of the room, in a recess of the fireplace, and sat down and waited. Nothing came, however, and as we began to feel chilly we wrapped our overcoats round our legs, and after a brief ceremony with a black bottle lay down, and were soon asleep.

*   *   *

I woke suddenly with that strange intuition of something about to happen. The night was as dark as pitch, and the rain, aided by the wind, rushed down in torrents; but above the roar of the storm I distinctly caught the sound of footsteps and noises in the room above.

The voices were those of a man and woman, and were evidently raised in furious quarrel; but I failed to catch the import of the words.

My friend was sleeping soundly, and knowing by experience the difficulty of awakening him during night time, I lay still and listened.

The voices continued to wrangle for some time, and then when they seemed to have reached the highest pitch possible I heard a short scuffle ended by the sound of a blow; a couple of uncertain footsteps and then a heavy fall on the floor.

I then heard nothing for a minute or so except the storm without, but my mind, as is often the case when one receives a severe shock, was in a curiously quickened condition, and I distinctly remember listening for the sounds of the weapon when the murderer dropped it or laid it down so that I might judge of its kind. If it sounded like a hammer then it was the ghostly representation of the first murder that I was witnessing, if like a knife then the second crime was once more being enacted. I also remember reasoning that in the first case the house was furnished and the murderer would probably lay his weapon down on a table to avoid noise, but in the second case the weapon would probably be dropped on the floor.

Presently sure enough I heard something fall, but it sounded like neither of the weapons above mentioned. It sounded more like an ordinary walking-stick and so quickened had become my hearing that concurrent with this sound I heard another which might have been caused by the fall of a short piece of rope on the boards.

Presently I heard the footsteps again and they seemed to be scraping the floor. 'He is lifting the body now,' I thought. The steps, sounding somewhat heavier than before, went in the direction of the room where I knew the door was leading out on to the landing.

And now my terror, which seemed to have been rendered helpless in the first instance, began to assert itself.

My heart seemed to have deserted my body; there was a dreadful sinking in my stomach, and my limbs became rigid as I turned involuntarily on one side and stared in the direction of the floor with eyes that seemed growing in their sockets.

My friend was still sleeping heavily, but I could not have made a movement to waken him had I tried. I was dumb and helpless with fear.

I heard those awful footsteps coming down. I could hear the first foot dropped heavily on a lower step, and the scrape and lighter landing of the last as it left its step and was brought down on to that occupied by the first. These sounds were repeated with monotonous regularity, broken only where, as I knew, a step was missing by a heavier fall on the next step.

Nearer and nearer it came, and at last the steps ceased at the foot of the stairs. I felt that my brain could stand it no longer. Oh, God! how I prayed for the oblivion of a swoon and an awakening from this horrible nightmare!

Presently I heard the scrape of a match on the stair rail, and the sudden blaze in the darkness almost blinded me.

I saw standing at the foot of the stairs a tall, roughly-clad man with a brutal-looking face that was ghostly white in contrast with his jet-black hair and beard. His cruel upper lip was clean shaved, and the beard hung down like a fringe from a thin-lipped mouth, which had the appearance of a black line drawn across his lower face. His eyes were very small, and glittered like a snake's as he moved the match round in front of him, and peered about.

He was carrying the woman breast-upwards with his right arm passed round her left side and under her back. Her face, which was turned towards me, hung down almost perpendicularly, the long black hair falling down to the boards. Her eyes were wide open and staring, and the matchlight glittered on the surface of their glazed pupils. There was a jagged black shape on her temple, which I knew was the death wound, and a black-looking something crawled out of it and crept down through her hair, standing out here and there like dewdrops, and shining in the light of the match. This I knew was blood. The match went out, and the steps seemed to come opposite to the door and pause there. I was in deathly terror lest the ghostly apparition should come into the room instead of passing down into the cellars beneath, and then the room seemed to become like a furnace, and anon like a refrigerator. The floor seemed to rise up like the deck of a ship towards the floor of that awful murder room above, and then to sink down, down into the cellars underneath.

I threw out my arms to save myself from going down, and then with a chilling rush, oblivion came over my senses.

* * *

I woke at daylight with a splitting headache, and feeling very stiff and sick all over – the result, I supposed, of the wetting and the nightmare – to find my friend sitting on the floor putting on his boots. He did not seem in a very pleasant humour, and told me to hurry up as we were expected at the camp early, and so we left the building without delay, and started for the camp. I refrained from mentioning my awful dream until my friend broke ground.

'Well if that cursed house isn't haunted, it ought to be. I've been dreaming all night of murder going on in those top rooms and bodies being carried down into the cellars, and – '

'Good God!' I exclaimed, 'I also had a terrible dream too, full of the same things; there must be something in this double nightmare; it must mean – '

'There's nothing in it,' he snapped rather impatiently, thinking, no doubt, that I begrudged him a monopoly of nightmare; 'it means nothing but that we're double idiots.' So I thought it best to let the matter drop.

I left New South Wales shortly after the incident of the haunted house, and knocked about over the world generally for some years. The ghost business had completely vanished from my memory, when one day in San Francisco I came accidentally across a Victorian newspaper about a year old. I turned it over curiously, and my eyes caught the following item of news which I read half through before the full meaning of it burst on my mind. You may judge the effect it had upon me.

THE LOWTHER MURDER
From our Sydney Correspondent

The carrier, Marston, who was hung on Monday last for the murder of his wife in an old deserted building near Lowther, where the body lay hidden for nearly four years, made the following confession on the day preceding his execution.

'In 18— I, Stephen Marston, was travelling with a horse team between Mount Wombat and Reynold's Marsh, where I lived. Some time in January I took the team into town for a load of fencing wire for Blackman's run. My wife went in with me to buy some things. Both my wife and I were in the habit of drinking, and we brought some liquor out with us on the back trip. I think we had two bottles of brandy and half a bottle of rum.

'We reached the old Lowther estate the first night, and camped about half a mile from the place on the main road; we were then about seventy miles from home.

'It looked like rain in the evening, and we decided to camp in the old stone house for the night. We had tea at the dray, and after seeing that the horses were right we started for the house, taking some blankets with us. We chose one of the upper rooms because the lower ones were close, and smelt bad. There were a lot of corn husks in the place, and I carried some upstairs for a bed.

'Neither I nor my wife were perfectly sober, and we had more drink before turning in, and so got too drunk to undress and lay down in our clothes.

'Some time in the night we woke up and had a quarrel about something of no matter now. She was more under the influence of drink than I. She scratched my face and bit like a cat, and I caught up my horse-whip and, as she struck me in the face again, I lost all control over myself, reversed the whip, and struck out blindly in the dark with the butt end of it. It was a heavy whip with a steel rod running through the handle, and the binding had frayed away at the big end and left the steel bare. I didn't think of this at the time, for as true as God's above me, I never meant to kill my wife.

'She fell and lay still, and I began to feel frightened. I struck a match and saw an awful gash on her forehead, from which the blood was running, and when I tried to raise her I saw that she was dead.

'I was terribly shocked; I drank some brandy and carried the body down into the cellars, intending to bury it there. I left the body in the cellar and went out through the front door, intending to bring a spade from the dray to dig the grave with. But when I returned the day was breaking, and something prompted me to look in through the window of one of the lower rooms. I was startled to see two men asleep among the corn husks on the floor.

'I immediately returned to the team and started for home, which I reached the following night, and there gave out that my wife had left me again – she had run away twice previously and of course the neighbours believed me.

'I buried the body (which had not been disturbed) on the next trip, and as soon as I could threw up the lease of the farm which I was living on and went up country, where I was arrested last May. I have no children living nor any relatives that I know of.'

*   *   *

The most curious feature of the confession is the statement as to the presence of other persons in the house at the time of the murder. It will be remembered that Marston made this assertion in his defence and tried to turn it to account, but the police who investigated the matter discredited the whole story.

The Death Child

Guy Boothby

Guy Boothby (1867–1905) is well known for his supernatural thrillers involving Dr Nikola, a magician searching for the elixir of life. He was born in Adelaide and became private secretary to the Mayor of Adelaide before settling in England in 1894 to pursue his literary ambitions. Apart from the Dr Nikola series, he wrote several supernatural novels, including *Pharos the Egyptian* (1899) and *The Curse of the Snake* (1902). He was also an amateur farmer and dog breeder. Boothby died from influenza at the age of 38 at his home at Boscombe in Hampshire. His short collections include *Bushigrams* (1897), *Uncle Joe's Legacy and Other Stories* (1902), *The Lady of the Island* (1904) and *For Love of Her* (1905), all of which contain supernatural stories. 'The Death Child' appeared in *For Love of Her*, and 'A Strange Goldfield' in *Uncle Joe's Legacy*.

One summer night, about three years after I took to the pearling trade in the Pacific, five of us – John Browdie, a Yorkshireman, standing six feet two in his socks; a Londoner, whom we called the scholar, more on account of his mannerisms than his learning, I fancy; Harry the Digger; Sailor Jim, and myself – sat yarning on the fo'c'sle of the lugger *Waterwitch*, anchored off the New Guinea Coast. It was about the hottest night of the year, and save for the gentle *flip-flap* of the water alongside, and the wear of the cable in the hawse hole, everything was so still that you could even distinguish the sound of the waves breaking on the beach more than two miles away.

The lights of Port Moresby winked at us over our starboard quarter, while away to port shone the riding light of the *Merrie England* Government steamer. The stars shimmered like gold dust strewn across the sky, and, as if to show that there still remained some sort of touch with England, the Great Bear just lifted above the northern horizon.

On three occasions the Yorkshireman had embarked upon the narration of a mysterious story, which we had all heard a dozen times before, setting forth, at interminable length, the adventures of his grandfather at a certain West Riding race meeting; but we invariably managed to stave him off in time.

As the talk slackened he saw his opportunity, and commenced at once –

'Yo' see, n'out would do for gran'fer, but 'e mun see t' Leger run, an' as 'e was a'goin oop t' moor – '

I drummed my foot against the hatch, while the scholar, who had been ashore that afternoon, said hastily from the cable range –

'Do any of you remember the wreck of the *Kate Kearney*?'

The Yorkshireman saw another chance in the silence that followed, and hastened to make the most of it.

'Ho'd tha tongue, lad!' he said, 'Wha's t' use o' bringin' that oop now? It's rude to interrupt, and you mun first 'ear tell o' ma gran'fer an' – '

'But what about the *Kate Kearney*?' I asked quickly.

Before the north countryman could get another word in, the scholar had begun his story –

'It is rather a curious story, and it was something that happened to me ashore today that made me think of it. First and foremost you must bear in mind that this yarn is not make-believe. At least a dozen men now on their road to – well, never mind where – are convinced of its truth; and all I can say is, if you want further proof, well, you have only to adopt Papuan Lizzie yourself, and see what comes of it.

'She was, or *is* I should say, since she is still very much alive, a New Guinea native from the Lakoli River; fifty miles or so away down there under the moon. "The Yankee Pirate" (shot last year in the Solomon Group) blackbirded her by mistake, when she was about six years old, in spite of a curse from her infuriated hag of a mother who raced the party down the beach, swearing that whoever had to do with the child would surely die. It was a beautiful curse, so the Yankee told me, and on it the story I'm going to tell you hangs.

'Of course the whole ship's company laughed at the idea of anything happening to them – it would have been strange, if they hadn't – but just mark how perfectly the curse worked out!

'Before I go any further I must explain to you that these things happened at a time when Government agents were unthought of, and when an adult *kanaka* landed in Port Mackay meant a solid gain of nearly twenty pounds to the man who brought him over. Legalised slavery it may have been, but the money was there safe and sound nevertheless.'

'Lad! I'm jealous tha knaws't too much about yon times,' said Browdie with emphasis.

The scholar glanced over the side to where the copper sheathing glittered in the moonlight, and then up at the motionless vane upon the mast-head, before he continued –

'Most of the *kanakas* out of that shipment went to the Eureka Sugar Company's plantation on the Pioneer River, and with them went Lizzie. The manager's wife, a kind-hearted soul, took pity on the miserable coffee-coloured little urchin, and allowed her to spend the greater part of her time playing with her own children. Within a week, two of them found their way into the sugar house and were killed in the machinery, and the mother, who saw the accident, is now in a Brisbane lunatic asylum.

'Three months later the company was in liquidation, the plant-ation was shut up, and the *kanakas* were dispersed to the four winds of heaven. Nobody seemed to want Lizzie, so she passed from hand to hand up the coast, stopping here and there for a few weeks at a time, but always being moved on by the fatalities that followed in her wake. At last she reached Townsville, the capital of the North, as you know its inhabitants grandiloquently term it. Here it looked as if she were going to be allowed settle down for a while. But the kind lady who was struck by her forlornness and took charge of her, developed typhoid fever in some inexplicable fashion within a month of her arrival, and died a fortnight later, throwing the child upon the world once more. Her executors were at a loss to know what to do with the brat, so they were only too grateful when a kind-hearted gentleman came forward and said that he would take her off their hands, and carry her home to England as a present to his wife. He left Townsville in the mail boat *Carrysfort*, and as the world has good reason to be aware, that ill-fated vessel struck an uncharted rock off Cape York, and went to the bottom in some-thing under three minutes, taking with her every living soul on board save four.

'Papuan Lizzie was one of the four who did not find a watery grave. She was thrown to three Lascars who were clinging to a spar alongside. How it came about it is impossible to say, but the men were never heard of again; Lizzie, however, was picked up by a *bêche-de-mer* schooner a few hours later, and carried to Thursday Island. Unfortunately her fame had preceded her, and it was there that she received for the first time the name of the "Death Child". For some days no one would have anything to do with her, and consequently she wandered about the beach as miserable an urchin as could have been found in the whole Western Pacific. Then a zealous missionary, anxious to prove how idle and wicked such suspicions were, gave her a home.

'For nearly six months all went well, and bit by bit the ugly little creature developed an affection for her guardian that was as grotesque as the cause of it was pathetic. He had begun, and would have finished, her education if the curse had not uncoiled itself, and led him to interfere in a drunken street brawl; during which Rhotoma Sam stabbed him to the heart for his pains, and thus deprived Lizzie of another protector.

'After this, for three months or so, the record of her movements is more or less uncertain. I believe she went down to the D'Entrecasteax Group in the trading schooner *Skylark*, and probability is given to the theory, by the fact that the *Skylark* left Port Moresby, and was never heard of again.

'When next I saw her Lizzie was back in Thursday Island, uglier and more impish than ever, and so convinced was everyone of her Satanic association that not a mother's son or daughter would take her in, or befriend her in any way. Consequently she was compelled to live by herself in Tommy Burns's old hut in the gully behind the Chinese Gardens.

'Now, among the multifarious inhabitants of the Island at that time was a former mate of the *Kate Kearney*, the vessel we were speaking of just now, a vindictive sort of a fellow named Benman, who had a great and undying hatred for Captain Edwards, of the same craft. He used to say that the captain had concocted a plot to get him discharged from the company's service, and he vowed that come what might, he would be even with his enemy before many years had passed. The captain, in total ignorance of this hatred and believing that Benman liked him rather than otherwise, wrote in a friendly sort of way, asking him, as a personal favour, to find a suitable black maid for his wife.

'Seeing his way to as devilish piece of mischief as ever was planned, Benman chuckled to himself and began to make enquiries.

'When, a month later, the *Kate Kearney* put in for stores he hunted up Papuan Lizzie and sent her aboard with a polite little note, recommending her, and saying how glad he was to have a chance of being useful to his old friend. Mrs Edwards, who was an invalid, took a great fancy to her new handmaid and as soon as they were at sea, set about completing the education the unfortunate missionary had begun.

'Leaving Thursday Island the *Kate Kearney* sailed on a trading cruise among the Islands. The ship's company included the captain, his mate, a supercargo, an Englishman fresh from home, three Solomon boys, and a half-caste Philippine Islander. Also Papuan Lizzie, who detested lessons or work of any kind, and spent most of her time on the main hatch, huddled up like a native idol, blinking at the sun. Then the curse, which had not made any visible mischief for well-nigh three months, began to think about business once more. On this occasion it took the form of a mutiny.

'One sunny afternoon the *Kate Kearney* lay becalmed off Arurai in the Kingsmills. The sea alongside was as smooth as glass, and almost as transparent, while overhead the spars and rigging stood out double-sized against the azure sky.

'The skipper and mate were pacing the deck, wondering from what quarter they might expect the wind, and talking of things in general. Coming aft they leaned over the taffrail to watch a shark struggle astern.

'Then the half-caste Portuguese, who had been lolling against the wheel with nothing to do, save to hatch mischief and to dream of the spree he intended having when next he got ashore, suddenly received a signal from the fo'c'sle, made up his mind, and drawing a revolver from his belt, shot both men dead. Next moment the vessel, from being an inanimate mass upon the sunlit waters, became surcharged with life. The supercargo, who was below, asleep, alarmed by the noise, ran up the companion ladder, rifle in hand. But the murderer, who had the advantage of him, fired as soon as his head appeared, and the white man fell backwards down the ladder into the cuddy, dead as a doornail, shot through the skull.

'By this time the ship was in an uproar. The remainder of the hands made their appearance from their hiding places and set to work to throw the bodies overboard to the sharks they had been watching less than half an hour before. When this was done, the half-caste assumed command. The Englishman was given the chance of serving, or of sharing the fate of his companions. Naturally he chose the former alternative. Mrs Edwards terminated an interview with the ringleader by throwing herself overboard, while Papuan Lizzie sat on the hatch and cried very bitterly, for she loved her kind benefactress, and would willingly have put a knife into the back of the half-caste, only she was afraid. She was not of course to know that she was the cause of all the trouble.

'For three months the *Rolling Wave*, alias the *Kate Kearney*, did an amazing trade among the Islands. At the end of that time her hold was full to bursting, of pearl shell, copra, tortoiseshell, and dried *bêche-de-mer*.

'Then, quite by chance, for there was no navigator aboard worthy of the name, they reached Ponape, a Spanish settlement of the Caroline Group, and anchored outside the reef. When all was snug the half-caste went ashore, leaving the crew to gamble and quarrel among themselves as they pleased. Though he did not know it, they were hatching another mutiny among themselves, and this time against himself, for they had come to the conclusion that he was carrying things with far too high a hand.

'As soon as he returned, and dusk fell, the Englishman, who was friendly with neither party, seized his opportunity, slipped down the cable, and also made for the shore. It was a long swim, and the sea was running high under a freshening gale.

'Ponape, with its few hundred natives and sprinkling of Spaniards, is not by any means a big place, so he discovered the Governor's residence without very much searching, and poured his thrilling tale of mutiny and murder into that official's ear.

'The Governor immediately ordered out his state army, an officer and ten men, all as zealous as himself, and with great pomp and circumstance issued the command that the schooner *Rolling Wave* should be boarded and seized.

'In spite of the increasing storm, the army put off and eventually got alongside without resistance from the mutineers, who at the time were below. The only visible occupant of the vessel was Papuan Lizzie, who was crying under the lee of the deckhouse aft.

'Having placed sentries at the entrance to the companion ladder, the Governor went below with the balance of his men. He found the ship's company engraved on cut-throat euchre, and you can imagine their astonishment when they saw the soldiers enter.

'They fought like wild cats, but it was only to discover that sheath knives and bare fists are of small avail even against Spanish swords and derelict muskets. Having ironed them, the Commander-in-Chief placed them under a strong guard and then searched the ship.

'While he was occupied in this fashion he forgot to take stock of the weather. When they had come aboard it was working up for a storm; now it was such a night as you seldom see. A cyclone was sweeping down upon the Island, and even the usually placid water inside the reef was white with driven foam. By the time those on board arrived at an understanding of their position, it had torn up the schooner's straining cables, and was racing her along the treacherous line of rocks, at more than racing pace. Eventually she went to pieces close in shore, and out of the eighteen souls aboard her, including the Governor, the soldiers and their prisoners, only two escaped alive. One was the Englishman I have already mentioned, who had accompanied the boarding party to see what happened, the other was Papuan Lizzie, who, strange to relate, was landed high and dry on the beach without scratch or injury. Two days later the Englishman left in a schooner for Tahiti, and for the time being that was the last he saw of that queer little atom we used to call the "Death Child".'

Harry the Digger, put down his pipe.

'Hold on, my lad,' he said very quietly, 'you haven't told us how you learnt these things.'

'Well,' said the scholar with a quiet chuckle, 'it seems to me I should know something about them, considering I was the Englishman who gave the information to the authorities, and who was allowed to live on condition he joined the mutineers.'

'A neatly worked out yarn,' I continued; 'and pray did you ever hear what became of the Death Child after that?'

'She remained in Ponape for upwards of two years, I believe, and then managed to make her way, how I cannot explain, across the Pacific until she reached Port Moresby once more.'

'Here?' we cried in astonishment. 'You don't mean to say she's in Port Moresby at this moment?'

'Most certainly I do,' he replied. 'I saw her only today when I went ashore. It was my meeting with her that made me think of telling you the story. But you mustn't run away with the notion that she's the same Liz. She's a changed character altogether.'

'In what way is she changed?'

'She's grown up and a married woman. You remember Pat Dolson, the man who was in Thursday Island a year or two back, who claimed to have been an Oxford Don, and who had the reputation of being able to drink more mixed liquor at one sitting, and to be able to swear in a greater variety of tongues than any other white man in the Pacific? You do? Well, then, he's her husband. They were married a month ago.'

'Surely you're joking. What on earth made him marry her? Is the man mad?'

'It looks like it, does it not? At any rate, he's gone to pieces now. I never saw such a wreck of a man in my life before. Lives out in the bush among the niggers, dresses in the native style, and if ever I saw a man on the borders of the jumps he was that one. He talked an awful lot of nonsense to me about Fate-Destiny-Powers of Darkness, and goodness only knows what all, mixing it up with Greek and Latin quotations. Said he was bewitched by Liz, and that it was ordained from the first that he should marry her – so how could he help himself? I told him he was a fool for his pains, and that he deserved to come to just the sort of ends he prophesied. All the time I was talking Liz sat at the door of the hut, watching me out of half-closed eyes, with that devilish smile of hers upon her face. When I left she stopped me in the bush, and showing all her teeth in a grin, asked me if I didn't think she would make him "*one big all the same first-class wife*".'

'What did you say?'

'I can't remember exactly, but I fancy I consigned her to the place where wives who make promises before marriage and don't fulfil them afterwards are popularly supposed to go. As it was, she – '

The scholar stopped suddenly, and held up his hand.

'Hark!' he cried. 'What was that?'

We sat silent, listening, but all we could hear was the soft murmur of the water alongside, and the gentle creaking of the spars as the tiny vessel rocked at her anchor. Then there was a sound a short distance away on our starboard bow, that made us all leap to our feet like one man. It was the cry of a person in sore distress.

'It's someone drowning!' cried sailor Jim, who was always ready to jump to a conclusion. 'I've heard that cry too often not to know it. Here! let's get the boat away at once, or we'll be too late to rescue him.'

As he spoke he ran to the davits, but before he could let go the falls the sound reached our ears again, and this time it came from close under the counter.

'Schooner ahoy!' it said. 'Take me aboard.'

A moment later we were all at the taffrail, craning our necks over the side in an attempt to discover who the man might be, and to render him any assistance that might be in our power.

He did not seem to be in need of so much help as he had led us to believe, for he presently scrambled on board, and having gained the deck shook himself like a Newfoundland dog. He was stark naked, and had long black hair that trailed upon his shoulders. Taken altogether, he did not make a pretty picture.

'Good heavens, Dolson!' cried the scholar with a gasp, as he recognised the man before us. 'You don't mean to say it's you? What on earth has brought you out here like this?'

But Dolson only gave a queer sort of grunt, and threw down upon the deck a native basket constructed of some sweet-smelling reed. After that he sat down on the main hatch, and hid his face in his hands. We stood round and watched him, unable to make head or tail of it all. Undoubtedly he was crazy.

'She said she had bewitched me,' he began after a pause. 'Because I beat her she cursed me only this evening. "You shall not find your death on land," says she, "nor shall you be drowned in water. Your death shall come to you through me, and though I be dead yet shall I be there to see you die." It's a lie! She *is* dead, it is true, for I killed her myself. But she will not see me die. Of that I am certain.'

So absorbed were we in watching him and listening to his ravings, that we entirely failed to notice a canoe which had come softly up alongside, nor the black figure which had made its way aboard over the bows. Had we done so we should probably have warned Dolson, but it was Fate that kept us otherwise employed so that we should not see. An arm went up, and then a poisoned spear came aft, travelling straight for the naked figure seated on the hatch. It caught him full and fair in the chest, between the shoulders, and a few minutes later Dolson was squirming upon the deck, and his murderer had disappeared into the night again. In his agony Dolson chanced to touch the basket he had brought on board with him, and under the impetus thus given to it the contents rolled out, and into the circle of light made by the lantern which someone had thoughtfully brought up from below. To our horror, we discovered that the black ball rolling and bobbing towards the bulwarks was neither more nor less than the head of Papuan Lizzie – the Death Child – severed at the trunk. The eyes were open, and the mouth was set in a diabolical leer. As I noticed this horror, the man whom we called Dolson gave up the ghost, and thus his wife's prophecy came true. He had not died on land, nor was he drowned in water; his death came to him through her agency, and though her body was not present, still her eyes were there, and saw him breathe his last.

And yet there are some people who, having read this story, will say they do not believe in witchcraft, nor will they own that they have any faith in the power of a curse.

A Strange Goldfield

Guy Boothby

Of course nine out of every ten intelligent persons will refuse to believe that there could be a grain of truth in the story I am now going to tell you. The tenth may have some small faith in my veracity, but what I think of his intelligence I am going to keep to myself.

In a certain portion of a certain Australian Colony two miners, when out prospecting in what was then, as now, one of the dreariest parts of the Island Continent, chanced upon a rich find. They applied to Government for the usual reward, and in less than a month three thousand people were settled on the Field. What privations they had to go through to get there, and the miseries they had to endure when they *did* reach their journey's end, have only a remote bearing on this story, but they would make a big book.

I should explain that between Railhead and the Field was a stretch of country some three hundred miles in extent. It was badly watered, vilely grassed, and execrably timbered. What was even worse, a considerable portion of it was made up of red sand, and everybody who has been compelled to travel over that knows what it means. Yet these enthusiastic seekers after wealth pushed on, some on horseback, some in bullock waggons, but the majority travelled on foot; the graves, and the skeletons of cattle belonging to those who had preceded them punctuating the route, and telling them what they might expect as they advanced.

That the Field did not prove a success is now a matter of history, but that same history, if you read between the lines, gives one some notion of what the life must have been like while it lasted. The water supply was entirely insufficient, provisions were bad and ruinously expensive; the men themselves were, as a rule, the roughest of the rough, while the less said about the majority of the women the better. Then typhoid stepped in and stalked like the Destroying Angel through the camp. Its inhabitants went down like sheep in a drought, and for the most part rose no more. Where there had been a lust of gold there was now panic, terror – every man feared that he might be the next to be attacked, and it was only the knowledge of those terrible three hundred miles that separated them from civilisation that kept many of them on the Field. The most thickly populated part was now the cemetery. Drink was the only solace, and under its influence such scenes were enacted as I dare not describe. As they heard of fresh deaths, men shook their fists at Heaven, and cursed the day when they first saw pick or shovel. Some, bolder than the rest, cleared out just as they stood; a few eventually reached civilisation, others perished in the desert. At last the Field was declared abandoned, and the dead were left to take their last long sleep, undisturbed by the clank of windlass or the blow of pick.

It would take too long to tell all the different reasons that combined to draw me out into that 'most distressful country'. Let it suffice that our party consisted of a young Englishman named Spicer, a wily old Australian bushman named Matthews, and myself. We were better off than the unfortunate miners, inasmuch as we were travelling with camels, and our outfits were as perfect as money and experience could make them. The man who travels in any other fashion in that country is neither more nor less than a madman. For a month past we had been having a fairly rough time of it, and were then on our way south, where we had reason to believe rain had fallen, and, in consequence, grass was plentiful. It was towards evening when we came out of a gully in the ranges and had our first view of the deserted camp. We had no idea of its existence, and for this reason we pulled up our animals and stared at it in complete surprise. Then we pushed on again, wondering what on earth place we had chanced upon.

'This is all right,' said Spicer, with a chuckle. 'We're in luck. Grog shanties and stores, a bath, and perhaps girls.'

I shook my head.

'I can't make it out,' I said. 'What's it doing out here?'

Matthews was looking at it under his hand, and, as I knew that he had been out in this direction on a previous occasion, I asked his opinion.

'It beats me,' he replied; 'but if you ask me what I think I should say is it's Gurunya, the Field that was deserted some four or five years back.'

'Look here,' cried Spicer, who was riding a bit on our left, 'what are all these things – graves, as I'm a living man. Here, let's get out of this. There are hundreds of them and before I know where I am old Polyphemus here will be on his nose.'

What he said was correct – the ground over which we were riding was literally bestrewn with graves, some of which had rough,
tumbledown head boards, others being destitute of all adornment.
We turned away and moved on over safer ground in the direction of
the Field itself. Such a pitiful sight I never want to see again. The
tents and huts, in numerous cases, were still standing, while the
claims gaped at us on every side like new-made graves. A bullock
dray, weather-worn but still in excellent condition, stood in the
main street outside a grog shanty whose sign-board, strange incon-
gruity, bore the name of 'The Killarney Hotel'. Nothing would suit
Spicer but that he must dismount and go in to explore. He was not
long away, and when he returned it was with a face as white as a
sheet of paper.

'You never saw such a place,' he almost whispered. 'All I want to do
is to get out of it. There's a skeleton on the floor in the back room
with an empty rum bottle alongside it.'

He mounted, and, when his beast was on its feet once more, we
went on our way. Not one of us was sorry when we had left the last
claim behind us.

Half a mile or so from the Field the country begins to rise again.
There is also a curious cliff away to the left, and, as it looked like
being a likely place to find water, we resolved to camp there. We
were within a hundred yards or so of this cliff when an exclamation
from Spicer attracted my attention.

'Look!' he cried. 'What's that?'

I followed the direction in which he was pointing, and, to my
surprise, saw the figure of a man running as if for his life among
the rocks. I have said the figure of a man, but, as a matter of fact,
had there been baboons in the Australian bush, I should have been
inclined to have taken him for one.

'This is a day of surprises,' I said. 'Who can the fellow be? And
what makes him act like that?'

We still continued to watch him as he proceeded on his erratic
course along the base of the cliff – then he suddenly disappeared.

'Let's get on to camp, 'I said, 'and then we'll go after him and
endeavour to settle matters a bit.'

Having selected a place we offsaddled and prepared our camp. By
this time it was nearly dark, and it was very evident that, if we wanted
to discover the man we had seen, it would be wise not to postpone
the search too long. We accordingly strolled off in the direction
he had taken, keeping a sharp look-out for any sign of him. Our

search, however, was not successful. The fellow had disappeared without leaving a trace of his whereabouts behind him, and yet we were all certain that we *had* seen him. At length we returned to our camp for supper, completely mystified. As we ate our meal we discussed the problem and vowed that, on the morrow, we would renew the search. Then the full moon rose over the cliff, and the plain immediately became well-nigh as bright as day. I had lit my pipe and was stretching myself out upon my blankets when something induced me to look across at a big rock, some half-dozen paces from the fire. Peering round it, and evidently taking an absorbing interest in our doings, was the most extraordinary figure I have ever beheld. Shouting something to my companions, I sprang to my feet and dashed across at him. He saw me and fled. Old as he apparently was, he could run like a jack-rabbit, and, though I have the reputation of being fairly quick on my feet, I found that I had all my work cut out to catch him. Indeed, I am rather doubtful as to whether I should have done so at all had he not tripped and measured his length on the ground. Before he could get up I was on him.

'I've got you at last, my friend,' I said. 'Now you just come along back to the camp, and let us have a look at you.'

In reply he snarled like a dog and I believe would have bitten me had I not held him off. My word, he was a creature, more animal than man, and the reek of him was worse than that of our camels. From what I could tell he must have been about sixty years of age – was below the middle height, had white eyebrows, white hair and a white beard. He was dressed partly in rags and partly in skins, and went barefooted like a blackfellow. While I was overhauling him the others came up – whereupon we escorted him back to the camp.

'What wouldn't Barnum give for him?' said Spicer. 'You're a beauty, my friend, and no mistake. What's your name?'

The fellow only grunted in reply – then, seeing the pipes in our mouths, a curious change came over him, and he muttered something that resembled 'Give me.'

'Wants a smoke,' interrupted Matthews. 'Poor beggar's been without for a long time, I reckon. Well, I've got an old pipe, so he can have a draw.'

He procured one from his pack saddle, filled it and handed it to the man, who snatched it greedily and began to puff away at it.

'How long have you been out here?' I asked, when he had squatted himself down alongside the fire.

'Don't know,' he answered, this time plainly enough.

'Can't you get back?' continued Matthews, who knew the nature of the country on the other side.

'Don't want to,' was the other's laconic reply. 'Stay here.'

I heard Spicer mutter, 'Mad – mad as a March hare.'

We then tried to get out of him where he hailed from, but he had either forgotten or did not understand. Next we inquired how he managed to live. To this he answered readily enough, 'Carnies.'

Now the carny is a lizard of the iguana type, and eaten raw would be by no means an appetising dish. Then came the question that gives me my reason for telling this story. It was Spicer who put it.

'You must have a lonely time of it out here,' said the latter. 'How do you manage for company?'

'There is the Field,' he said, 'as sociable a Field as you'd find.'

'But the Field's deserted, man,' I put in. 'And has been for years.'

The old fellow shook his head.

'As sociable a Field as ever you saw,' he repeated. 'There's Sailor Dick and 'Frisco, Dick Johnson, Cockney Jim, and half a hundred of them. They're taking it out powerful rich on the Golden South, so I heard when I was down at "The Killarney", a while back.'

It was plain to us all that the old man was, as Spicer had said, as mad as a hatter. For some minutes he rambled on about the Field, talking rationally enough, I must confess – that is to say, it would have seemed rational enough if we hadn't known the true facts of the case. At last he got on to his feet, saying, 'Well, I must be going – they'll be expecting me. It's my shift on with Cockney Jim.'

'But you don't work at night,' growled Matthews, from the other side of the fire.

'We work always,' the other replied. 'If you don't believe me, come and see for yourselves.'

'I wouldn't go back to that place for anything,' said Spicer.

But I must confess that my curiosity had been aroused, and I determined to go, if only to see what this strange creature did when he got there. Matthews decided to accompany me, and, not wishing to be left alone, Spicer at length agreed to do the same. Without looking round, the old fellow led the way across the plain towards the Field. Of all the nocturnal excursions I have made in my life, that was certainly the most uncanny. Not once did our guide turn his head, but pushed on at a pace that gave us some trouble to keep up with him. It was only when we came to the first claim that he paused.

'Listen,' he said, 'and you can hear the camp at work. Then you'll believe me.'

We *did* listen, and as I live we could distinctly hear the rattling of sluice-boxes and cradles, the groaning of windlasses – in fact, the noise you hear on a goldfield at the busiest hour of the day. We moved a little closer, and, believe me or not, I swear to you I could see, or thought I could see, the shadowy forms of men moving about in that ghostly moonlight. Meanwhile the wind sighed across the plain, flapping what remained of the old tents and giving an additional touch of horror to the general desolation. I could hear Spicer's teeth chattering behind me, and, for my own part, I felt as if my blood were turning to ice.

'That's the claim, the Golden South, away to the right there,' said the old man, 'and if you will come along with me, I'll introduce you to my mates.'

But this was an honour we declined, and without hesitation. I wouldn't have gone any further among those tents for the wealth of all the Indies.

'I've had enough of this,' said Spicer, and I can tell you I hardly recognised his voice. 'Let's get back to camp.'

By this time our guide had left us, and was making his way in the direction he had indicated. We could plainly hear him addressing imaginary people as he marched along. As for ourselves, we turned about and hurried back to our camp as fast as we could go.

Once there, the grog bottle was produced, and never did three men stand more in need of stimulants. Then we set to work to find some explanation of what we had seen, or had fancied we saw. But it was impossible. The wind might have rattled the old windlasses, but it could not be held accountable for those shadowy grey forms that had moved about among the claims.

'I give it up,' said Spicer, at last. 'I know that I never want to see it again. What's more, I vote that we clear out of here tomorrow morning.'

We all agreed, and then retired to our blankets, but for my part I do not mind confessing I scarcely slept a wink all night. The thought that that hideous old man might be hanging about the camp would alone be sufficient for that.

Next morning, as soon as it was light, we breakfasted, but, before we broke camp, Matthews and I set off along the cliff in an attempt to discover our acquaintance of the previous evening. Though, however, we searched high and low for upwards of an hour, no success rewarded us. By mutual consent we resolved not to look for him on the Field. When we returned to Spicer we placed such tobacco and stores as we could spare under the shadow of the big rock, where the Mystery would be likely to see them, then mounted our camels and resumed our journey, heartily glad to be on our way once more.

Gurunya Goldfield is a place I never desire to visit again. I don't like its population.

Sea Voices

Roderic Quinn

Roderic Quinn (1867–1949) was born in Sydney and educated at Catholic schools. He worked at a variety of jobs, including produce merchant and school teacher, before becoming the editor of the *North Sydney News*. He began publishing verse and short stories in the *Centennial Magazine* and *The Bulletin* in the 1890s, and quickly established a reputation as a leading Australian poet. His first and only novel, *Mostyn Stayne* (1897), is an account of a pirate marooned on Australia in 1720 and includes a terrific storm in which it rains blood and a haunted wood where skeletons are chained to the trees. Quinn is best known for his poetry and he produced several volumes of verse. His first collection, *The Hidden Tide* (1899), was well received and attracted positive comment from W. B. Yeats. He never married, living with family members and in a boarding house for the last twenty years of his life. 'Sea Voices' appeared in *The Bulletin* in November 1933 and is an evocative meditation on the supernatural and Sydney after dark.

Recently towards midnight I awoke to hear the sound of breaking waves. Low, insistent and ever-even, it stole up to my room over a mile of streets and lanes from the sands and rocks of Bondi and Tamarama.

Through my open window I could see that the sky was starless, and as full consciousness came to me I realised that save for the rumble of a distant tram, bearing late folk from the city homewards, all else but the articulate sea was silent. Listening to that sound it somehow seemed to me that I did not wish to fall asleep again, but only to lie at ease and think, to let one's thoughts wander where they pleased. With me lying warm abed they straightway trooped back to the first long-ago night on which I heard Bondi roaring.

I lived then in a long, low, weather-board house situated between a gaol and a hospital. The house stood in a fair green field, surrounded by tall trees. The house no longer stands there. The ground on which it stood is now a public park, and the gaol over the way from it has become a college. Thus much has happened since as a child waking in the darkness on the heights of Darlinghurst I first heard Bondi roaring.

At that time, judging by its voice, the sea seemed very much nearer to me than it does now, though then I dwelt miles away from the coast, whereas now I live within a half-hour's easy stroll of it. Roar as it might after the wildest of storms, the waves breaking on beach and cliff would now be inaudible to the keenest of ears of one living on the heights of Darlinghurst. This will be understood by anyone who pauses to think that the green, leafy medium of smokeless, noiseless air through which the sea sent its sounds in those far-off days no longer exists, and that those sounds, losing their way among streets and alleys, are downed and drowned by man-made tumult.

Now in that long, low, weather-board house, waking as a child in the night, it was not the sea only that I heard. There was, for instance, the chorusing of crickets singing in the darkness, singing without pause, ceasing not to sing even when the warders from their watch-houses on the near-by gaol walls called for hours, telling each to each that all was well within those walls.

'Twelve o'clock and all's well!'

I remember how, as hour succeeded hour, I used to lie and shiver, lost in wonder, dreaming that strange things were happening in the world outside – strange, dark things that would shame and shock the light if they happened by day – when I heard that call go up; heard it solemnly voiced and repeated – now close at hand, now in the distance, now remotely sounding. But always when it died away, bringing me back to the sweet things of earth, I heard the crickets singing.

I recall that once, when they sang as a great host, I threw my blankets aside and got out of bed and went stealthily out into the night, thinking to find out what it was that made them so voiceful. A late moon was shining whitely, and it occurred to me that maybe it was her light that was inspiring them. Not only were the crickets singing but, also, there was a heavy scent of honeysuckle on the air. Very pleasant was that honeysuckle perfume, and strangely thrilling it was to be out there in the night all alone. In such a scene, at such an hour, anything might happen.

Walking to the garden gate I softly opened it and looked across the road towards the gaol. On the bright footpath opposite, her face turned to the tall stone wall of the gaol, stood a woman. At the sight of her I lost all thought of the crickets and the honeysuckle.

She wore a cloak and a veil, both very black in the white light. Her head was thrown back, her face uplifted, and it seemed to me that her hands were joined in prayer. She seemed very strange and very lonely standing there with hands and face upraised. Not liking the sight of her at all I drew back, and was closing the gate when a voice called out above her.

'One o'clock and all's well.'

Seven hours afterwards they hanged a man in the very gaol before which that woman stood with such strange appeal in her attitude.

*   *   *

Low, insistent and ever-even sounded the waves breaking at midnight on the rocks and sands of Tamarama and Bondi. Because of the character of their appeal I knew that no wind was hurrying them, but that they were sent in by a sea which was returning to the coast from which it had been driven by a recent westerly gale. Had a wind been at work on them theirs would have been a subdued roar, intervalled by notes of clamour and tumult; for the many-mooded sea has many voices, and for those who love the elemental every voice has a message.

Warm abed in my room on the heights of Bondi, I recalled many days and nights of thrilling and delightful associations with it. Memories of days spent on the harbour, on salt-lakes and on almost landlocked waters flocked back on me, making me forget that slumber was good and should not be denied its appointed hours. Memories, too, were mine of nights when, greatly venturing with other urchins of a like age and a like mind, I sought out some cave on the coast, and there cowered over a fire of grass-tree root and tea-tree limb, talking of strange things, listening to the wash of the waves, and ever and anon peering out into the darkness, half-hoping and half-fearing to catch a glimpse of Big Ben.

Yet, peer as we would, such a glimpse was denied us. Much would have been our glory if it had been vouchsafed us, much fine food for after talk among our fellows, for Big Ben, like some Old-World legend of werewolf or Black Huntsman, was reputed amongst the youth of the waterside to be the most savage monster that ever roamed the coastal seas – a great, grey shark, renowned for his cunning and ferocity. It may be that Big Ben was but a creature of the imagination, but with us the very mention of him made the flesh creep and the blood grow chill.

Less than an hour's journey from the Quay lived a fisherman whom I visited frequently. Like many fishermen, he was wise in the ways of sea and wind, but he was nearer to Nature than most, having the blood of the aboriginal in his veins; blood which in spite of his white grandfather and father, still held cells in it that were stored with strange secrets, and knowledge not taught in schools.

He knew by the feel of the water and the sound of the sea what the weather would be like on the following day, or before the following day should come to dawn. He knew, also, what fish to expect at certain seasons and at certain phases of the changeful moon, and what shoals the sea in a generous mood would send him. Mullet rich with oil, slim garfish or silver-sided trevally.

His home, a two-roomed hut, tin-walled, bark-roofed, stood at the head of a cove which was saved from the hard usage of the open sea by a curving point of land, timbered to the water's edge. Though visited by few, time seldom lay heavily on his hands, for though there might be nothing to do there was always something to see. Always daily and nightly something that appealed to him as of more than passing moment was happening. Sometimes it was a rolling, rollicking school of porpoises that he saw; sometimes a flock of silver gulls skimming over the surface of the cove in pursuit of a swarm of fish that moved swiftly through the undertide.

One night a shoal of sharks filled the underwaters with lines and curves of silver fire as, darting here and there, they played havoc with a school of mackerel, and one night he could not sleep for the snorting and splashing made by a strayed whale at the mouth of the cove. But stranger even than these were some of his experiences.

Once as we idled together, watching a streaked and yeasty sea that rolled landward before a nor'-east wind, pointing to a long reef that lay low to the northward, he told me that it was haunted.

'Haunted!' I breathed.

'Yes,' he answered gravely, 'but not at all times.'

'Haunted by what?'

'By things that sing.'

He turned and faced me, and in his eyes I saw a look as though they were listening.

'Again and again,' he said, 'fishing wide of the reef I have heard them, but always it was at night, and always when a nor'-easter was blowing.'

'What was it they sang?'

'I cannot tell you; I do not know. They sang, they chanted, and that is all I can say. No words could I make out, and always the singing came from far away, and always the wind fought against the voices.

He said no more but left me, and, going down to his boat, set about drawing the wet heap of his net from it, so that stretched on the sands of the beach it might be dried by the hot sun of midday, whilst I – of a sudden coming back to the world and a consciousness of the time of day – grew somewhat startled to find myself murmuring: 'Yes, indeed, Horatio, there *are* more things . . . '

The Cave

Beatrice Grimshaw

Beatrice Grimshaw (1870–1951) achieved considerable fame in the first decades of the twentieth century as a writer of novels and travelogues about the South Pacific, where she travelled extensively. Born in Cloona, County Antrim, Ireland, Grimshaw was educated at Caen, Normandy; Victoria College, Belfast; and Bedford College, London. She worked as a journalist in Ireland before embarking on her first expedition to the South Pacific in 1903. Grimshaw subsequently became a professional traveller and wrote numerous books about her experiences, both non-fiction works and tales of romance and adventure. She spent most of her time in Port Moresby, until she settled in Kelso, near Bathurst, in 1936 where she continued to write until she retired in 1940. Amongst her numerous stories are several tales of supernatural horror which are worth seeking out. Some are published in *The Beach of Terror and Other Stories* (1931) and *The Valley of Never-Come-Back* (1923), but many are uncollected. 'The Cave' first appeared in the *Blue Book* in 1932.

Over Rafferty's Luck – misnamed – the wind seemed always blowing. Perhaps it did not really blow as much as I imagined. Perhaps, for the first time in my life, I merely had leisure to observe such things, and to be impressed by them.

To see how the long grasses shivered, showing the footmarks of the wind, it strode over them like Peter striding on the sea; as it suddenly failed and sank – like Peter – leaving behind it a flurry of stirred leaflets that made you think of flaws on water . . . How, in the tide of the grass, always rising higher against the few doomed buildings, there streamed and wavered, like wonderful seaweeds, long strands of bishop-purple bougainvillea, and *allamanda*, all gold-wreckage of the creepers that used to climb over the roof and wall. How a loose door, in office, or bungalow, would suddenly give itself to the wind, and shut with a thunderous noise, making one think, for a distracted moment, that somebody had returned . . .

Nobody did. It had not been anticipated that anyone would, when the owners of the bankrupt mine had hired me to stay there. I was to hold the place by doing a little work, while they went afield looking for capital – which they hardly expected to get. There was just enough chance of it, however, to make it worth their while to send me to the island, and leave me there at a negligible salary, with six-months' stores, and the freedom of the whole place, on which there was not so much as a native or a dog. Only myself and the deserted shaft and the rotting bungalow, and the wind that blew continually, complainingly, through the grasses and through the fallen creepers, wine-coloured and gold.

There were these, and something else. There was a shadow on the island: the loom of a strange and eerie story but half-told.

Rafferty's Luck had not failed from the usual causes – not altogether, that is. It had gone through the common history of little, remote mines; supposed at first to be very rich in copper; it had turned out to be a mere pocket, with a problematical vein behind it, that might or might not be worth developing when found.

It had been worked by the partners – there were three – in turns. The island was far out of the track of ships; it had been visited accidentally, by a shipwrecked crew. Three of these had found the copper, and kept silence; and later on, two had gone up to work it.

They had worked it, won enough ore for a good show, and waited confidently for the returning boat. But – when it came, it found only one man. The other had killed himself. Without any reason, he had cut his throat.

The third man took his place, and arranged, as before, that a passing schooner should call. It called within a few days, and found one man. The other, without any reason, had leaped over a precipice, and died.

Upon this, the third went away, and stayed so long that the mine – which was on British territory, and under mining laws – had nearly been forfeited. At the last moment the men now interested in it got me to go and hold the place, while the third partner went to London for capital.

They were candid enough – they told me that the island was under a shadow; and when I asked just what they meant, they said: 'Exactly that. Rafferty and Wilder' (the two who had died) 'both said something about shadows.'

'What?' I asked.

'Nothing that anybody could understand. Rafferty had cut almost through his windpipe, and Wilder's face was smashed in by the fall. As like as not,' went on the third partner – France was his name – 'as like as not, drink had something to do with it; they were neither of them sober men.'

'But you are – and you didn't come to any sort of grief?'

'I am – and I didn't.'

'Yet you don't feel like staying. You only had a few days of it.'

'Haven't I told you I must go and scare up some cash? Are you on, or not?'

'I am on,' I said.

'Good. A man with an M.C. and a D.C.M. like you – '

'Hang the M.C. and the D.C.M. I'm going because I'm broke, and because I want to know what it's like to be really alone. As for your shadows, they won't make me jump over cliffs. I take one spot after sundown, never more.'

'Good,' said France again. He looked at me as if it was in his mind to say something more, but whatever the thing was, he kept it back . . . 'About the journey,' he continued . . .

Six weeks later I was left at Cave Island by a whaleboat – the last step in a decline that began with an ocean liner, continued through inter-island schooners and trading ketches, and ended in the last ketch's boat, sent off to ferry me through a network of reefs too dangerous for any sizable ship.

'If there is payable ore here,' I thought, 'small wonder it's been overlooked; God-forsaken and Satan-protected the place is, and out of the way of the world!' And I began to wonder, as the whaleboat stemmed green shallows, making for the hummocky deserted bay that stretched beyond, whether I had done well. I am from Clare; I have seen the dread sea-walls of Moher, and felt, on their high crowns, the 'send' of that unknown evil that men of Ireland, for the confounding of strangers, chose to personify as the frightful Phooka. 'This too is an evil place,' I thought, and on that account, I said a small prayer. Now mind you, it was well done, as you shall afterwards know.

Then we beached, and began unloading my gear; and I was too busy with that, and with carrying most of it up to the bungalow, before dark should fall, to think of anything else. By and by the boat was back at the ship's side, a long way out, and the ship had made sail, and when I looked at her, in the last of the light, and saw her fading away like a ghost that has given its message, and goes back to its tomb, I knew that I was indeed alone – pressed down and running over, I had my wish!

After a day or two, I began to wonder what all the trouble was about, if indeed there had ever been any trouble except drink and the consequences of it. Cave Island was a windy spot, as I have said; not very large or long, only a mile or two at biggest, it was swept by all the winds that blow across the immense, lonely spaces of the central Pacific world, where almost no land is. In the mornings and at nights it was cool; during the day nothing but the wind saved it from most torrid heat. It was a barren place, and full of stones, some of them black and spongy and as big as houses. There was coarse grass, that never seemed to be still, almost as if things unseen ran under it, and kept it moving even in a calm. There were a few flowers that Rafferty had planted in his time, and there was the iron bungalow, and a storing shed, and a shaft with bucket and windlass dangling over, and tools abandoned by the side. For the rest, there was the sun wheeling over the island, at night the myriad unpitying stars, and always sea and sea. So lonely it was, that you could hear yourself breathe; out of the wind, you could listen to your heart beating. When you got up in the morning you took the burden of yourself upon your shoulders, and carried it, growing heavier and heavier, all day; even at night, it was with you in your dreams. Yet I liked this, as one likes all strong, violent experience. Solitude is violent; it is delicious, it is hateful; and as surely as a snake unwatched can strike, so it can maim or kill . . .

What do you know, you who think that solitude is a locked room in a city, or a garden with the neighbours shut away?

A week or so went past. Every day I went to the workings, did a job with pick and shovel; wrote in my diary what I had done, and for the rest, was free. I liked to be free. Not since the war – and certainly not in it – had I been my own man; if I was not filling one of the blind-alley jobs that confront the untrained, hardly educated man of near forty, I was harder at work than ever, hunting another.

But if I was free, I was not at ease. I could see, after the first few days, that there was not much in the mine – worse, that there was never likely to be. I had worked copper before, and I judged that the worst of it was better than the best of this, once the surface show had been removed. In fact, it was nothing but a pocket. And how was a mere pocket going to give me a brick bungalow with an arched veranda, in Bondi or Coogee, and a garden behind it and a little touring-car, and a tobacconist's business somewhere near the surf beaches, to keep all going; and in the garden, behind the window-panes of the bungalow, in a long chair on the veranda, at the wheel of the car, or swimming brown and bonny through the surf – always there, in my heart and in my life, the girl of my hopeless dreams.

No, I had not told France all the truth. He is a good fellow, but one does not give him confidences. Being broke was nothing new to me; being alone, the spice of it, the strangeness, I could have done without. But Rafferty's Luck offered the one and only chance I had of making my dream come true, and I would have taken it if it had led halfway to hell.

Instead, it seemed to lead to nothing.

I was so disappointed, so sore against France – whom I now perceived to be engaged in the familiar trick of unloading a hopeless venture upon a public too far away to understand – that I set my teeth, and resolved to hunt the island from coast to coast – to comb it through for a better show, and if found, to take that show myself. I don't know that this was moral; I only know I was prepared to do it.

By this time, I had forgotten all about the 'shadow', and the suicides. Men who have roughed it, who own little, are not particularly shocked at suicide, or sudden death of any kind. You must have much to lose before you shudder at the passing breath of the storm that has swept another from his hold on life, and that will one day sweep you too.

So I did not think about Rafferty, or about Wilder – until the day when I found the cave; and after that it all began.

I had been prospecting over the summit of the island, without much success. On this day, I went down to the beach, and began patiently to circle the whole place, resolving, literally, to leave no stone unturned in the search for something better than Rafferty's Luck. It takes longer to walk all around an island than you'd think, even if the island is no more than a mile or two across. I spent all day upon the job, eating a biscuit for dinner, and drinking, once or twice, from the little streams that ran out of the crevices. If any of them had tasted ill I should have been glad; but they were all fresh as milk, no tinge of metal in them.

Toward sunset I came upon something that I hadn't noticed before – a cave. It was at the foot of an immense wall of rock; you could not have seen it from above, and the only way of reaching it was the way by which I had come, a painful climb along the narrow glacis of stones on the windward side. The beach and the anchorage were of course on the lee side. Ships wouldn't, for their lives, come up to windward; I was therefore almost sure that nobody, save myself, had seen or visited the cave.

That pleased me – you know how it is. I was glad that I had brought my torch with me – a costly big five-cell, like a searchlight, that She had sent me when I sailed; she hadn't sixpence to rub against sixpence, but she would have given her head away – and so would I; that was why we both were poor, and likely to remain so . . .

I had a good look at the cave. It was very high; seventy or eighty feet at least. It was not quite so wide, but it seemed to run a good way back. The cold stream of wind that came out of it had a curious smell; I could not describe it to myself, otherwise than by saying that the smell seemed very old. I stood in the archway, in that stream of slightly tainted wind, examining the rocks about the mouth of the cave. There was not much daylight left now, but I could see, plainly enough, that here was small hope of a better find. I kept the torch in my hand as I went on into the interior of the cave; time enough, I thought, to turn it on when I had to; there were no spare batteries on the island.

By and by I began to go backwards; that is, I went on a little way, and then turned to look at the ground I had passed, lit up by the stream of light from the entrance. Coral, old and crumbling underfoot; limestone; a vein of conglomerate. Nowhere any sign of what I sought. It was getting darker; the cave, arching high above me, seemed to veer a little to one side, and the long slip of blue daylight was almost gone. Now, with half-a-dozen steps, I lost it altogether; I stood in complete darkness, with the cool wind streaming about me, and that strange, aged smell, now decidedly stronger.

'Time for the light,' I thought. Something made me swallow in my throat, made me press my foremost foot tight to the ground, because it seemed, oddly enough, to have developed a will of its own; it wanted to move back, and the backward foot wanted to swing on its toe and turn round . . . I will swear I was not afraid – but somehow my feet were.

I snapped on the light, and swung it ahead. It showed a narrow range of rock wall on each side, a block of velvet darkness ahead, and in the midst of the darkness, low down, two circles of shining bluish green. Eyes – but what eyes! They were the size of dinner-plates! They did not move, they only looked; and I was entirely sure that they saw me. If they had been high up, I do not think I should have minded them – much. But they were, as I have said, low down, and that was somehow horrible. Lurking. Treacherous . . .

I had shot crocodiles by night, discovering them exactly as I had discovered this unnamed monster, by the shine of their eyes in torchlight. But I had had a sporting-rifle to do it with, and knew what I was shooting at. Now I was totally unarmed; the futile shotgun I had brought with me for stray pot-hunting, was up at the bungalow. I had not the vaguest idea what this creature might be, but I knew what was the only thing to do under the circumstances, and I did it: I ran away.

Nothing stirred. Nothing followed me. When I reached the outer arch of the cave, all glorious with sea and sunset, there was not a sound anywhere but the lifting crash and send of the waves upon the broken beach. I stood for a moment looking at the magnificent sky that paled and darkened while one could quickly have counted a hundred. 'I shall have to come back,' was my thought, 'with a charge of dynamite, and a bit of fuse. Shotgun just as much use as a pea-shooter.' I told myself these things, but now that I was out of the cave, I could not for the life of me believe in what I had seen. 'It wasn't the sort of smell it ought to have been,' I said aloud weakly, and kicked the stones about aimlessly with my foot. Something rolled. I looked at it, and it was a skull.

'Peter Riordan,' I said, 'this is not your lucky day.' And I picked up the skull. There were bones with it, all loose and lying about. 'I can make a guess what happened to Mr Bones!' I said, peering through swiftly falling twilight at the skull. It was like a shock of cold water to see that it was old beyond computing – almost fossilised, dark and mossy with the passage of incalculable time. As for the bones, they crackled like pie-crust when I put my foot on them. I could see where they had fallen out of the rock; they must have lain there buried, for a long time.

'I don't understand,' I thought. 'Things don't fit together. This is a hell of an island.' It seemed good to me to climb the cliff as fast as I could, making for the solid walls of the bungalow, and leaving behind me in the inhospitable twilight those queer bones now unburied, and the cave, and the immense green eyes that did not move.

The bungalow was a good way off; in order to reach it, I had to cross the empty rolling downs on the top of the island, with their long grass that never was still, and their heaps of hummocks of black stone. By this time it was so late that I could only see the stones as lumps of indefinite darkness. Some of them were big even by daylight; by night they looked immense. They were queerly shaped, too; once, when I paused to get breath (for I can assure you I was going hard) I noticed that the biggest one in sight looked exactly like the rounded hind-quarters of an elephant, only no elephant ever was so big.

I leaned against a boulder, and mopped my face. There was a rather warm wind blowing; it brought with it the sort of scents that one expects by night – the dark-green smell of grass wet with dew, the curious singeing odour of baked stones gradually giving out their heat, little sharp smells of rat and iguana, out hunting. And something else . . .

'Peter Riordan,' I said, 'you quit imagining things that aren't there. Rafferty did, and Wilder did.' And I propped myself against the stone, and took out a cigarette.

It was never lighted. Just as I was feeling in my matchbox, I looked at the giant boulder again, and as I hope for heaven, I saw it walk away. That is, it did not walk – it hobbled, lurching against the sky.

For obvious reasons I didn't light the cigarette, but I put it into my mouth, and chewed it; that was better than nothing. 'We aren't going to be stampeded,' I said (but noiselessly, you may believe). 'We are going to see this through.' And, being as wise as I was brave – perhaps a little wiser – I got inside a sort of pill-box of loose stones, and peered out through the openings. By this time it was as dark as the inside of a cow; you could only see stars and stars. And the ink-black blots made against them by one thing and another. And the great black thing that wasn't a boulder, and wasn't an elephant, went lurching and lumbering, smashing through Orion, wiping Scorpio off the sky, putting out the Pointers where the Cross was waiting to come up; it seemed to swing all over the universe.

'It's chasing something,' I thought.

It was. One could see it tack and turn with incredible swiftness, swinging behind it something that might have been legs and might have been a tail. Clearly, it was hunting, like the rats and the iguanas, and now I could see – or thought I could see – the thing it hunted: something very small, compared with the enormous bulk of the beast; something that dodged in and out of the stones, running for its life. A little, upright thing with a round head, that scuttled madly, squeaked as it ran.

Or had I fancied the squeak? The whole amazing drama was so silent that I could not be sure. It seemed to me that if there had been a cry, a queer thin cry, I had heard it inside my head, not outside. I can't explain more clearly, but there are those who will understand. At any rate, I was sure the thing had cried, and that it had cause. The end was approaching.

There was another frantic doubling, another swing around of the immense hobbling beast, and then the little creature simply was not – and the enormous shadow had swept to the edge of the cliff and over, and was gone.

I felt my forehead wet. My breath was coming as quickly as if it had been I who had squeaked and doubled there, out among the night-black grasses and the stones . . . The shadow! They who died had seen shadows.

'But,' I found myself saying argumentatively, to the silent stars, 'I am real, and that wasn't. It's like things in a dream, when you know the railway engine can't run over you, because it isn't really there.'

Something obscurely answered: 'Rafferty is dead, and Wilder is dead. Death is real.'

I got out of the pill-box. 'I shall say the multiplication table all the way home,' I told myself. And I did. But when I had got home to the bungalow, I said something else – I said a prayer. 'Perhaps they didn't,' I thought. Then I went in, and cooked my supper. It was quite a good supper, and I slept very well.

Next morning nothing seemed more impossible than the things that, I was assured, had not happened last night. All the same, I decided to go and have another look at the cave, with plenty of dynamite, and the shotgun, for what that might be worth. I could not forget that Beth, who would give her head away – and who had given her heart – was waiting for that brick house, and that little car, and those Sunday mornings on the surf beaches. And I was resolved that she should not miss them.

It was now about ten days since I landed, and I began, for the first time, to count the days that remained. France would have to reach London, find a simpleton who would finance his venture (I knew he'd do it – he could have squeezed money out of a concrete pillar), return to Australia, and make his way to the island. Six weeks; three weeks; six weeks; three or four weeks. Nineteen in all. And I had put one week and a half behind me. There remained seventeen and a half. Four months and a half. A hundred and twenty-two days, if I succeeded in keeping my senses. If I did not, it was a hundred and twenty-two minus x.

I could see the x in front of me; a black, threatening thing, big as a garage door. But I defied it. 'You won't get me,' I said. 'I'm bound for Bondi and the brick bungalow.' And, whistling 'Barnacle Bill' to keep my spirits up, I began to cut lead piping into slugs. 'Ought to have brought a rifle,' I thought, 'but never mind; I can do something with these, and a bit of dynamite and a fuse.'

It took me about fifteen minutes to cut up the slugs. When I raised my eyes from the table on which I was working, I saw, through the window of the cottage, a steamer – a small trading-boat with a black and white funnel. She was out in the roadstead, and she was just preparing to let go anchor.

I let off a shout; you should hear a Clare man do it!

'X, I've got you,' I cried. 'Dead as a doornail – stabbed with your own beastly minus!' And I sent the lead pipe flying across the floor. I just had to make a noise.

In the roadstead, the little steamer was making a terrible row with her roaring anchor-chains, and a whaleboat was rapidly being lowered. Within ten minutes, France and I were shaking hands.

'Never went to London at all,' he told me at the top of his voice. 'Got the whole lump of expenses right in Sydney, from two or three splendid chaps who were staying at my hotel. Loads of money. Country fellows.'

'They would be,' I thought, remembering France's local reputation.

'Brought the machinery up with me. Brought a geologist. Get a start, get a nice report, go down again and float the company.'

'Leaving me in charge?'

'That's right.'

'It isn't – not by a mile! France,' I said, looking him straight in the eyes – he had candid, jolly blue eyes, the little beggar, and he had a smile under his toothbrush moustache that would have wiled cash out of a New York customs-officer – 'France, I don't like this affair of yours any too well, and I'd prefer to be out of it.' For I knew, now, that the little car and the Sundays in the surf would have to come by some other road.

'Got the wind up?' he asked, cocking his hat on one side of his head, and looking at me impertinently.

'I don't know about that,' I said – and indeed I did not know; it was a puzzling matter – 'but I do know that there isn't enough payable copper here to sheet a yacht.'

'Oh, you're no expert,' he said easily. 'Let me introduce Mr Rattray Smith, our geologist. Mr Peter Riordan.'

'Why not a mining engineer?' I asked curtly, glancing with some distaste at the academic-looking youth who had followed France out of the boat.

'Came too high,' explained France with a charming smile. 'Smith knows copper when he sees it.'

'I reckon he knows which side his bread is buttered on,' I commented, without troubling to lower my voice over-much. I simply could not stand that geologist; he was such a half-baked looking creature, fairly smelling of chalk and blackboards.

'Quite,' was France's answer. 'And he's got all sorts of degrees; look lovely on a prospectus.'

'Maybe,' was all I answered. I heard afterwards that Smith's degrees were more showy than practical, from our point of view – B.Sc., F.G.S., and something else that I forget; palaeontology was his special game, and he knew next to nothing about metals. France had got him cheap because he had been ill, and needed a change. France, it appeared, meant to make full use of Mr Rattray Smith's shining degrees in the forthcoming prospectus; meantime, as he somewhat coarsely put it to me, he intended to 'stuff the blighter up for all he was worth'.

'You go and take him for a walk,' he said to me now. 'Show him the workings, and help him with his notes. I've got to see the machinery ashore.'

I didn't want to see that machinery land; I knew only too well what it would be – old, tired stuff that had been dumped on half-a-dozen wharves, for the deluding of share-holders, in many places; stuff never meant to be used, only to be charged at four times its value in expense accounts...I took Smith to the workings; showed him the ore, lowered him down the shaft, displayed the various tunnels. I said not a word. He could delude himself if he liked; I meant to have no hand in it.

Perhaps he was not such a fool as he looked; perhaps, I cynically told myself, he was more knave than fool. At all events, he said very little, and took only a few notes. I began to like him better, in spite of his horn-rimmed glasses and his academic bleat.

'Look here,' I said, as we were returning to the house. 'I've been all over the damned island, and I'll eat any payable stuff you find.'

'All over?' he said, cocking one currant-coloured eye at me through his glasses.

I began to think he might not be such a fool as he looked. Clearly he had sensed a certain reserve that lay behind my speech.

'Well,' I said, not caring enough about him to mince words, 'there's a warren of caves down on the wind'ard side of the island and I tried to investigate the biggest one the other day.'

'What did you find? Any indications?' he squeaked.

'Couldn't tell you. I was stopped by a beast. Nightmare beast, with eyes as big as plates. Hadn't a gun with me, but I meant to have a go at it later on.'

'But that's – but that's most – ' he began to stammer eagerly.

France, who had gone to the house for a drink, looked out of the window, and interrupted me.

'What's this about beasts, and why are you making slugs for your silly old shotgun?' he demanded.

I told him.

'You've got 'em too,' was his only comment.

This, for some reason or other, made me desperate.

'That's not the whole of it,' I said. 'Last night I saw a thing as big as six elephants chasing a little thing in the dark.'

'You would,' he said. 'Have a hair of the dog that bit you, and take some bromide when you're going to bed.'

'Look here – will you come down to the cave yourself?' I pleaded.

'With all that machinery to land, and the ship bound to clear before sun-down? Not much.'

'Very well. Will you come for a walk on the top of the island after dark?'

'Oh, yes,' he said, casually. 'Never saw anything when I was here for a fortnight, and don't expect to now. But I'll come.'

'Was it moonlight when you were here?' I shouted after him as he started for the beach.

'What's that to – Yes, I reckon it was.'

Rattray Smith began deliberately: 'The influence of light on all these phenomena – '

'What d'ye mean?' I asked. 'Are you a spiritualist? Surely you couldn't be.'

'In the excellent company of Sir William Crookes and Sir Oliver Lodge, I certainly could,' he answered. 'I suppose you think that the modern man of science is necessarily sceptic, like his – his – '

'I think he believes either a darn' sight too little, or a devilish sight too much, if you ask me,' I said. 'But wait till tonight.'

We waited. And after dark, we all went up to the top of the island and posted ourselves in the 'pill-box'. There was an enormous sky of stars above us; all round us the faintly smelling, feebly rustling grasses, and standing up among them, big as cottages and railway cars, were the silhouetted shapes of gigantic rocks.

I had thought we might have hours to wait, and after all might see nothing; but I was wrong. We had not been in the pill-box ten minutes, before a whole mass of stars before us went suddenly black. It was just over the biggest of the cottage-sized rocks, and I had a nasty idea that the rock itself – or what we had thought to be rock – was part of the rising mass.

Have you ever seen an innocent stick turn into a serpent, a log in a river show sudden crocodile-eyes and swim away?

If you have, then you will know how I felt.

Up went the monster, half across the sky; and now it began to lurch and hirple with that strange movement I had noted before, covering immense areas of ground with every lurch. I heard Rattray Smith draw in his breath with a sort of whistling noise.

'I don't think it'll touch us,' I whispered, with my lips on his ear. 'Keep quiet.'

'Man,' he said. 'Oh, man!' and seemed to choke.

France kept quite still.

I smelled the queer smell of it, not the sort of smell it should have been; strangely old and non-pungent. I saw a small shadow, round-headed, come out of nowhere and scuttle away. I saw the great shadow hunting it. Smith saw too; for some extraordinary reason, he was crying, in broken, half-suppressed sobs.

'I don't reckon it can – ' I began, in a cautious whisper. He interrupted.

'Man,' he said, 'You – you – don't know. I've seen discarnate spirits; I've seen – I – No matter. This is beyond everything one ever – *Woop!*'

They were out of the pill-box, like rats breaking cover, and I after them, going I didn't know where. I had seen what they had – and even though I didn't believe it, I ran. The big shadow had turned toward us, suddenly rearing itself up, up, until it stood a hundred feet high among the stars. It leaned a little forward, like something listening; it was semi-erect, and in its enormous forepaws it held a small dark thing that kicked and then was still.

'I – I – ' stuttered Rattray Smith as we ran. 'Discarnate dinosaur – spirits if they get angry – Where's the house?'

'Wrong way,' I panted, seizing his elbow. I had caught a pale grey glimmer in front of us, and realised we were heading for the sea. We stopped and looked back. Something immense rocked heavily against the stars, coming up with appalling swiftness. I saw that it was between us and the bungalow. Not that that mattered; by its size, it could have cracked the bungalow like a nut – and that it meant, for sport or for spite, to drive us over the cliff. I knew – I don't know how – that it was powerless to treat us as it had treated the little black ghost of prehistoric man, in that strange reproduction of an age-old drama, but that it was an evil thing, and would harm us all if it could. And I knew too, in the same swift enlightening moment, why one man of the two who died had fallen over the cliff, and why another had slain himself. The last had not been able to endure this terrible rending of the veil . . .

'Smith,' I panted, 'stand your ground; you'll break your neck. It can't harm us. It's only the fear.'

'Discarnate spirits – ' he babbled. I did not heed him. I was busy doing what the soldier did for Joan of Arc, in her evil moment – making a Cross of two sticks, with a stem of grass twisted round them. I held it in my hand, and I said – no matter what. Those who know will know.

By ever so little, the giant shadow missed us, lurched forward and with one toppling leap, went down the cliff.

'Come on,' I shouted to Smith and France, though I could not see the latter. 'I've got my torch and a plug of dynamite; we'll see the whole thing through.'

'What are you going to do?' squeaked Rattray Smith.

'Put out those eyes in the cave,' I shouted. I was exhilarated, above myself – as one used to be in the war. I scrambled down the cliff in the transparent dark, feeling my way; slightly surprised, but not much, to hear Smith coming after, I found the cave.

We stood for a minute gaining breath, and looking about us. There was nothing to be seen anywhere; nothing to be heard but the steady slapping of waves on the beach.

'I'm with you,' declared Smith squeakily. 'As a palaeontologist – '

'A which?' I said. 'Don't trip over those bones, and don't stop to pick them up now!' – for he was stooping down and fumbling. I added, without quite knowing what I meant, 'The dinosaur's ghost didn't have eyes.' But he seemed to know; he said: 'That makes it all the more – ' I did not hear the rest; we were too busy picking our way.

Round the corner, we stopped. The eyes were there. Low down, unmoving, unwinking in the ray of the torch as I threw it on. Big as plates; blue-green, glittering –

'Hold the torch while I fix this,' I whispered. Smith took it; his hand was unsteady, but I could not blame him for that. I bit off my fuse as short as I dared; lit it, and tossed the plug . . .

There was a boom that almost cracked our ear-drums; immediately after, stones and dirt came smashing down in such quantity that we found ourselves staggering wildly, bruised and cut, beneath a hundred blows.

'Are you hurt?' I called to Smith.

'Bring your damned torch here,' was his only reply.

I came forward, and found him on hands and knees in the midst of an amazing raffle of half-fossilised bones; some of them were as big as the masts of a ship, though partly smashed by the explosion. Almost falling loose from the cliff above our heads was the most astounding skull I had ever dreamed of, a thing far bigger than an elephant's, with huge eye-sockets set well forward, and the tusky jaws of a tiger. Behind the eye-sockets, as I waved the torch, shone a mass of something vivid, greenish blue.

'Oh, God,' cried Smith – who didn't believe in God – 'you've broken up the finest dinosaur skeleton in the world!'

I was too busy to trouble about him. I had climbed a little way up, and was scraping at the mass of iridescent, green-blue crystals in which the skull was set; which, through uncounted ages, had sifted down through various openings, filling the huge orbits of the eyes, so that they gleamed in the light as if alive.

'I'd break up my grandmother's skeleton,' I told him joyously, 'if it was bedded in copper pyrites. We've found the paying stuff at last!' It was not the dark roof of the cave that I saw, as I said that, not the glittering pyrites, or the amazing great bones, or the scrambling, complaining figure of Smith, on the floor of the cave. It was St Mary's in Sydney, on a summer morning, with a white figure coming up the aisle 'on her father's arm' – to me!

Rattray Smith, I understand, has written a great deal for different scientific magazines about the curious happenings on Cave Island. In one, he told the story of the great skeleton; how it was found, and where, and how put together again. He doesn't say what he got for it, but I believe that was something to write home about; good dinosaurs come high, with or without incredible ghost stories attached. The spiritualistic magazines simply ate up his account of the prehistoric ghost and its sinister activities. Especially did they seem to like his conclusions about the skeleton acting as a sort of medium, or jumping-off point, for the apparition. He may have been right or wrong there; at all events, it is certain that after the removal of the bones, no one engaged in working the mines ever saw or heard anything remarkable.

France? We found him in the bungalow, drunk, and under a bed. He says, and maintains, that we were all in the same condition. A man must save his face.

The Cave of the Invisible

James Francis Dwyer

James Francis Dwyer (1874–1952) was born in Camden Park, New South
Wales. His father was a gifted story-teller and this probably influenced
Dwyer to write. In 1899, while working in a post office, he was convicted
of forgery and sentenced to seven years prison. While in prison he con-
tributed verse and short stories to *The Bulletin*. Dwyer was released in
1902 and left Australia altogether in 1906, travelling widely in the United
States, Asia and Africa. He became a prolific novelist and short story
writer, most of them tales of mystery and adventure in the Haggard
tradition. His short story collection, *Breath of the Jungle* (1915), contains
a number of supernatural tales, many of them involving Hochdorf, the
German naturalist. The following tale, an unusual ghost story, was first
published in *The Blue Book* in April 1939.

Jan Kromhout, the big Dutch naturalist, lowered himself into a huge
rattan chair and looked out across the green swath of palms and
canarium trees. Kromhout's camp, in which I was a guest, was close
to the village of Brajonolon, in central Java; and from the terrace of
the bungalow we could see the great Temple of Bororboedoer. In
splendid majesty it rose before us; the mighty Tjandi Bororboedoer,
'Shrine of the Many Buddhas'.

Not as large as the monuments of Angkor Wat, Ajanta and Alara,
the Temple of Bororboedoer is considered more beautiful in archi-
tectural design. Its carvings, still intact after twelve hundred years,
bring thousands of tourists to stare at the bas-reliefs. Those bas-
reliefs, if placed in a straight line, would extend for more than three
miles. Here was the centre of Buddhist influence in Java in the sixth
century . . .

'Belief is a strange thing,' said Kromhout, his eyes upon the temple.
'There are many places throughout the world where the atmosphere
has been charged with a definite spiritual quality put into it by the
reverence of believers. Buddhism in Java is dead – Mohammedanism
has throttled it; but a blind person who came close to this sanctuary
would sense the awe and mystery that is still here. Still here after

centuries have passed. *Ja*. Into the mixture of oxygen, hydrogen and carbon dioxide has filtered a spiritual compound that does not react to the instruments of the scientists. It is Faith.

'Do you know that argon, one of the constituents of the atmosphere, was only discovered forty years ago? It is present in seven or eight parts to a thousand in the air we breathe; but we did not know it was there till Lord Rayleigh and Sir William Ramsay discovered it toward the end of the last century. That discovery makes me hopeful. Sometimes – sometimes I think that in the days to come, we might have instruments so delicate that we could measure the spiritual intensity of places like this temple. Measure the degree of faith, of hope, of longing for a better world. I would like to measure the holy dreams that fill the Oude Kerk in Amsterdam, that was built in about 1300, or the air of St Paul's and St Peter's, or that place in the Mosque of Saint Sophia at Stamboul that is called "The Holy Wisdom".'

For a long interval the big naturalist remained quiet; then with a strange eagerness in his voice he went on: 'If such an instrument were perfected, one might also be able to measure the devilish quality of places. Of demon-filled places that I have visited in the Malay.'

In silence we sat and stared at Tjandi Bororboedoer. The sun had set: and a soft rose tint spread slowly over the porous trachyte and lava blocks of which the temple is constructed. This tint deepened to a gorgeous crimson, changed to a dark red; then with a fierce suddenness the tropic night plunged upon the building and blotted it out.

Filled with black gloom now were the interminable galleries with their two hundred scenes of Buddha's spiritual experiences. Invisible were the thrilling bas-reliefs beginning with that of Mâya, the mother of Buddha, watching the white elephant descending on a lotus flower from heaven to symbolise the conception of her son, and ending with the last thrilling scenes that show the weapons of the Prince of Darkness turning into flower petals as they fall upon the head of the saint.

From the soft dusk came the voice of Jan Kromhout. The great Buddhist sanctuary seemed to be nearer now. It was, I thought, squatting just beyond the row of flame trees whose red flowers perfumed the night.

'At times,' said the big Dutchman, 'the East frightens me. I become the victim of terrors. Then I pack my things and take a trip home to Amsterdam, so that I can get my courage back. There is sanity in Holland. Much sanity. I am nearer to God when I put my feet on Kalver Straat. I go and sit in the Oude Kerk, and those stained-glass windows of the Lady Chapel make me feel clean and good. There is a lot of faith in stained glass. And I go to the Ryks Museum and look at the fine pictures by Frans Hals and Rembrandt and Rubens, and so I cure myself. *Ja, ja*. I cure myself.

'Five years ago I went back to see my sister and her husband. I stayed a month; then the East came in the night and whispered to me. I thought that the whimperings of little animals came up to my room from the Leidsche Kade. My sister cried 'and begged me to stay, but I could not.

'On the ship that brought me to Batavia, I made friends with a strange man. He was a Russian named Andrey Ilyin, and he was an archaeologist. He was but thirty-four years of age, and he was big and strong and bold-looking. And he was a dreamer. A great dreamer. Someone has said that there is no rest for the man who is both a dreamer and a man of action, and this Russian was of that type. He knew the East. He thought it the cradle of life, the home of all the mysteries. He had many ideas that were disturbing; and in the hot, heavy nights crossing the Indian Ocean we stayed up on deck and argued till the dawn.

'He put forward theories that were not supported by scientific evidence; but that lack of evidence did not trouble him. *Neen*. He just jumped across the gulfs, and when you asked him how he got to the other side, he laughed. He thought that scientists lacked imagination, that they spent too much time building bridges instead of hopping mentally to the other side. It may be so. Dreamers see many things.

'One of his theories I had big cause to remember. I will never forget it. He thought that longevity was a matter of breathing the same atmosphere that we had started to breathe. That life depended on the constancy of the atmosphere. You see, we did not know what the atmosphere was composed of, till Cavendish made his tests at the end of the seventeenth century. And Cavendish did not know of argon and of other substances.

' "The atmosphere we are breathing is not the same as the Pleistocene or the Neolithic man breathed," said Ilyin. "It is not the atmosphere in which the mammoth and the dinosaur lived. We know nothing of its composition in those days. A change in it might have killed them off. Then again the longevity of Methuselah might be accounted for by the air he breathed. Some special brand."

'Sometimes he made me laugh; sometimes he puzzled me. When we were near Tandjong Priok, he told me the reason of his visit. He was searching for old atmosphere! Old. *Ja, oud!* Atmosphere that had not changed for hundreds of years. Air which was the same air that blew over the Malay in the days when King Asoka sent a piece of Buddha's body to Java as propaganda for Buddhism. They were good propagandists in those days.

'"How can you find such a place?" I asked Ilyin.

'"There might be an old temple bottled up and forgotten," he said. "You know how wine gets better with age? If I found such a place, the atmosphere might have improved."

'I said goodbye to that Russian at Tandjong Priok. I was not sorry. He talked too much. We Dutch say, *Der gaan veel woorden in een zak.* Many words go to one sack.'

Kromhout rose from his chair as a soft whimper came from within the bungalow. The black ape was on the point of becoming a mother, and the big naturalist went inside to comfort her. I could hear his voice assuring her that he was close by, and that no harm could befall her.

Returning to the veranda he took up his story. 'I went here and there in my business of collecting specimens. I made a trip to Samarinda in Dutch Borneo, and I went from there to Makassar and on to the little San Miguel group in the Sulu Sea. Now and then I thought of that Russian and his theories. It was not easy to forget him. Ideas that are a little crazy stay in our heads when we forget matters that are founded on common-sense.

'I came back to Batavia, and I got a commission which took me to the volcanic country near Padjagalan. It is bad. The sulphur fumes and the carbonic gas kill birds and animals that are fool enough to stay around. It is a little piece of country that looks as if it might blow up at any moment, when some of the old volcanoes start their fires again.

'I had been there two weeks when that Russian fellow Ilyin walked into my camp. "It is old *Tête-de-Fromage*!" he cried. "Old *Tête-de-Fromage* who will not be convinced!"

'He told me that he was camped some fifteen miles away, and that he was quite happy and contented. "I heard that a Dutchman was trapping here, and I thought it might be you," he said. "I'm pleased because I wanted to tell you something. You remember our talks about atmosphere? Well, I have found proof of what I said to you on the ship."

'"What have you found?" I asked.

'He grinned at me. "I have found a place where the air is six hundred years old," he said. "Six hundred years old, and pure."

'"Pure?" I asked.

' "That is what I said, Dutchman," he answered. "Dry and pure. It has been bottled up for centuries. Six centuries or more. There has been no opening except one small door that is not used once in a century. The things living there, toads and lichen, die immediately when in contact with modern air."

' "You mean that they are killed by the light?" I said.

' "No, by the air," said Ilyin. "I have moved them in the night. It is the air that kills them."

'I sat silent, waiting for Ilyin to tell me more, and he did. "There is something else about this place," he said. "Something extraordinary: the Past is there."

' "How?" I snapped.

' "In the atmosphere," he said quietly. "The air of the place is impregnated with old memories. It has clung to them. They have been held in a sort of atmospheric solution because there has been no fresh air to disturb them. At times – at times you can feel and see enough to reconstruct what happened there."

' "*Ja*," I said, "I know all about those spots. They are not good. They are vicious. If you go trying to reconstruct events that have happened here six hundred years ago, you will get yourself into the crazy house, and the Dutch will ship you back to Russia."

' "Imagination," said that fellow, "is one of the greatest gifts of God. The straight back-heads of the Dutch and the Germans make it impossible for them to carry the gift. If you feel inclined to come over and visit me, I will show you all the proof that you want."

'Of course I was curious to know what that fellow had found. My skin prickled with curiosity. He had given me directions; and three days after his visit, I went along the Jungle path that led to his camp. That part of Java has many old temples. Quite close are the ruins of Brambaran, which was a Brahman temple dedicated to Vishnu and Siva. I found that Ilyin's camp was alongside a small temple so completely covered with crawling vines that you might pass it, thinking it was a green hill.

'Ilyin grinned when he saw me. "I knew you would come," he said; "I have been watching the road for three days. Cheese and mystéries are great things to attract Dutch naturalists. Tell me, Kromhout, why you people put carraway seeds in your cheese?"

' "To make fools ask the reason," I snapped. "Where is your old atmosphere that you were bragging about?"

' "You must not approach it in that spirit," said Ilyin. "You see, there are reasons. I am not the owner or the real discoverer. I will introduce you, but if you please, try to look as if you believed, even if you lack the imagination to see beyond your nose."

'I was annoyed, but I had come to see what I could see, so I followed Ilyin through the jungle till we came to a thatched hut. In the hut were an old man and a girl of about eighteen. First I will tell of the man. He was a Sundanese; and when I saw him, he was what is called *latah*. His eyes were glazed and his nostrils distended. I did not like the look of him.

'The girl – *Ach*! the girl was something that the gods of the jungle had made to peep at. She was just meeting womanhood. Her skin was of beaten gold, and all the dreams of the world were in her big frightened eyes. Eyes like the little musk deer that spoke to you, saying, "Do not harm me; I am nice and innocent and I will be good." *Ja*, they were wonderful eyes. And she had little teeth so white and beautiful that you wished that she could get annoyed and bite you with them. And she was dressed as she should be dressed. She had a six-foot strip of scarlet silk wound tightly around her waist, then thrown loosely across her bosom and over one of her shoulders. Sometimes that sash slipped from her shoulder, or maybe the little devils of the jungle pulled it away. In her left nostril she had a small ruby that winked at you as much as to say: "Wouldn't you like my job?"

'Ilyin spoke to the Sundanese, but that fellow was in dreamland and did not hear. The girl answered for him. She said we could not visit the temple that day. The man was *latah*; I would have to wait. That Russian tried to bully her, but she would not give way, although she was afraid of Ilyin, who was big and strong and did not think much of women. When that scarlet sash slipped from the girl's shoulder, Ilyin would grin like a tiger that meets a young antelope.

' "Dutchman, you must stick around," he said. "It will be worth it. You will know things after you have seen what I have seen."

'For three days we waited. And we argued a lot. When I spoke of Hanne's *Handbuch der Klimatologie* or Woeikof's *Die Klimate der Erde*, that Russian would laugh at me. "All the fellows that have written about climate and atmosphere write of them in relation to health and industry and crops," he said. "Not one of the idiots writes about the relation of climate to the soul. They tell how altitude affects the circulation and respiration of the body, and how winds are bad for persons with certain complaints, but they say nothing of the effect of places on the vital principle, on the spirit. Look at this place! Wouldn't the atmosphere of this spot transform a man? Wouldn't it get into his blood?"

' "If the damned leeches left him any blood!" I snapped. There was a strange quality around that place, but I would not let that Russian bully me. There is something that you say in the United States. *Ja*! That is it: you say "I am from Missouri." Well, I was from Amsterdam, and I wanted to be shown too.'

Again the black ape called to the naturalist. Kromhout hoisted himself from the chair and hurried to comfort her. As I listened, I detected a whispering accompaniment to his words. Other small captives knew of the condition of the black ape, and were troubled.

'On the fourth day that Sundanese got over his bout with hashish,' continued Kromhout, as he returned. 'He did not like me. He said the place was *krámat*; that meant it was too sacred and magical for me to put my big feet inside it. Ilyin swore at him. At last the Sundanese gave way.

'First we entered the temple proper. That was only an antechamber to the real place. But we entered quick, so that not much fresh air could get in, and that no old air could escape. It was quite dark, but the Sundanese took my hand and led me. I would sooner have had the little hand of the girl, but that Russian had grabbed her as a guide.

' "Why not a flashlight?" I asked.

' "There is no need for one," said Ilyin. "There is light in the vault where we are going."

'That puzzled me, but I said nothing. We came to the far end of the temple and climbed down a stone stairway. I could see nothing, but I understood that we were in front of a stone doorway. Ilyin spoke to me. "It is necessary to enter quick," he said. "When the old man pulls the lever, the stone will swing back. It will be light then. Sava, the girl, will go first, then you, then I and the old man. But move quick! *Poskorēe! Poskorēe!*" He was all excited.

'I could not understand how it would be light when the stone door opened, but I said nothing. Then the door swung back, and I found that Ilyin had spoken the truth. Through the lighted space hopped the girl; I stumbled after her, and after me came Ilyin and the old man.

'We were twenty feet underground, and there was no opening to that vault except the door through which we had come, but the place was illuminated. It was lit up like a phosphorescent sea. I thought for a moment that the light came from millions of fireflies, or the luminous beetles of the *Lampyridae* that are related to glow-worms. I was wrong. The light came from a type of lichen that I had never seen. A variety of *Lecanora calacarea* that is mentioned by Engler and

Prantl in their book *Die natürlichen Pflanzenfamilien*. It sweats in the dark places where it grows, and its sweat is phosphorescent.

'That lichen covered the walls and the roof of that big vault – covered them like a silver tapestry. Lichen is strange stuff. Some day when the world dies, the lichen will make a death shroud. *Ja, ja*. And it will be very pretty. The blue-green algae, the red and yellow *Agyrium*, and the phosphorescent *Lecanora* that covered the walls and roof of that great vault. Lichen is the beard of death.

'After I got over the shock from that growing stuff, I noticed the air. It was heavy, very heavy. It was so thick that you thought you could chew it, but it was not unpleasant. Not at all. It was soothing. Have you ever tried opium? *Neen*? Well, the air of that place brought to me the nice loosening of the nerves that you get after the first whiffs of an opium pipe. It rubbed against my face like an invisible kitten. It touched my hands and my bare calves. It got into my hair and tickled my scalp. It had the ways of a bazaar woman. Now and then I swung round with the belief that someone had touched me with a finger on the back of the neck.

'There were small toads hopping about on the stone floor of the vault – the jerboa type of toad, with long legs. Ilyin, the old man, and the girl Sava took care not to step on the toads; and when the girl saw that I did not take much care, she spoke to the Russian, and he whispered to me: "Please be careful," he said; "the old man will get annoyed if you squash them."

' "Why?" I asked.

' "The old man speaks to them," said Ilyin. "When he wants to show me something extraordinary, he tells them to keep close to the wall so that they will not be trodden on by the others."

' "What others?" I snapped.

' "You'll see," he grinned. "You'll see, Dutchman."

'He was full of mystery, was that fellow. It was bubbling out of him. And the air that had fingers, and the phosphorescent lichen, were the hypodermic syringes with which he tried to squirt it into my system.

'We walked the length of that place. It was enormous. The pillars were beautifully carved with figures of birds and monkeys, and at the bottom of each pillar was a square stone box like those at Brambanan, that are filled with the dust of the dead. We did not speak. The only sounds were the *slap slap* of the toads as their bellies hit the floor. It was not nice. The only sweet thing in that place was the girl. I thought she was afraid of that vault – quite a lot afraid of it.

'We came out from that place in the same manner as we went in – slipping quickly through the door at the bottom of the stairs. For an hour or so I felt that I had been drugged; then I was myself again, and able to argue with that Russian. I had to admit that the air was curious, but more I would not admit.

' "You have no imagination!" cried Ilyin. "The French named you Dutch well when they called you *Têtes-de-Fromage*. Cheese-heads you are! You could not feel the Past in that place?"

' "I felt the air, and I heard the jerboa toads," I said. "Not more than that. It is good to have belief, but it is not good to have too much of it. That is the way to madness."

' "Wait around," said the Russian; "you will see what you will see. The girl has promised me."

'He smacked his lips when he spoke of that girl. There are two nations that strut when they speak of women – the Germans and the Russians; but the Russian has more charm. He is more dashing. He is a little mad, and women like madmen.

'I wanted to go away from that place, but I could not. It held me there because I felt that something would happen, something big. Have you noticed that lots of tragedies have been photographed? Those photographers have been there with the machines aiming at the spot where an automobile turns over, or some race-horse falls down, or that Balkan king is shot. You think it is luck? It is not. The man with the camera sensed the accident before it happened. That is what makes the good press photographer. Some time I will tell you a story about that business of sensing a smash.

'Each day I would see that Russian stalking the girl. *Ja*, stalking her like a black panther stalking a mouse deer. Whenever I saw the flash of her scarlet sarong in the jungle, I would see Ilyin close to her. And I would swatch her eyes and watch those of the Russian. The fear was growing greater in hers; in his was the belief that he would conquer. He would pull his moustaches and brag about the girls that had loved him in Moscow when he was at the university. He made me sick with his talk.

' "You had better watch that old man," I said to him.

' "Pooh!" he cried. "He is nothing. The girl – ah, the girl is some-thing precious. Do you know, Kromhout, that she believes she is a reincarnation from other days. She speaks as if she was around here when things were happening."

' "Then she will know too much for you," I snapped.

' "No woman knows too much for me," said that fool. "At the university they called me 'Little Andrey, the Fisher of Souls'. She will be mine very soon."

'Men are fools. We Dutch say: "Roasted pigeons do not fly through the air." It is a good proverb.

'One morning I saw that old Sundanese creeping through the jungle on his hands and knees. I could not see Ilyin or the girl, but I guessed that old man was hunting for them.

'That afternoon Ilyin was very gay. He sang little Russian songs that were all about girls who loved very much and who were willing to kill themselves for fellows. He sang them in his own language, but he translated them for me. I thought them foolish. Dutch girls would not do the things that those songs told of. Not much. Dutch girls keep their feet on the ground very hard.

' "Tonight, Kromhout," said Ilyin, "something might happen. It has been a big day for me. Sava loves me. *Da*! She loves me a lot. And she has promised me that she will make old sulky Mokhan put on a show tonight to celebrate our love-pact. In that vault we might see the Past." '

The naturalist paused in his narrative. He sat silent in his big chair. I thought he might be marshalling the events of that evening of long ago, putting them in order, shaping them so that they could be intelligible. Or perhaps he thought that the pause might let the caressing fingers of the Malayan night bring to my mind the capacity for belief. Belief in the strange tale that he wished to unfold.

'It happened as that Russian thought it would happen,' he said, and his voice was lowered as if afraid that the Tjandi Bororboedoer, squatting out in the thick darkness, might be annoyed at hearing him tell of the secrets of the long-buried past. 'The girl persuaded the old man to put on a big show. *Ja*, a big show. And he did!

'When we climbed down into that vault, I thought the lichen was more phosphorescent than the first time. It might have been just fancy. I don't know. Perhaps I was excited. The air was that air that had fingers which tickled the back of my neck and rubbed my scalp.

'The Russian did not know what was going to happen. I do not think the girl knew. It was just the business of the old man. He was not *latah* now. He was alive. His black eyes were sparkling, and at times I thought there was a grin of delight on his face.

'We had walked about twenty paces when the noise started. *Ja*, the noise. It started at the far end of the vault, some hundred feet from where we were standing; and it came creeping toward us, eating up the silence. Eating up the silence like a great invisible mouth. It was funny. At first it was not a great noise. It was soft and rather soothing, but as it crept nearer and nearer, it became louder. Much louder.

'Now and then it would stop for a few seconds – stop as if it had been throttled. And all our eyes were turned to the spot where it had halted. Do you understand? We knew, although we could see nothing, that it had a certain point. It was near this or that carved pillar that supported the roof. A noise made by something that we could not see. Moving and stopping, moving and stopping.

'It grew louder. Much louder. New noises joined up with it. Noises that I could not place, noises that had been lost to the world when that temple went out of business. There was a devilish rumble that seemed to be the backbone of the clamour. It came at intervals. It seemed to shake the temple. And it carried a poisonous fear with it. Drums of hell was that noise. *Ja*, drums of hell!

'When that big queer noise came, I thought the veins in my head would burst. It led the others to a sort of crescendo; then it snapped off quick so that it hurt your head. And you could see nothing. Nothing at all. In that vast underground vault there was only the old man, Ilyin, the girl and myself. *Ja*, and the toads. Those toads were banked now inches high around the walls and around the pillars. They were afraid – those toads. Possibly they saw things that we did not see. That *bufo-jerboa* is clever. Very clever.

'Closer and closer came that racket. Bulging its way toward us! I leaned forward, pop-eyed and sweating, in an effort to see something. I have heard all the noises of the jungle, but I have never heard noises like those. They were devilish. They were beyond the intelligence of man. They woke memories of things that were snaky and shiny, things of the past when the bull-roarer struck fear into the hearts of those who heard it.

'In the bones of our ears are echoes that have been asleep for hundreds of years. Frightening echoes. They are in the cells of our brains. They are part of us. We collected them in our climb out of the dark womb of the world. This civilisation of ours is a small thing. It is of yesterday. It is the thin scum of conceit that we have placed upon the terrors of other days. And when we are frightened, that scum that is civilisation, that is modernity, that is law and order and smugness and silly pomp and humbug, is broken by those memories that are mostly hooked up with sounds.

'They come out of the depths. The beat of the tom-toms, the clang of the devil-gongs, the hiss of big serpents, the whirring of the wings of vampires and pterodactyls. *Ach*! This memory of ours is a terrible thing – for the subconscious is filled with sounds. There is stored the bellow of the mammoth and the sound made by the shine dripping from the scaly legs of the plesiosaurus!

'Now, years after, I can hear those sounds of that vault when the world is quiet. I will always hear them. They are in my flesh, in my bones, in my blood. They are a fear-poison that has got into my body through my ears.

'I wished to run, but I could not. My legs had lost their power. They were boneless, and I was afraid that I would fall to the floor. The noise had swung a little to the left of us, and for that I was glad. You bet I was. If it had swept over us, I would have died from fear.

'The old man, the girl and the Russian did what I did – turned their heads to follow the sound. It was now surging between two great pillars of the vault, surging through them like a cataract of clamour!

'It was then that the girl cried out. She shrieked and pointed. Pointed at nothing that we could see, but something that was plain to her. Something or somebody. Somebody, I think. *Ja*, I am sure that she saw someone, at that instant.

'She shrieked again, and sprang forward; but that Russian was not going to let her get into that racket of noise. He grabbed hold of her waist and tried to hold her. He was strong, as I have told you; but she wished to touch something in the stream of noise. She was slippery like a snake. Her sarong was almost torn from her body as she wrestled; then as she leaped forward again, she and the Russian were in that frightening river of noise. They were in it! We knew!

'That Russian was six feet and a little bit. He weighed two hundred pounds, and he had muscles of steel. But his size and his weight did not matter much then. They were nothing to the forces that were around him. Nothing at all. Something picked him up. For an instant he was held horizontally at about three feet from the floor; then he was jerked head high and thrown across the vault, thrown across with such force that he struck the wall some twenty feet away. Struck it and dropped to the floor.

'That noise stopped then. Stopped with a suddenness that made me think I had become deaf. We did not move till we heard the *slap-slap* of the toads as they moved away front the walls and the pillars. It was comforting to hear those jerboa toads moving about.

'I went over to the Russian. He was quite dead. His head had struck the wall, and his skull was fractured. I remembered his face for a long time. There was fear on it. A great fear. I have often wondered if he saw what it was that picked him up and tossed him across the vault . . .

'*Ja*, there was an inquiry. The Dutch were angry about that business. They sent a magistrate from Djokja, and police came from Soerakarta. I told what I had seen and heard, and those police grinned. They were stupid fellows who could not believe anything unless they saw it with their little piggy eyes. And the fat magistrate from Djokja was so stuffed with *rystaefel* that there was no room for imagination.

'The girl would not speak. She was a little frightening. That fat magistrate asked her if the Russian had seduced her; and she looked at him in a way that gave him cold shivers. She did not like that question.

'The old man would not say much. When the magistrate asked him what had made the noise in the vault, he gave a funny answer. He said: 'They are the dead, that the years have eaten their bodies, but whose souls walk.'

'The police ruined that vault. They smashed down a part of the wall, and all that phosphorescent *Lecanora calacarea* shrivelled in an instant when it met the air of the day. And those jerboa toads turned over on their backs and died with little croaks. It was a pity. I would have liked that some big man, some scientist of the order of Regnault or Angus Smith, should study the air of that chamber. Now it is too late.'

The big Dutchman rose and went within the bungalow.

I sat silently looking out across the dark stretch to where Tjandi Bororboedoer, 'Shrine of the Many Buddhas', rose imperially. That foolish idea that the temple had moved closer to hear Kromhout's narrative was still upon me. I was a little afraid.

The big Dutchman reappeared. 'The black ape has got a little one,' he said, and his voice was soft with tenderness. 'Come and look at it. She thinks it is the most wonderful baby ape that the Malay archipelago has ever seen.'

Hallowe'en

Dulcie Deamer

Dulcie Deamer (1890–1972) was a New Zealander who became a well-known figure in Sydney Bohemian society in the 1920s and 1930s. She wrote several historical novels and a collection of fantastic historical tales, *In the Beginning: Six Studies of the Stone Age and Other Stories* (1909), from which the following story, an evocative werewolf tale set in an imagined middle ages, is taken.

Hevar sat up – not suddenly, but with a cat-like movement, that left the weight of the woollen coverlet still on her knees. The close, shuttered darkness was difficult to draw breath in, and there was a smell of clothing. On her left side rose the loud, nasal breathing of a man, flavoured with the fermented drink of his last meal, and his nearness was witnessed by the coarse, human odour of one whose skin is never touched by water, and who has grown warm between blankets. A masculine odour with a hint of milch cattle and manure in it. It was on the stroke of midnight, and Hevar was more awake than at high noon. She drew up her knees listening, and from the bed foot came the wordless moan of a sleeping child. Then, very far away, a long, long howl was lifted, nearing and nearing until it seemed to touch the shutter and whimper at it, nose against the fastening. The child cried out in its sleep, half-sobbing, and beat with its fists. Hevar's nostrils widened. 'It is time, it is time,' said a sharp voice within her, and she got out of bed, slipping her pillow stuffed with hen's feathers into the place where she had lain, that it might keep the warmth of her body. Again the child struck the sides of its carved wooden chest. Hevar felt as it were cords that drew her, and she yielded to them with gladness. She went surely with no feeling hands, treading only on her spread toes after the manner of a cat. The door opened and was latched. Then she lit a taper of yellow wax, and set it in a candlestick on the floor. The airless room was empty, with many shelves, and bunches of dried sage hung from a rafter. Hevar unbolted the hinged shutter, and hooked it back. A square of cold darkness looked in, but there was no wind, and the taper burned steadfastly on the stone floor. It was the midnight of Hallowe'en. Standing in the centre of the room, she loosened her white night-shift. It slipped to her breast, to her waist, to her knees, and lay around her feet. Hevar glanced once at the shadowy corners; then she laughed soundlessly with a show of teeth. The metal cross she took quickly from her neck, and laid it under her right heel, and the heavy, dark plaits were shaken loose. Dipping her fingers in a jar, she began to moisten her body from the head to the feet. The jar held poisonous liquid, distilled from the leaves of rue, foxgloves, hemlock and monk's head. As she rubbed herself, the place where the chrism of baptism had marked her forehead burned as though a red coal were held to it. But when the poison touched it, the burning ceased. Then she put out the taper, and in the darkness belted herself with a girdle cut from the hide of a black wolf, into whom a devil had entered. Immediately she was gripped with strong shuddering; the girdle held about her like a cincture of fire, and the sight behind her eyes seemed to go out. She had a muffled sensation of sinking, sinking, sinking, to a place that is beneath the bottom of all bottomless things – a something less than the span betwixt hell and heaven, but far enough. There was light – but the light was black, if such might be – and the uneasiness of great activity. A flame, dark as the smoke of burning pine logs, went upward, and those that served moved in it, coming and going. Something was said, and she saw an inverted cross . . . Then her eyelids lifted, and she knew that the sight of the flesh had returned to her.

Hevar the she-wolf stepped from the circle of a dropped night-shift. The nature of the darkness had changed, and she could see easily the tokens of mice by the wall-chinks. She crouched, sprang through the window-place, and alighted on silent feet. Some tiny thing that bore a green glow-worm light ran, threading the thin grass by the house wall. A number of fat, velvet-backed spiders, having drawn a single thread from the eaves to the gateway post, filled in a planned design of wheel-shaped openwork, and hung a dew-drop to each silvery spoke. Immediately a flight of midgets on wings transparent as diamonds and shot with greenish sheen, alit on the stretched thread, dancing the length of it, while three death-watches ticked in concert, keeping some sort of time. Hevar could see these happenings, and the thatched sheds of the steading, and the tops of the orchard of plum trees as though it were full day. And the night was awake and busy. A waft from the sheep pen, where ewes on the verge of early lambing were folded, stirred the hair on Hevar's spine, and sent an anticipating quiver to the tip of her bushy, inward-curving tail. She padded through the gateway, where the farm-gate swung on its hinges. On the gate sat a black impet with its forked tail over its shoulder. It pointed at her, and began to whirl round and round the top bar. The dog that was tied by the fold-fence lay close with eyes of fear, and his mane stood up. When the fold bleated with one voice and pushed hither and thither, and crowded foolishly from side to side, it was as though he did not hear. . . Hevar the she-wolf tore at the bloody gullet of the last just-killed ewe. In either of her lives there was no pleasure like this throat-ripping, this worrying of warm wool. Her open mouth grinned, and the tongue flickered between the white dog-teeth. The dead ewes lay everywhere on the fold floor, and the thick blood crawling to the centre had sunk, leaving the imprint of a dark cross.

Hevar the woman was wont to take feeble lambs into her lap, giving them milk from a heated pipkin... 'Look up-up-up!' sang the house kobold, from the sloped thatch of the hen-roost. 'Tomorrow you will weep because a wolf – a wolf, huh! has been in the sheep-fold. Till cockcrow, and I – I – I will tweak the rooster's longest tail feather, and tickle him with a barley straw. Huh!' Below, two flames of evil fire moved in the sheep-pen. Then a shadow leaped back into the mystery from which it had come.

Hevar stole down by a field edge, her belly low in the sweet, soaked grass. A mild glow lay on the face of the field, as though the patient, hidden earth were breathing, and the breath was luminous. Twice a great owl skimmed the grass-heads with some semi-human, prick-eared, slit-eyed atomie hunched between the motionless wings. Where the soil turned peaty and rich-smelling, and the grass coarse and mixed with reeds, a row of pollard willows slanted outward over the widening of a mill-brook that had scooped itself a mysterious depth. Grass-green fire flickered on the water, and the nixy of the hole, lividly pale as the undersides of some fishes, with full blue lips, and great soulless whitish eyes, had risen to below her woman's breast, and was plucking at the almost sunken body of a man. The water-fire dripped from her hair in which little eels were knotted, and all over the pool phosphorescent bubbles rose and burst. The she-wolf crossed a shallow matted with cress and mint. In the flat meads many stooping figures moved, gathering and gathering. A woman, with her apron filled with poisonous meadow saffron, was culling fool's parsley. A huge piebald cat rubbed against her hands, purring with pleasure.

'Luck to you, neighbour,' she said to the tongue-lolling wolf stealing through the tall, flowering weeds. 'You run tonight, I run tomorrow. The devil be with you!'

The cat purred louder, stretching and contracting its claws in pure delight.

An enormous golden-red moon was lifting above a shoulder of the tilth, and a string of bats passed across the uppermost half. As it grew to its full circle, the under rim on the edge of the ploughed land, the twin uprights of a gallows drew two black lines of the blank face of it, and between them hung something that seemed no larger than a dangling beetle. About it was the circling flicker of crow's wings. At the gallows foot a pick-axe rose and fell, minute as the claw of an insect against the vastness of the ruddy, lightless moon. It stopped in the mid-height of its tiny swing, and a thin scream, like the voice of a child in agony, shrilled up, and snapped, as though a heel had been set upon the child's throat. Then a dog howled. To draw forth the man-shaped root is death. The she-wolf that was Hevar slid into the midnight within midnight of a close wood. Here it was all astir, and so crowded that the palpable air had thickened. Troops of will-o'-the-wisps hopped in and out of the contorted tree-roots, as like to white candle flames as pea is to pea, save that they were evil in their very essence, and knowingly. Slimy shapelessnesses, akin to the one-night growths of spotted fungi, coated with a yellow mucus, sprawled and crept, leaving the silver trail of slugs. Bubbles of wan fire, in which milky light churned, wandered close to the earth, and pigmies, some prickly as a burr, some legged like hunting spiders, swarmed. Suddenly a pure glowing grew out of the quickened dark, broadening and broadening, softer and more pervading than keen daylight. Down the wood-path moved a girl in her night smock, holding a lit candle, whose flame she shielded with her other hand, and her darkened eyes were expressionless as the glass stare of a doll. Only her baptismal mark showed as if a forehead diamond lay just below the parting of her plaited hair. But on her right, and behind, a shape that was like a spear of intense white light moved with her, and before them the path thickened with close grass, bright as a good folk's dancing-ring, and the fungi blackened away, and the nameless spawn lapsed back to the scum from which they bred. The light and the sleeping girl passed slowly; then the two walls of malignant darkness rushed in and met rejoicing, and the place seethed. But Hevar had fled swiftly, ears flat, and tail tucked between hind legs, and when the sharp voice within that screamed, 'Run! – this is no place for us!' was silenced, she was on the grey high road, and the sow-thistles behind the grave-yard wall nodded their tops at her, though the night was airless. About the open belfry, spiked with an iron cross, where the church bell hung as if the bell-rope had been turned to rigid stone, a ring of linked impets circled swiftly as a top spins, and on the church roof they were – thick as starlings. A figure moved on the road, but after the manner of no living thing, and Hevar checked to watch. It was a woman, or what had once been a woman, in the brown shroud of her burial. She was yellow-grey – the colour of the second day of death – and her eyelids were sealed down as though the coins still weighed upon them. But her mouth was redder than any girl's, and to the full underlip hung a tear of blood. Her naked feet moved woodenly in the dust, and her arms were stiff at her sides as they had been put by the layers-out. She passed in by a wicket in the wall. Somewhere in the tangle of hideously-rank weeds there would be a narrow, open pit.

Hevar had trotted on the cross-ways. Here there were only vague suckings in the water meadows, and a splitting of the earth above a suicide's burial-place, that closed and drew apart again, She sat on her haunches, waiting. From beyond the turn of the road two sounds came to her – human, for they were coarser and had more body to them than the sounds of that night – a man's voice, and a man's heavy-footedness. Now he was round the turn, and a swinging lantern tossed light back and forth. The length of the stride was a trifle overdone, as was the working arm. As he came he bawled the Te Deum at the top of a voice throaty from fatigue and fear, and with his free hand dragged after him by its leash a most unwilling dog that whined anxiously, its tail completely out of sight.

'This,' said the sharp voice that spoke in Hevar, 'is a fool. A coward also. He has not even the courage to tell himself that he is afraid. See to him.' The she-wolf flattened herself, trembling.

The man who bawled a triumphant hymn in his nervous terror was very close. The water-meadows had silenced, and the earth-crack shut like the halves of a touched oyster.

'Now!' said the voice.

But Hevar leapt one little moment late, and the man had seen the eyes of a she-wolf.

'Holy Saint Nicholas!' howled the singer of *Te Deum*s, with blue panic clutching his entrails. Then, from pure brute instinct, and with the force of his almighty fear, he swung and crashed the lantern on the beast, dropped it, and bolted, bellowing to the countryside to save his life, while the dragged dog yelped. Far and far away the first cock crew faint as an elfin horn. A pause of breathlessness, and the next took up the challenge, nearer, and the next, and the next. The world turned in its sleep, muttering, and now every dung-hill, straw-stack, and rick-yard rail blew a defiant trumpet.

'The day is coming!'

In the cross-ways lay the unclad body of a woman with a bloody head, and having a strip of some dark hide about her waist. A heavy lantern was cast in the stained dust. It had the look of a most abominable murder.